MINE

Visit us at www.boldstrokesbooks.com

Acclaim for Georgia Beers's Fiction

"Sales Call" (in *Erotic Interludes 2: Stolen Moments*)

"'Sales Call' is an artfully well-developed and credible vignette. So often there is a fantasy aspect to erotica, but this reviewer prefers a kind of reality wherein the story could happen to anyone in similar circumstances. Beers delivers that expectation in a delightfully satisfying manner." —*Independent Gay Writer*

Too Close To Touch

"Beers knows how to generate sexual tension so taut it could be cut with a knife…[in this]…tale of yearning, love, and lust." —*Midwest Book Review*

"*Too Close To Touch* is about a woman who has dedicated her life to trying to please 'Daddy' and lost herself in the process. Beers doesn't tie the story up neatly at the end either. She leaves some questions open, which is appropriate for her character. Gretchen herself becomes an open question looking for a lot of answers. This is a very satisfying and thought provoking book." —*Just About Write*

Lambda Literary Award Winner *Fresh Tracks*

"…a story told uniquely by Beers with a clear and strong voice. If you are looking for a story where two women fall in love, have some misunderstandings along the way, and then move on to a committed relationship, *Fresh Tracks* is not that book…It is a meaty and challenging story with an ensemble cast where the lines between lovers and friends are sometimes blurred. Beers…rises above the pack of romance novelists [and her] love of her craft shines through with this bold and successful move." —*Just About Write*

By the Author

Fresh Tracks

Too Close to Touch

MINE

by

Georgia Beers

2007

MINE

ISBN 10: 1-933110-95-3
ISBN 13: 978-1-933110-95-0

This Trade Paperback Original Is Published By
Bold Strokes Books, Inc.,
New York, USA

First Edition: November, 2007

Credits
Editors: Cindy Cresap and Stacia Seaman
Production Design: Stacia Seaman
Cover Design By Sheri (GRAPHICARTIST2020@HOTMAIL.COM)

Acknowledgments

First and foremost, I need to thank my dear, dear friend Erin Fennell. She has one of the sweetest souls of anybody I've ever met, and she gave me free rein to pick her brain as well as her heart so I could try to understand the issues, emotional roadblocks, and internal doubts and questions a young widow must face. Her honest and invaluable guidance about grief and surviving the loss of a spouse, as well as her unending friendship, mean more to me than I can possibly put into words. I love her with all my heart.

Thank you to Sue Lasher for all the insight, information, and education on bereavement groups, what they do, and how they're run.

Great appreciation to my friend Chris DelConte for his extremely helpful suggestions and pointers regarding the wonderful world of real estate.

As always, I owe huge thanks to my beta reading posse—Stacy Harp (who's been with me since my very first book), Steff Obkirchner, Jackie Ciresi, and Paula Tighe. Their encouragement, nitpicks, and pats on the back did what they always do: helped me write a better novel.

This is the first time I've worked with Cindy Cresap as an editor, and she took her life in her hands by offering me some very radical suggestions in order to improve the book you're holding right now. And though I confess to initially harboring some rather violent thoughts about her, in the end, she ended up being right (which is why she's the editor and I'm not). So I want to say thank you to her for having the patience and courage to show me a better way to craft this story.

Not for the first time, and certainly not for the last, big, big thanks to Len Barot and Bold Strokes Books. I am lucky, proud, and extremely grateful to be in such cool company.

Dedication

To Bonnie
I don't have to tell you. You already know.
I love you.

CHAPTER ONE

The sun beat down mercilessly on the worn wood of her back deck, and Courtney McAllister knew she'd be spending the day in the pool again. Not that she minded. There were worse ways to spend a day. She glanced out the kitchen window at the thermometer mounted at an angle for viewing from inside. Eighty-seven. At eight o'clock in the morning. Another scorcher.

It was cool enough in the house, though. She'd been against getting central air, but on days like this, was blissfully glad she had it. It wasn't all that great at cooling the upstairs and the bedroom often seemed a bit stuffy, but as she wandered the first floor with her coffee cup in her hands, she was happy to be comfortable. Breaking into a sweat first thing in the morning was not her idea of fun. Unless she was sweating for the right reasons, of course… which hadn't happened in a really long time. Sometimes, Courtney was certain it would never happen again, and the idea of spending a steamy afternoon floating in the pool alone seemed suddenly sad and pathetic.

She stood in the middle of the living room, slowly turning in a circle and taking in everything there, trying not to panic about the changes she was about to set in motion. She loved this room. The ceilings were high with two skylights that threw sunlight down onto her head and created funky geometric patterns on the thick beige carpeting. The chocolate brown leather couch was buttery-soft and inviting even if you were just looking, practically screaming for you to come and sit on it. In the corner by itself sat Theresa's overstuffed reading chair and matching ottoman. Courtney never sat in it, choosing instead to let it sit abandoned yet spotlit, like some shrine to the way things used to be. The scratched and marred oak coffee table sitting solidly in front of the couch was something that really needed replacing. But it was the first piece of furniture Courtney and Theresa had purchased together and they'd been loath to give it up. Some weird, sentimental reasoning that neither could put her finger on. Now that Theresa was gone, Courtney was even more hesitant, as if getting rid of the old table would be akin to tossing away a part of her old life.

She flopped onto the couch and propped her bare feet up on the object of her worry. She should be used to this by now, this wavering, this back-and-forth. She'd been doing it for almost three months. The summer was more than halfway over. She'd have to start preparing for school soon and she knew if she let herself get to that point, she'd put things off for another year. Who wanted to sell a house in the middle of winter?

She could hear Amelia's voice very distinctly, as if her best friend was still standing right in front of her, scolding gently like she had the day before.

Honey, this place is too damn big for just you. First of all, you don't even use half the rooms. Second of all, it's way the hell out here in the 'burbs and you never see any of your friends. You're becoming a hermit. You need to get out there, to mingle. Her tone had softened at that point. *It's time to move on, sweetheart. Theresa wouldn't want you to be stuck like this.*

Although Courtney knew Amelia was right, she still prickled at the assumption that she was turning into a recluse. She'd dated. She'd dated more than once. Just because she hadn't found a woman who curled her toes, did that mean she wasn't trying? That she was perfectly happy being alone and lonely in her big house that she'd purchased with her dead girlfriend?

Shaking her head in dismay, she sighed loudly, wishing somebody—anybody—was nearby enough to hear it and sympathize with her plight. Directly across from her, she scanned the shelves on either side of the large television. She studied the myriad of framed photographs and souvenirs from what felt like—and what was—a previous life. There was Theresa on the whale-watching boat during their trip to the Cape. She smiled when she recalled that just moments after snapping the picture, Courtney turned to her left and promptly threw up in the garbage can. Theresa never let her forget it. The next shelf down held an 8 x 10 in gorgeously bright color of Theresa and Polo. The adopted beagle mix had been Theresa's pride and joy and she was devastated when old age had claimed him several months before Theresa's accident. Courtney had lost them both within a year. Sometimes, she wondered how she'd survived.

She set down her mug, stood, and crossed the room, reaching out to pick up a black-and-white picture in its sturdy wooden frame. She held it with care, lovingly running her fingertips over the round, smiling face of her beloved partner. It was the day of their union ceremony and they'd both looked gorgeous and ridiculously happy. Their white dresses were simple. Theresa's short dark hair was glossy and tucked behind her ears. Courtney's—longer and a lighter brown—was up in a French twist. Even in a photograph, the glimmer of ecstasy was visible in Theresa's rich brown eyes. She'd always told Courtney it was the happiest day of her life.

Courtney set the frame back in its place as she felt the threat of tears. "Damn it," she mumbled. She'd gotten much better at reminiscing without getting overly emotional. It seemed that people were right: time does help heal. But the wedding picture got her every time. She retrieved her mug and escaped back into the kitchen where a slice of buttered toast lay abandoned on a plate at the table. She sat down and her eyes were pulled to the newspaper ad she'd spread out last night.

The woman staring back at her looked coldly beautiful. Blond, with a smoothly chiseled face and prominent cheekbones. Even in black and white, the blue of her eyes was obvious. They were an icy shade, which seemed like the perfect adjective, the darkness of her lashes making the color even more apparent. Courtney reached a hand out and tilted the page so she could see it more clearly.

Rachel Hart, Million Dollar Producer.

Most realtor ads Courtney had seen had some kind of catchy phrase, something corny like "I've been around the block," or "I won't just find you a house, I'll find you a home." Apparently,

Rachel Hart, Million Dollar Producer, didn't need catchy. She had those eyes.

"Carl says she's one of the best around," Amelia had said a couple days earlier, referring to her mortgage broker husband. "She'll sell this place in a heartbeat. And look." She'd pulled the newspaper out of her bag, folding it so Courtney could see the title page and note that it was the local gay rag. "She advertises in the paper of your people." Her expression filled with affection and humor, she tossed the section at Courtney. "Just think about it."

Courtney had thought about nothing else since then. The pros and cons, the benefits and the drawbacks. She made lists, for Christ's sake. She hated the idea of giving up her dream home. It was the house she'd picked out with Theresa, that they'd purchased and decorated lovingly together. They'd only been there for a year before Theresa's accident and they'd had plans for this house. But Amelia was right. It was too big for only one person, and the thought of getting a roommate just to take up space was depressing. It wasn't *that* far into the suburbs, but even the thirty-minute drive from downtown could become grating, especially in the winter. Most of the evening activities Courtney took part in—and there were fewer than there should have been—took place in the city. More often than not, she found herself driving the thirty-minute commute after work, then turning around an hour later only to drive another thirty minutes back into the city for whatever she was doing that night. Then another thirty minutes to get home again. It was tedious. There was a definite appeal to finding something smaller and closer.

But Theresa...

Courtney knew the problem. She knew it exactly. After more than a year and a half of therapy after Theresa's death, she knew exactly how to analyze her own feelings and reactions. Of course, knowing the source didn't make such things any easier to deal with, but awareness was good, wasn't it? Wasn't it good for her to understand that she was worried about selling the house because deep in her heart, she felt like she'd be leaving Theresa behind?

She dragged her attention back to the picture of Rachel Hart, Million Dollar Producer. She didn't exactly look warm and fuzzy, but she advertised in the gay paper, so she got points for that in

Courtney's book. "Million Dollar Producer" was impressive, she had to admit. If Courtney got technical with the details, she'd also have to admit that she'd stand to make a healthy profit from selling. Theresa's life insurance policy had paid off the entire mortgage, which had been a huge relief since there was no way Courtney could have afforded it alone. Not that she was all about the money, but making some to put away for retirement definitely held an appeal.

She picked up the cordless phone from where it sat on the table, dialed the first three numbers listed on the newspaper ad, then clicked off with a sudden surge of panic. She pressed the phone to her forehead and closed her eyes, willing her breathing to steady. Her coffee now cold, she took a large gulp anyway, wet her lips, and dialed again. This time, she didn't hang up.

❖

Rachel Hart held the MapQuest directions in her right hand and read as she maneuvered her BMW into a left-hand turn. Satisfied she was on the right street, she set the sheet down and took in the neighborhood as she drove. *Nice*, she thought. *Good-sized houses, roomy yards, lots of trees, cul-de-sac.* She nodded, knowing she could sell any one of these houses in a matter of days. It was an up-and-coming area of suburbia, new developments going up all over the place. Everybody wanted to be out here, to send their children to this particular school. She could already think of six different clients who'd be interested in one of these houses. She was sure Danny probably had a few, too, though she wasn't sure she even needed to mention it to him. Why share the profit if she didn't have to?

She swung the car into the driveway of number thirty-seven, pleased to note it was at the end of the cul-de-sac…prime location. It was probably very quiet. The only traffic this house saw was either destined for its driveway or lost. It was perfect for a family with children.

Rachel picked up her leather portfolio off the passenger seat and got out of the car. She smoothed the jacket of her black pantsuit and mentally went over the details she had researched earlier that day. The house was purchased nearly four years ago by two women:

Courtney McAllister and Theresa Benetti. A little over a year later, the ownership had been transferred to Ms. McAllister alone. She had been the one to call and set up the appointment, and since there had been no "we" in any of their conversation, Rachel assumed this was yet another lesbian couple who'd purchased up and then broken up. She saw it happen all the time; it was frighteningly common. The good news was that Rachel was sure—assuming the interior of the house had been maintained—that she could sell this place for a good twenty-five to thirty thousand dollars above the original purchase price. The area was flourishing. Maybe the extra profit would ease the pain of the breakup.

She shrugged and headed across the walk to the front door. None of it was any of her concern. Her job was to sell this house, and that's what she was going to do. Quickly and for the most money.

She gave her hair a fast finger-comb and then rapped on the big oak front door, noting with pleasure the leaded glass embedded into it. A nice front door made a great first impression. She was still thinking about that as it was pulled open and an attractive brunette with a warm smile said hello.

Courtney McAllister was not what Rachel had expected, though she wasn't sure why. Maybe it was the lack of bitterness, that hardening around the eyes that women get when they've been left or they're being forced out against their will. This woman seemed...resigned, but pleasant. She was dressed casually in a pair of well-worn, soft-looking cargo shorts and a navy blue T-shirt and had an athletic air about her. Her chestnut brown hair was pulled back off her face, which was devoid of any makeup, and she was barefoot. Her handshake was firm and she invited Rachel inside with a friendly wave of her arm.

"Can I get you something to drink?" she asked, her green eyes looking directly into Rachel's. "Coffee? Beer? Wine? A Coke?"

Rachel shook her head. "Thank you. No. I'm fine."

"Well...here it is." Courtney tried for a smile, but it came across as more of a grimace and Rachel nodded, noting that her prospective client had drifted from seeming comfort to slight unease.

They stood in the middle of the high-ceilinged living room, Rachel scanning her papers and Courtney nervously shifting from foot to foot and rubbing her hands together. Rachel looked up and squinted at the skylights, then jotted a few notes on her paper. "Do you know how old these are?" She pointed up.

"They were here when we bought the place." Courtney shrugged. "They don't leak, though," she added as an afterthought.

Rachel nodded again and wandered to the front windows, peering behind the sheer curtains. The only sound in the room was the scratching of her pen on paper as she made some more notes.

"So…" Courtney said in an obvious attempt to fill the silence. "How do we do this? Do you want to wander? Do you want me to show you around? Tell me what the process is. I'm kind of new to all of this."

Rachel had found in more than ten years as a realtor that there were two main kinds of sellers. There were the people who couldn't wait to sell. They were the ones who were having a new house built or were moving up in the world or were moving out of town. They were generally happy and gave Rachel free rein, listening to her suggestions raptly and carrying them out without question. Then there were the people who didn't want to sell. They were being forced to because of finances or they'd been through a breakup or divorce and didn't want the memories. Courtney was hard to pinpoint and Rachel found that intriguing, deciding she must fall somewhere in between. She rarely asked for details, though they were often offered up anyway. She preferred to use the clues given to her to figure out the situation on her own. Sort of a solo brain teaser, a challenge she issued herself.

Twenty minutes later, she'd wandered the house unescorted— she always chose to make her first trip alone, without the narration of her client to cloud her judgment—and returned to the living room with her notes. Courtney sat at one end of the leather couch looking decidedly more nervous than she had earlier, like a deer caught in the headlights of an oncoming car. Rachel took the other end of the couch and sat at an angle so her knees pointed toward her. She placed her business card on the table and then consulted the scribbles she'd made during her perusal.

"Okay, here's what I've got." She looked up from her notes to be sure Courtney was paying attention. The expression on her face was hard to read, but Rachel pushed forward, launching into her usual introductory spiel. "You've got a beautiful place here. I don't think we'll have any trouble at all selling it. A couple suggestions: Do whatever you can to get rid of the clutter. Clutter makes things look smaller, and you want everything to appear as large and roomy as possible. The closets are a little crowded. See if you can thin stuff out a bit. The guest bedroom has a bunch of boxes labeled 'Clothes to Salvation Army.' Get those out of here. They look messy. The upstairs office? You need to thin some of that out, too. That shelf of trophies needs to go, the certificates on the wall. Maybe replace them with one simple painting. And here." She gestured to the entertainment center with her chin. "You need to get rid of some of the pictures. I always suggest that my clients depersonalize as much as possible. People want to walk through the place and be able to picture themselves in here. With all your stuff lying around, they'll end up picturing themselves in *your* house instead of *theirs,* and I've found that doesn't guarantee a sale as well."

Courtney blinked at her, the look on her face clouding over with…something Rachel couldn't put her finger on. Anger? Pain? Rachel studied her. "Ms. McAllister? Are you okay?"

Courtney stood abruptly and Rachel followed suit. "You know what? I think I've changed my mind."

Rachel felt her head spin from the unexpected change in direction. "I beg your pardon?" She barely registered Courtney's hand on her elbow, almost pulling her through the living room and steering her toward the door.

"I've changed my mind," Courtney said again, almost breathless as she opened the front door. "I don't think I'm ready to sell. I'm really sorry to have wasted your time, Ms. Hart. Please forgive me."

Before Rachel knew what was happening, the front door closed and she was left standing on the front stoop of number thirty-seven, blinking in confusion. She stood there for several long minutes, trying in vain to figure out exactly where things had gone so terribly wrong and wondering how on earth she'd misread Courtney McAllister so badly.

She took a deep breath and blew it out. In a gesture of frustration, she lifted her arms out and dropped them to her sides, the portfolio banging against her thigh. She finally conceded defeat and got back into her BMW, still feeling somewhat dizzy from the weird turn of events, though now annoyance had begun to creep in. She started the engine and stared at the dashboard, not really seeing anything but Courtney McAllister's anxiety-ridden face.

As she backed out of the driveway, she growled with irritation, "Well. *That* was a first."

CHAPTER TWO

Y ou did *what?*"
      Amelia's voice was so shrill, Courtney had to hold the phone away from her ear, certain her friend had reached frequencies only dogs could hear. "I couldn't help it," she said, sounding like a whining six-year-old. "I panicked."

"Panicked? Girl, you freaked out. What the hell is the matter with you?"

Courtney sighed and rubbed her forehead. She could picture Amelia, her dearest friend since college, sitting at her own kitchen table, her dark brown eyes sizzling with fire, her black hair glossy and brushed back from her face, which was probably etched with disapproval. Courtney fought to explain what she'd felt the previous evening. "I don't know, Meel. I don't know. I just...she was so... detached, you know?"

"Detached? How do you mean?"

"She wanted me to get rid of stuff...pictures and things. You know?" Courtney didn't like the memory or the idea of what Rachel Hart, Million Dollar Producer, suggested she do. "She told me to get rid of my pictures of Theresa and me, her trophies and certificates in the office..." She trailed off.

"She said that?" It was more of a statement than a question. "She said, 'get rid of these pictures of your dead girlfriend, as well as her awards and stuff'?"

"She said I needed to depersonalize," Courtney said, knowing she wasn't really answering the question.

There was a pause and she knew Amelia was nodding, processing. "Let me ask you something. And tell me the truth."

"Okay."

"Did she know Theresa had passed away?"

Courtney scratched at an invisible spot on her chest and nibbled on the inside of her cheek. "Um…"

Amelia sighed. "Damn it, C. What the hell am I going to do with you, hmm?" Her tone was quiet, which in many ways was worse than when it was shrill. Courtney knew it meant Amelia was frustrated and disappointed with her, so she sighed, too.

"Love me forever?" Courtney said, feeling small.

"That's already a given, you bonehead." There was a beat of silence. "You're going to call her back, right?"

Courtney grimaced. "Do I have to?"

"Yes, you absolutely have to. You need to get her back there—if she's willing to even give you the time of day, which I have to admit, I wouldn't be—and you need to apologize to her."

Courtney groaned.

"And you need to tell her the truth. The poor girl deserves to have all the facts before she's judged on her behavior, don't you think?"

"I suppose. But she's so…cool."

"That's bad how? I've seen her picture. Remember?"

"No, no. Cold. Cool as in cold. As in not friendly. She was beautiful, that's for sure." Courtney thought back to the strikingly tall figure that had stepped into her house like she owned the place. The perfect hair, the impeccable suit, not a wrinkle or a piece of lint to be found. "Beautiful and cold."

"Are you trying to sleep with her or do you want her to sell your house?"

"Amelia!"

"I'm just trying to understand you, that's all. She's a *realtor*, Courtney. Have you met many of them in your life? Because I have and I'm sorry to say, the majority of them are cold, conceited, and bitchy. But I'm also thinking cold, conceited, and bitchy is probably going to get me more money for my house, am I right?"

Courtney grinned in spite of herself. "Are you ever not right?"

"It's rare, sweetie. It's rare."

"Can't I just call a different realtor?" Courtney winced at the fact that she was still droning on like a toddler.

"Sure you can. After you call and apologize to Ms. Icy Cool."

They debated for several more minutes, but Courtney's arguments became less and less vehement because she knew Amelia was right. She owed Rachel Hart an explanation and an apology at the very least. They hung up with Amelia claiming victory.

Courtney sat for long moments at the kitchen table, staring at the business card Rachel had left. She held it up and ran her thumb over the small photograph, a duplicate of the one in the paper, but this one in full color. The realtor stared confidently into the camera lens, as if she was certain the picture would be perfect. Only the barest hint of a smile touched her full, pink lips, and Courtney found herself wondering what Rachel Hart, Million Dollar Producer, would look like if she actually laughed outright. She imagined possible lines crinkling at the corners of her eyes; she imagined the almost-dimples that dented her cheeks deepening just a bit. Shaking her head, Courtney took in a big breath and blew it out.

"Time to eat crow," she said with a sigh and dialed the phone, thankful when Rachel's voice-mail message came on. She listened until the beep, then took a deep breath and dove in.

"Um…Ms. Hart. Iii. This is, um, Courtney McAllister. You remember me, I'm sure. I'm the one who wigged out on you yesterday and practically tossed you out of my house? Yeah. Well. Um, I wanted to apologize. I was very rude and I'm really, really sorry. It's just…" She had no idea how detailed she should get, but couldn't seem to stop herself once she got started. "It's just that my, um, my partner was killed in a car accident not quite three years ago, so…the whole 'take the pictures and stuff down' aspect of your visit…I took that a little too personally, I'm afraid. I'm really sorry." She exhaled, feeling relieved to have gotten it out. "Anyway. If you're still interested in selling my house, I'd love to start over. If not, I understand completely and maybe you can direct me to another realtor." She left her phone number and signed off, feeling a weird sense of pride and accomplishment.

❖

"God, I want to take a nap."

Rachel looked across the room at her officemate, Danny Boyle, and grinned. "I told you to lay off the chardonnay during lunch, didn't I?"

Danny laughed, taking the chastisement in stride. "You did. I can't help it. James doesn't understand the idea of a quick lunch. He likes to eat at nice places."

"And nice places mean a glass of wine."

"Absolutely."

"Just like a couple of gay men." She winked playfully at him as she dialed the voice-mail retrieval number on her cell and listened. Closing her eyes as she absorbed the words, she muttered, "Oh, Christ." The sound of her snapping the phone shut cracked through the air like a whip.

Rachel could feel Danny's curious gaze on her, knew her face was flushing, and she was more irritated at the shame she felt than she was about the overall situation. Not an emotion she was familiar with, embarrassment flooded her like some internal dam had just broken. The cell phone landed on the desk with a thunk. She dropped her head into her hands and groaned loudly.

Cocking a perfectly manscaped eyebrow at Rachel, Danny asked, "Everything okay?"

Rachel picked her head up from her hands and focused on him as she processed what she'd just heard. "That was my insane client from last night."

"The cute one who changed her mind at the last minute and tossed you out on your shapely behind?"

Rachel managed a smirk. "The very same one."

"And?"

"Remember when I told you that she started to get weird when I went through my depersonalization lecture?" Danny had taught that method to Rachel. Not all realtors used it because clients could be put off or become insulted, but more often than not, clients understood that the realtor just wanted to help create the best circumstances for selling the house. Before now, neither of them had ever run into an issue.

"She had a lot of stuff out. A lot of personal things," Rachel continued. Even though she'd already told him all this earlier, she felt like saying it again would maybe help her feel better now that she knew the root of the problem. She thought back to Courtney's upstairs office in particular. There were photos and volleyball trophies and some MVP award on a wooden shelf, and several certificates and awards mounted on the wall. She hadn't really looked all that closely, but she'd bet her entire savings account now that the name inscribed on each item was *not* that of Courtney McAllister.

"So you said," Danny prodded, willing her along with a hurry-up gesture of his hand.

"So her partner? The one I was sure must have moved out?"

"Uh-huh."

"Yeah, she's dead."

Danny blinked at her in shock. "Wait, wait, wait." He held up a finger, keeping her from continuing. "So…let me get this straight. No pun intended. You told her to take down and pack away all the pictures and personal items belonging to her *dead* girlfriend?"

"That's exactly what I did." Rachel nodded with a grimace.

"Oh, my God. Holy shit." Danny cackled with glee. "This is better than a soap opera."

"It's not funny, Danny. I didn't know," Rachel said in her own defense. Her stomach churned and she felt sick.

"She didn't think that might be a good thing to tell you?"

"Apparently not." She dropped her head back into her hands, mortified. "God, I'm so embarrassed. Was I just supposed to figure that out on my own? Do I look psychic to you?"

"Wow." Danny continued to chuckle, shaking his head. "I can honestly say in all my years in this business, *that* has never happened to me."

"Lucky you. Jesus."

"So…" He gestured to the abandoned cell phone with his chin. "Was that all she said?"

Rachel looked up at him. They weren't what she'd considered

close, but in all honesty, she wasn't really all that close to anybody. He was a decent guy; she liked him and his partner. They'd shared an office for nearly five years and they helped each other out with clients; he generally sent the lesbians to her and she directed the gay men to him. It was a relationship that seemed to work well for both of them. "She wanted to apologize."

Danny made a face of approval. "Okay. She gets points for that. A little late, but still a nice gesture."

"And she wants to know if we can try again."

Danny studied her as she chewed at her bottom lip.

"I don't know," she pronounced after several seconds of silence, as if he'd asked her a question. "I just don't know. Mostly because she's made me feel like an idiot and I hate that. I don't know if I can face her. I don't know if I *want* to." She looked at Danny. "What do you think?"

"Well," Danny said matter-of-factly. "Let's look at the most important aspect, shall we? Would you make any money on the house?"

Rachel pursed her lips before she spoke. "It's a nice, fairly new place out in Mendon. Yeah, I could definitely get a good price for it."

He shrugged. "Then go sell the son of a bitch."

❖

The more Courtney had replayed her conversation with Amelia, the guiltier she felt about how she'd treated Rachel Hart, Million Dollar Producer, earlier in the week. Unable to believe Rachel had actually agreed to meet with her again, Courtney had spent the last three days rehearsing what she would say to the realtor when she finally saw her. She knew she had a lot of ground to make up and she was determined to do so. She delivered her apologies directly into the bathroom mirror over and over again until the wording was just right—sincere, but not too corny. She practiced her friendly smile, her open and approachable expression, hoping to invite any questions or suggestions Rachel might offer. She made a few small hors d'oeuvres of a good, sharp cheddar cheese and some crackers, and had a bottle of white wine chilling in the fridge. As she glanced down at her outfit and smoothed a wrinkle out of her shorts, she chuckled not for the first time because she felt more like she was waiting for her date to arrive than her realtor.

"God, what does that say about me?" she asked aloud, not really wanting to deal with the answer.

She practiced her apology one more time, feeling confident that it was just right. When the doorbell rang at exactly seven o'clock, all the words flew right out of her head and left her feeling blank and empty. She wanted to scream.

Patting a hand over her hair one last time and wishing she'd pulled it back off her face instead of leaving it down, she took a deep breath and pulled the front door open. She felt the heat from the outside hit her like a wall, and all sound stuck in her throat.

Rachel Hart stood on the front stoop looking like she'd just stepped out of an upscale catalog for ladies' business attire and totally unaffected by the heat. Her suit was sage green and lightweight, a smart choice given the high temperature of late July. Rather than a pantsuit like the last time, this ensemble had a short skirt on the bottom and Courtney blinked, absorbing that Rachel's legs seemed to go on for days. Courtney took in the imposing figure, from the strappy sandals on up, admiring the shapely cut of the matching green jacket and how it accentuated a trim waist, filing away the wink of cleavage that peeked out from beneath the cream-colored silk camisole, and stopping on the icy blue eyes that stared right back at her. Courtney nearly choked on her own breath.

"Um." She cleared her throat, embarrassed that she'd been staring so openly. She thrust out her hand. "Ms. Hart. Thanks so much for coming back."

Rachel took the offered hand and shook it firmly.

"Please." Courtney stood aside. "Come in."

Rachel entered the foyer, briefcase in hand, heels clicking on the tile floor.

"Before we get started," Courtney began, her voice quivering just a touch, "I just wanted to apologize once more. Face-to-face." She looked directly at Rachel, wanting to be sure the realtor believed she was sincere. "I'm really sorry for the other day. I was rude and there's no excuse for the way I treated you. I hope you'll forgive me."

A beat of silence passed before Rachel responded. "It's fine. No big deal." She waved her hand dismissively and wandered off to the right, into the living room.

Courtney stood alone in the foyer for several seconds and wondered if her apology had actually been accepted or if she'd just been brushed off. With a mental shrug, she followed Rachel's path.

"Can I get you something?" Courtney asked as Rachel set her briefcase on the coffee table and popped it open. "I've got a nice sauvignon blanc chilling in the refrigerator. I've also got Coke, water, iced tea…"

"A glass of water would be great," Rachel said, not looking up as she rooted through her papers. "Thank you."

Courtney headed for the kitchen, wondering if it was true that the temperature was about ten degrees cooler in the living room or if it was just her guilty conscience. Well, what did she expect, anyway? She'd practically thrown the woman out bodily during their last meeting. It wasn't surprising that she'd be distant. *Rude, even*. Courtney filled a glass with ice and then water from the fridge door. She picked up the plate of cheese and crackers, took two steps toward the doorway, and then came back. She set everything down and pulled out the bottle of wine. Wielding the corkscrew with defiant determination, she poured herself a glass of the New Zealand white and returned to the living room.

She stopped before she entered Rachel's peripheral vision, staring in surprise at the change in front of her. Courtney had left the television on, hitting the mute button before answering the door. The screen was tuned to Animal Planet and some dogs were running an agility course. It wasn't the dogs that stole Courtney's attention and stopped her dead, though. It was the change in expression on Rachel Hart's face. Gone was the cool, detached professionalism, replaced by the ghost of an amused smile and a gentle crinkling around her eyes, just as Courtney had pictured in her mind. The overall softening made her look like a completely different person, and Courtney was stunned by the transformation.

Not wanting to startle her, Courtney cleared her throat softly and continued on her path into the room. She nearly whimpered in protest when the "realtor face" dropped back into place with an almost audible slam.

"Here you go," Courtney said, handing over the water glass. She set the munchies down on the table. Gesturing to the television, she ventured, "You have a dog?"

Rachel took a seat on the couch, seemingly absorbed once again in her notes. "No. I live in an apartment."

When it was obvious no further comment was coming, Courtney nodded and sat on the opposite end of the couch, leaving plenty of space between them. "Oh." She sank back into the leather and sipped her wine as Rachel scanned her notes from her previous visit. "Whereabouts?"

Rachel glanced up, a glimmer of irritation zipping across her face. "Pardon?"

"Where is your apartment?"

"In the city." Rachel pulled a pen from the top pocket of her briefcase.

Courtney sipped her wine. After a few seconds passed, she said, "Huh."

Rachel's shoulders sagged just a little and she looked at Courtney once more. "Excuse me?"

"It just seems weird to me. That's all. You're a realtor. You sell houses for a living. It's…unexpected that you live in an apartment." Courtney shrugged.

Rachel studied her for a long moment, holding her gaze. "I'm busy. It's easier."

"Okay." Courtney smiled, the smile fading to a grimace as Rachel finally glanced away. *God, she'd be so much prettier if she'd loosen up a little bit. And smile once in a while. What would that hurt?* Courtney let her gaze linger on Rachel's profile, noting the gentle curve to the bridge of her nose, the almost-black of her eyelashes. Her hair had several levels of color, various shimmering shades of gold, and its waves just skimmed the tops of her shoulders. The idea of dimples could be seen on her cheeks, her chin was strong, and her throat looked soft. Courtney sat up abruptly when she realized how much she wanted to reach out and stroke it with her fingertips, just to see how soft that skin really was. Then she thought absently that it would more likely be chilly to the touch, like caressing ice. That idea made her bite her lip to keep from grinning.

"All right." Rachel's voice cut through Courtney's musings and Courtney sat up a little straighter. It seemed to her that Rachel was trying to choose her words carefully. "My original advice still applies." Her tone softened as she looked Courtney in the eye. "Are you okay with that?" she asked quietly.

Courtney nodded, again surprised at Rachel's ability to change her entire demeanor in a split second. "Yeah. It's hard. It's hard to hear and it's hard to do. But…I understand what you're saying." She swallowed down a sudden lump. "It's time. I plan to work on that this weekend."

Rachel watched her for a long moment, as if deciding whether or not she was telling the truth. "Okay," she said finally. "We'll come back to that when we talk numbers." She flipped the top sheet of her pad over to a clean one. "Let's talk about this first: what are you looking for in a new house?"

Courtney blinked at Rachel and raised her eyebrows in surprised realization. "Oh, my God, I hadn't even thought of that. If I sell this house, I'll need to move, won't I?"

Rachel gave a genuine grin, its appearance causing Courtney to nearly do a double take. "That's generally how it works."

"Wow. Okay. Let's see." Courtney stood up with her wineglass and paced in front of the coffee table as she tried to organize her thoughts, feeling Rachel watching her movements. "Smaller," Courtney said, waving one arm to encompass the large room. "Definitely smaller. This is a bit too much for me." She looked at Rachel, who was scribbling notes. "And closer to the city. I feel a little far away. Disconnected. I'd like to be a little closer to the heart of things. You know what I mean?"

Rachel looked up and caught Courtney's eye. After a second, she nodded.

"I don't really have a particular neighborhood preference. Just keep me out of the scary parts, okay?"

"Okay."

Courtney drained her wineglass. She suddenly felt a little jittery and wasn't sure if it was the fact that she was actually going through with selling her and Theresa's house or if it was the brittle distance of the woman sitting on her couch. "That's not really much, is it? Does it help? At all?"

"Absolutely. We'll get more specific about what you like and what you don't after I find some places to show you."

They went over more particulars about the sale of the house, the listing date, the asking price, open house or no open house, and so on. By the time Rachel packed up her briefcase and stood to go, more than an hour had passed and Courtney felt a weird sensation of impending loss, which made no sense because Rachel Hart was about as warm and comforting as a coat hanger.

They walked to the door together. Rachel turned and stuck out her hand. "Ms. McAllister, it's going to be a pleasure working with you."

Putting her hand in Rachel's, Courtney was surprised to feel warmth, having expected a coolness to match her aura. "Please. It's Courtney. Thank you so much for your help. And for giving me a second chance."

"I'll be in touch." With that, Rachel pulled her hand away suddenly and was out the door.

Courtney stood in the doorway, watching the BMW back down the driveway and trying to get a handle on the weird sense of... something she couldn't quite put her finger on.

CHAPTER THREE

Courtney hit the bottom of the stairs and was heading for the door to the attached garage when the phone rang. She set the box down and wiped her dusty hands on her shorts before grabbing the handset.

"Hello?" She was a tad out of breath.

"Been jogging?" Peter Manning's tone was deep and cheerful, laced with a comfort and friendliness that never seemed to go away. Courtney's breath whooshed from her in a quiet sigh of relief.

"Never," she answered good-naturedly. "Jogging is for crazy people."

"How have you been, Courtney?" There was an underlying seriousness to the question. "I got your message."

The simple sound of Peter's voice seemed to center Courtney and she inhaled deeply. He'd been her therapist for nearly two years after Theresa's death and he'd helped her through the most difficult and painful part of her life. She'd missed him terribly when he'd finally pushed her out of his nest and told her she was ready to face the rest of her life on her own, and she asked if she could reserve the right to come back for a mental tune-up every so often. He'd agreed with a grin. She called him periodically just to check in and let him know she was still surviving.

"I'm doing okay," she said honestly. "I'm selling the house. Finally."

"That's great. That's a big step."

She could see his smile in her mind just as clearly as if she'd been sitting across from him. "It is. I almost chickened out, but I pulled myself together. It's just too big for me here. And I feel... stuck. I feel stuck here, Peter." She lowered her voice. "She's been gone for two and a half years, and some mornings, I feel like it was yesterday and that I've made no progress at all moving forward with my life."

"And the other mornings?"

The smile came when she knew her answer was totally honest. "The other mornings are great. I feel good. I feel like I have a life of my own."

"Perfect. That's what I hoped to hear. You know this stuff is all perfectly normal, right?"

Courtney nodded into the phone. "Yeah. I do. I really do. It doesn't keep the weird feelings away, though."

"No, it doesn't."

There was a beat of silence. She'd always had trouble with those in her sessions with Peter. He liked to leave the conversation open, knowing she'd fill the silence eventually. An old therapist's trick, she was sure, designed to get the patient talking, but there were times when it made her want to scream. This time, though, she took the opening, surprising herself. "I was thinking...didn't you tell me a while back that there was a group for people whose spouses have been gone for a while? That they meet a couple times a month?"

"I did."

"Does that group still exist? And are they open to new members?"

"I can find out for you, but I'm sure they are. I thought you didn't like the idea of a group meeting."

She knew he was leading her, wanting to make sure she was up to this. He'd suggested she sit in on a bereavement group a few months after Theresa's death. He thought it would help her to see that she wasn't alone in her situation, that others were going through the same thing and helping one another cope. She'd agreed reluctantly, had attended the meeting in the basement of a church, wary and uncertain. And she'd left less than halfway through, feeling beaten and bombarded, taken off guard by so much raw grief. She couldn't stand it, all that pain floating around the room like a big, black cloud of anguish. She ran out of the church and promptly threw up into a nearby shrub. She'd never gone back.

"I think I'm better able to handle such a thing now," she said with confidence. "I just need to know that what I'm going through is common and that it'll pass. I'd like to be able to talk to somebody else who's in the same situation. I think I'm ready for that."

"I think you are, too," Peter agreed, and she could sense his pride in her progress. "I'm happy to hear all this, Courtney."

She had wandered into the living room as she talked and now plopped down onto the couch. The entertainment center seemed a little bare without the pictures, but she didn't let herself dwell on it. "I miss her, Peter. I miss her every single day. But I don't want to be stuck in the same place for the rest of my life, you know? I don't think she'd want that for me."

"I don't think she would either," Peter agreed.

"I'd like to date. I mean, I've dated. A little. Here and there." If she could even call them dates. "But I'd like to date the same person more than once or twice." She laughed softly at that, as did Peter. "I'd like to have sex again, for God's sake. Sex that means something. I'm only thirty-five years old. I want to fall in love again. I'm too young to be a widow forever."

"These are all very healthy, very normal feelings you're having, Courtney. They're good signs. You're making progress."

Courtney crossed her legs at the ankle on the coffee table. "Yeah? Well, it certainly doesn't feel like it sometimes."

"I know. But trust me. You're doing great. Let me get the information for you on the group and I'll get back to you, okay?"

"I'd appreciate it."

"You're doing great," he stressed again. "You really are."

"Thanks, Peter."

She hit the Off button on the phone. Fatigue suddenly settled on her like a lead blanket. She knew there were three more boxes upstairs that needed to go out to the garage, but she couldn't seem to command her body off the couch. She'd been working nonstop all weekend and now it was Monday morning. Already. And she was exhausted. All the things Rachel asked her to pack away or neaten or hide or change had been taken care of. Boxes of Theresa's stuff were labeled with black marker and piled neatly in the garage, something she didn't want to dwell on. There was a part of her that felt like she'd just relegated Theresa to cold storage, and that made her heart ache.

In addition, the For Sale sign was going up today. She wondered if she was ready for that. Not that it mattered at this point.

"Too late to turn back now," she said with a sigh, hauling herself up off the couch, determined to take care of the last three boxes before her limbs protested completely.

❖

"Holy cow, you're a big guy, aren't you?"

Rachel scanned the chart on the clipboard that hung from the chain link gate. The dog was a mix of German shepherd and Lab and he was huge. He was almost five years old and his owner had passed away suddenly. No family members could take him and he'd ended up here at Happy Acres. His fur was falling out in clumps, which Rachel knew was due to his nervousness, and she immediately felt sympathy for him. She opened the gate slowly, murmuring reassurances to him. He watched her warily, his big brown eyes taking her in. She didn't approach, though. She squatted in the doorway, leash in one hand, treat in the other.

"Come here, buddy. Want to go for a walk? Get a little air? It's kind of stuffy in here." She held the treat out so he could get a good whiff. "You can have this if you want. Come on, Rex."

He looked from her face to the treat and back again, then scooched toward her one small inch at a time, watching carefully.

Rachel made no sudden moves, knowing how scared Rex must be, how confused. *First, he loses his master. Then he loses his home.* Rachel's heart broke for him. At his age and size, it would be next to impossible to find someone to adopt him. But if there was one thing Rachel Hart loved, it was a challenge. She also loved Happy Acres because it was an animal shelter that gave dogs like Rex a chance. There was a strict no-kill policy. He could stay here as long as necessary and Rachel would pay for it herself, if need be.

His nose got closer to the treat. Rachel didn't move it. He sniffed, glancing up at her every couple of seconds as he stretched his body as far as he could, ready to spring back to the corner at the slightest provocation.

"It's okay, Rex. You can have it. Go ahead."

He was close enough now. He nibbled at the treat, but Rachel held on, forcing him to stay close. He was surprisingly gentle and she smiled at him, reassuring him with soft words until she was able to scratch under his chin. He didn't pull away, but let her touch him as he chewed, still watching her closely.

She spent close to fifteen minutes stroking him and talking to him before she clipped the leash to his green Happy Acres collar and stood. "What do you say, buddy? Want to feel the sun? It's damn hot, I'll tell you that. You probably won't want to be out there long."

He fell into step at her left in a perfect heel. She did a double take at him, surprised by his obedience. Rex's owner had obviously spent time with him. That just made his situation seem even sadder to her.

She took him out the back door and into the blazing early morning sunshine. This was how Rachel Hart started her day. She woke up early, had her coffee and ate breakfast as she read the newspaper. She went through her list of the day's appointments, which generally didn't begin until mid- to late-afternoon. Then she dressed in comfortable clothes and drove out to Happy Acres where she walked dogs for two or three hours, rain or shine. It was the best way she'd found to clear her head, organize her thoughts, plan sales strategies. The other volunteers there said she had a way with the animals, that she was somehow able to reassure them and earn their trust. She shrugged those comments off regularly, saying she was just nice to them, that was all, it was no big deal. They just shook their heads and smiled knowingly.

The grass was barely dewy at all this morning. The temperature had only dropped to the low seventies last night, and people were starting to get cranky. The heat didn't bother Rachel much, but she knew the forecast end to the heat wave would bring welcome relief to western New York. There were people who'd never left this area their entire life who would still complain about the weather. Rachel's mother was one of them.

She willed the thoughts from her head. It was too early in the morning to deal with thoughts of the woman who'd brought her into the world. Instead she focused on Rex as he sniffed at a nearby clump of grass. Thinking of him and his situation of loss logically brought her mind to her newest client.

Rachel wasn't impressed easily, but Courtney McAllister had impressed her. Not that Rachel had let on that she thought so. Frankly, she was still annoyed that she'd been made to feel like such a moron, but she'd get past it. She did feel, however, that it had taken some balls for Courtney to call and apologize and ask her for a second chance. Rachel had a hard time imagining what it must be like to lose a partner. It was difficult to look at somebody like Courtney—young, vibrant, very attractive—and think of her as a widow, but that's exactly what she was. What Rachel had suggested she do in order to better sell her house must have cut through her skin like a razor. She shook her head in disgust, annoyed at herself for not being better prepared, for not having that vital piece of information.

The thing that surprised her the most, though, was the seeming lack of bitterness Courtney showed. Her smile seemed genuine. She was friendly. Granted, Rachel knew nothing at all about her relationship with her late partner—for all she knew, they might have been miserable together. But here Courtney was, no older than her mid-thirties, and she was now forced to start life all over again. Most people at that age were looking forward toward the future, toward a second home or a yearly vacation or newer, bigger investments. Courtney McAllister had no choice but to go back to square one and start from the beginning. Again.

I'd be furious, Rachel thought, inexplicably angry for this woman she barely knew. Life could be so unfair. *I'd be mad at the entire world and I'd let everybody know it.*

"Just like Mom," she said aloud, shaking her head with a knowing grimace of realization. If you looked up the word "bitter" in the dictionary, there would be a picture of Alice Sullivan, Rachel's mother. She'd taken the definition and made it her own after Rachel's father left her. The sweet, gentle, loving woman Rachel remembered from her childhood had vanished, leaving in her place a sour woman full of anger and hostility. Now that Rachel was an adult, she was able to step back and see things a bit more clearly. She was able to understand what her mother had gone through and how she'd felt. But that had been many, many years ago, and not much had changed. Even remarried, nobody did embittered and resentful better than Alice. How Courtney had managed to avoid any semblance of cynicism, Rachel had no idea.

A bead of sweat trickled down the center of her back as the morning sun beat down on her. Rex began to pant as they walked, but he never once pulled on the leash; there was always slack.

"You're a good boy, Rex. We're going to find you a new home. Don't you worry." She scratched the top of his head and turned them back the way they'd come.

As she led him back inside, her thoughts still fleetingly on Courtney, she remembered that she had the For Sale sign in the trunk of her car. She was planning on swinging by Courtney's place to pound it into the front lawn on her way back from Happy Acres this morning. She absently wondered how Courtney would handle seeing it.

❖

"Hey there, good looking." Danny was dressed snappily in black chinos and a subtly patterned short-sleeve shirt of black and turquoise. He flopped into his chair and popped open his briefcase, then pulled some files out and set the case on the floor next to his desk. "How's things?"

"Not bad, Dan," Rachel replied, her attention turning back to her monitor. "How 'bout you? Business good?"

"It's slowing down. We're heading into the quieter season." The sounds of tapping keys filled the air as he logged into his computer. "And frankly, I could use the break. This summer has been crazy."

"Tell me about it."

The housing market had a fluctuation that was largely unpredictable, and Rachel had learned that it was almost always feast or famine. Either everybody was buying and selling or nobody was. She'd been a realtor for over a decade and she still had trouble getting a handle on the changeability.

She scribbled some notes on the paper in front of her. She was looking at recent listings, trying to match up possibilities with her clients who were in the market for new homes. Taking them from house to house was her least favorite part of the job. Most people tended to have a hard time seeing potential. Their first inclination was to pick apart all the negative aspects of a house rather than to see the possibilities. Trying to shift their perspective without sounding like a stereotypical salesperson could be very exhausting.

"So here's a weird coincidence," Danny said from across the office. "I've got a client who's looking to buy, right? He gives me his price range and I pick some possibilities out for him. I give him the list and one of the houses on it—which just happens to be two blocks from me and James—is the house he lived in with his first wife more than fifteen years ago. Can you believe that?"

Rachel made a sound of disbelief along with him and then went back to her monitor for several minutes before registering what he'd said. She glanced back at him. "Danny? Did you say a house near yours is for sale?"

"Yeah, it just went up last week. It's two streets over."

"Is there a listing on here?" She gestured to her computer.

"Yeah, but it's quite a bit cheaper than the places you're used to selling." He winked at her.

"I'd like to see it anyway."

"Okay, I'll link you. It's a great little place. Small for the neighborhood, but nicely maintained and cute as all hell. It'd be just right for one person or a couple." He punched some buttons on his keyboard, then hit Enter with a flourish. "There you go."

Rachel opened her e-mail, clicked on the link he'd sent, and took a look.

It was perfect.

❖

Courtney was nervous. She hadn't expected to be. After all, what was the big deal? She was going to simply sit in, listen, see if this was for her. That's all. She didn't even have to open her mouth if she didn't want to.

She sat in her Jetta in the parking lot and watched the kids on the nearby playground. The heat hadn't broken much, but it was definitely cooler than it had been. Children shrieked in delight as they ran through the shooting water of the sprinkler area to her left. She smiled, vaguely remembering what it was like to be that carefree, to spend the long, toasty summers howling with glee over something as simple as getting sprayed by cool water. She sighed wistfully.

The community center was a sprawling, one-story building made of neat and tidy brick. It wasn't large, but it was bigger than she'd assumed after years of driving by and seeing it from the street. Courtney was impressed by the center itself as well as the grounds. Everything was orderly, from the landscaping to the garbage cans. It was hard to believe she was in the city and not a suburb. Whoever managed this area did a nice job.

Steeling herself, she palmed her keys and exited her car, locking it, but leaving the windows cracked a bit. The walkway wound past the swing set and jungle gym, and Courtney took a deep breath to steady her nerves as she followed it, finally pulling one of the double doors open.

In the hallway, silence engulfed her immediately, surprising her with how thoroughly the doors and walls sealed out the sound from the playground. The shrieking was gone. The hum of passing traffic had dissipated. The air was so still that for a split second, Courtney wondered if she'd suddenly lost her hearing. She stayed completely motionless, noting the clean smell of the place, like somebody had wiped down the walls with a pine-scented cleanser. Then a door clicked from the hall, the murmur of voices filtered in her direction, and she was released from her seemingly frozen state. She stepped toward the sounds, her sandals slapping loudly on the hard floor.

She hadn't expected the building to be air-conditioned and she felt goose bumps break out along her bare arms. *There's never a happy medium in western New York, is there?* she thought with a grimace, not for the first time. *It's either sweltering or freezing.* She was not a fan of air-conditioning and wasn't looking forward to spending the next hour in a constant shiver. A jacket was the last thing on her mind in the early days of August, but she couldn't help thinking how much of a help one would be now. Her tank top was almost useless, and she wrapped her arms around herself in an attempt to ward off the chill. She scanned the doors down the hall, looking for number 217.

There were four people inside when Courtney peeked around the doorjamb. Three women and one man looked up as she approached and one woman walked toward her, hand outstretched, smile on her face.

"Hi there," she said cheerfully. "Are you looking for Beyond the Grief?"

Courtney inwardly cringed at the title of the group, just as she had the first time she'd heard it, but nodded and took the offered hand. "Did I find the right room?"

"You did. I'm Constance Mays. I facilitate." Courtney knew from the information Peter had given her that the job of the facilitator was simply to get people talking and keep any one person from monopolizing the floor. Constance seemed to have more than enough energy to do so. She was a petite woman in her mid-sixties with salt-and-pepper hair that she wore short and wavy. Her soft eyes were brown and kind. Her handshake was warm and more comforting than firm.

She guided Courtney into the room and introduced her to the others. Joanne was in her late sixties and looked very tired. Lisa was around Courtney's age, which surprised her, and her smile was friendly. Dave was a big hulk of a man who sealed his fate with Courtney when he scanned her up and down and smirked. She put him in his late fifties and then tried hard not to look at him again.

"We're just waiting for a couple more members who said they were coming," Constance informed her as she pulled some plastic chairs from the stacks against the wall. "Is this your first group like this?"

Courtney sat in the empty orange chair next to Lisa, and Dave sat directly across from them in the circle. "Um…well, I tried to attend a bereavement group a year or two ago, but…it wasn't for me."

Lisa smiled knowingly. "Me, neither," she whispered so only Courtney could hear.

"And how long have you been widowed?" Constance asked, completing her arrangement of the circle.

"Three years in January." She knew she should elaborate, would have to eventually, but couldn't manage to out herself within five minutes of meeting these people. And she was annoyed at her inability.

Before Constance could inquire further, three more people entered the room in fairly quick succession. A man with snowy white hair and the same tired look on his face that Joanne displayed, a woman in her seventies with the gentlest face Courtney had ever seen, and another man in his late fifties or early sixties with light, thinning hair and pale blue eyes.

Looking around the room, Courtney leaned toward Lisa and whispered, "Are we too young to be here?"

Lisa's shoulders moved in a silent giggle and she pushed her blond hair back from her face. "You have no idea how relieved I was when you walked in," she whispered back.

"Richard, Edith, and Ted," Constance said, stretching her arm in Courtney's direction. "This is Courtney. She's going to be joining us tonight."

They nodded in her direction, but said nothing. Edith smiled at her, as did Ted. Richard found a chair and lowered himself into it carefully.

Once they were all seated in the circle, Constance folded her hands together on her knees and looked at each of them with a gentle expression. "So," she said. "How is everybody doing?" Her attention stopped on each person for a few seconds. Courtney squirmed when it was her turn. Moving past her, Constance said, "Lisa? How was the date?"

Lisa shifted in her seat and looked down at her hands. They were nice hands, Courtney noticed. Pretty. Nicely taken care of, but not overly fancy. Clear polish. Smooth, unblemished skin. She wore a single solitary diamond on her right hand. Her left was bare. "It was nice."

"But…" Constance prodded, voicing the unspoken but very loud word that was hanging in the air.

Lisa blew out a breath. Her gaze strayed to Constance, then to Courtney, then back down to her hands. "But I kept comparing him to Stephen. I tried not to. I swear I did. But I just kept thinking, 'his hair is so different, his hands are too small, he's not listening to me, I don't think he gets me like Stephen did.' It really was unfair to the poor guy."

Courtney was unconsciously nodding in agreement. Lisa's description sounded just like every one of the dates she'd had since Theresa had died. It *was* unfair to her dates. And beyond frustrating for her.

"Try multiplying that feeling by ten or fifteen," Joanne said into the stillness of the room. "That's how it feels when you were with your husband for more than forty years. Try to even think about dating after that. *Then* you'll know true grief." Her eyes filled with tears, and Courtney felt a lump of sympathy and solidarity form in her throat.

Next to her, Lisa poked the inside of her cheek with her tongue and said nothing.

"I understand, Lisa." A surprising gentleness emanated from Ted. "I have the same problem comparing my dates to my late wife. I think it happens to all of us."

"It certainly does," Constance stated.

After a few beats of silence, the snowy-haired man named Richard spoke up. "Well." His voice was soft, kind. He reminded Courtney of her grandfather. "I took a lady friend to dinner last week. And I thoroughly enjoyed myself, though I, too, understand what Lisa is saying."

Constance's face bloomed into a grin. "Richard, that's wonderful. Tell us about it, would you?"

"Well." The tired look he'd sported on his way in was suddenly gone, as if his face was a chalkboard and somebody had simply come along with an eraser. "I've known her for quite some time. She lives one floor down at my complex. She lost her husband several years ago." He went on to talk about how the woman had asked Richard if he'd be interested at all in dining with her, how nervous he'd been, and what a terrific time they'd had just laughing and talking. He'd even managed to kiss her good night without dissolving into a quivering puddle of nervousness. Courtney found herself smiling as he told the story, inexplicably happy for this man she'd only met fifteen minutes earlier and about whom she knew nothing at all. She realized suddenly that the purpose of such a group was to offer hope. She realized it because it had been given to her simply by listening to a widower's story of a date. When the hour was over and she was helping to stack the chairs, Courtney felt better than she had in a long time. She silently thanked Peter for the gentle nudge to attend.

Bidding her thanks and good-byes to Constance, and promising to attend again, Courtney headed down the hall, strolling at an easy pace with Lisa.

"What did you think?" Lisa asked. "You didn't say much. Are you okay?"

"Yeah, I am. Actually, I think this is good for me. I've been feeling kind of…stagnant lately, you know?"

"And you lost your husband how long ago? Three years?"

Courtney wet her lips. "Three years in January. My partner. I lost my partner. My wife."

Lisa didn't miss a beat. "Then you and I really are kindred spirits as far as this group goes."

"What do you mean?" Courtney asked as she pushed the double doors open and they were smacked by the difference in temperature.

"Stephen was my fiancé, not my husband. Some of the older members of the group like to remind me of that every chance they get. That my grief isn't as strong or as devastating as theirs." Courtney gave a sympathetic smile to her new friend. "You may get a similar vibe, at least from the women."

"Seeing as Theresa wasn't my husband."

"Exactly. They usually segregate the members by age group, but this batch was so small, it didn't make sense. So here we are."

They laughed at the ridiculousness of the situation, but were content to shrug it off. When they reached their cars, Lisa asked, "Hey, Courtney? Do you think we could, I don't know, get some coffee sometime or something? It'd be nice to be able to talk to somebody about things who's not older than my mom, you know?"

Courtney was touched. "I'd like that."

They exchanged numbers and parted.

Chapter Four

It seemed like every year, Rachel was shocked at how fast the summer had gone. It felt like the flowers had just begun to bloom last week and now Labor Day weekend was on the horizon. She steered her slate blue BMW down the road, absorbing the sunny and pleasant absolutely beautiful day. The heat wave had finally broken and, aside from a few days of rain, the past two weeks had been blissfully moderate.

She felt good. She was pleased with the way this particular client transaction had gone. Courtney McAllister had immediately fallen in love with the small house Danny had recommended and put in an offer the same day she viewed it. Rachel had known the second she saw it online that it would be just the right fit for her client, and she hadn't been wrong. Selling Courtney's larger house had also been a nonissue. Once she'd made the changes Rachel had suggested, it had shown like an immaculate dollhouse and two potential buyers had entered into a bidding war within a week of it going up for sale. Courtney had ended up getting eight thousand dollars more than her asking price, something very pleasing to both her and her realtor.

Rachel was taking a bit of a detour, having just come from an appointment with another potential client referred to her by Danny. It was the Friday before the long weekend and it was going on two o'clock. Courtney's move was happening quicker than most cases, the new listing, the sale, the closing, and the move all happening within a month. Once she was in the right mindset, Courtney seemed to want to get into her new house as soon as possible. Or did she just want to get out of her old one? Since she was in the neighborhood, Rachel thought she'd swing by and see if she was able to catch Courtney before she was done moving out. They'd taken care of the closing that morning, but Courtney had some final things to take care of before she relinquished the keys; the buyers were understanding. Rachel needed to collect the keys and thought she might possibly be able to save Courtney a trip to her office by swinging by and grabbing them in person.

As she turned onto Courtney's street, she passed a moving truck. It was followed by two other cars, neither of which was Courtney's VW. Rachel kept going, wondering if she'd missed her.

At the end of the cul-de-sac, Courtney's gunmetal-colored Jetta sat like a lone boulder in the driveway. Rachel pulled in and parked next to it. The neighborhood was quiet, the sun shining down on the trees whose leaves showed tints of fall coloring along their edges. She inhaled deeply, the fresh air carrying the vague scent of the impending autumn, her favorite season.

The front door of the house was open, the storm door screened. Rachel shaded her eyes against it and looked inside, noting the emptiness.

"Courtney?" she called, the sound echoing through the vacant rooms. She tapped on the door lightly, not wanting to disturb the peacefulness. She called her client's name again, then reached for the handle and pulled the door open.

Despite the fact that she'd been in real estate for most of her adult career, Rachel still found empty houses to be just a little bit eerie, especially after she'd seen them full of furniture and life. She wrapped her arms around herself, trying to ward off the inexplicable chill she got as she entered. She didn't have to go far; Courtney was standing in the middle of the living room alone. Rachel wasn't sure whether or not to approach her and was filled with the sudden sense that she was intruding on a private moment.

"Oh, I'm sorry," she faltered. "I didn't mean to interrupt." As she turned to leave, Courtney spoke.

"It's okay." Her voice was soft and gravelly. "Stay. I'm just about ready to go, anyway."

"I…" Rachel hesitated, embarrassed that she'd walked in on such a personal scene. "I was in the area and thought I'd see if I could save you the trip to my office by just picking up the keys here." She shrugged, not knowing what else to say.

Courtney smiled at her, a gentle curving up of the corners of her mouth that told Rachel she was touched, even if she couldn't verbalize it at the moment. Then she lifted her face to the sun streaming in through the skylights and it shone down on her, bathing her in the warm light. Her hair was pulled back into a haphazard ponytail and the exposure of her throat made her seem so incredibly vulnerable that Rachel had to fight the sudden urge to move closer and protect her.

"Theresa stood just like this, right here, the first time we looked at this place." Courtney's eyes were closed as she reminisced. "Right here. The sun was shining in just like it is today. This spot right here is the reason we bought this house. Theresa loved the sunshine." She took a deep breath and lowered her face. When she turned to look at Rachel, there was a gentle shimmering of unshed tears. "Life turns on a dime, doesn't it?"

Rachel nodded.

Courtney cleared her throat as she dug into the pocket of her jeans and pulled out a set of keys. She crossed the room and placed them into Rachel's palm. "Thanks for saving me a trip. I appreciate it." With that, she took one last look around the empty room, nodded once, seemingly to herself, and exited through the front door.

Rachel was still standing there, the keys a warm weight in her hand, when she heard the Jetta's engine turn over and the car back out of the driveway.

❖

The Sunday before Labor Day was a gorgeous day, sunny, mild, and gently breezy. The lightweight curtains at the open kitchen window fluttered like feathers as Amelia put groceries away, checking with Courtney every few minutes to see where she wanted things.

"I've got to say, C., this place is really looking like a home. I can't believe how much you've gotten done in two days."

Courtney pulled her head out of the refrigerator and smiled. "It's good, huh?"

"It's great. I love it. And I'm glad you're closer now." She slid a box of cereal onto a shelf.

"Me, too."

The move had been one of the hardest things she'd ever done in her life, but she'd made it through. Once her friends had left her on Friday night, she'd cried herself to sleep in her new bedroom that Theresa would never see, feeling more alone than she had in months. But Saturday morning seemed to bring new vitality and she vowed to embrace it. She'd called Lisa from group and talked with her a bit, knowing she would understand. Then she'd spent the day unpacking, washing dishes, hanging pictures, and making the place into what she wanted. When Amelia had arrived late Sunday morning to go grocery shopping with her, her jaw had dropped to the floor like it weighed twenty pounds and she'd stared in disbelief at the living room that looked, well, lived in.

"Hungry?" Courtney asked now. "I'm going to make a sandwich."

"No, I can't stay," Amelia replied, smoothing back her hair. "I've got to get Kyle to the shoe store. I can't believe he waited until three days before school starts to tell me we forgot to get him new sneakers. The crowds are going to be ridiculous."

"There will be you and soccer moms everywhere." Courtney unscrewed the peanut butter jar and made herself a sandwich. "I, on the other hand, am going to sit on my ass on my new porch and have a glass of wine."

"I hate you," Amelia sneered good-naturedly.

"I know." Courtney smiled at her and bit into her late lunch.

The basement door opened with a start and they both jumped, Amelia letting out a little squeak. Mark Benetti peeked his head into the kitchen with a huge grin on his handsome face.

"Sorry about that." He had a toolbox in one hand and he set it on the counter. "Everything looks good down there."

Mark was Theresa's big brother, and he and Courtney had always been close. Their friendship had grown even closer after Theresa died; they'd leaned on each other and helped one another be strong through those first brutal months. Theresa's parents had been so devastated, it was all they could do to wake up each morning. They were no help for Mark. Courtney looked at him now, his curly brown hair rumpled, his dark eyes so like Theresa's, and felt indescribably thankful that she had him in her life. He meant the world to her.

She'd had an engineer's inspection before she bought the house—Rachel Hart had insisted upon it—but Mark still thought it would be a good idea if he checked things out himself "just to be sure." It was a sweet, albeit unnecessary, male gesture and Courtney loved him for it.

She handed over her sandwich and he took an enormous bite. "Thanks for checking, Markie. I appreciate it."

He wiped his hand on his gray T-shirt and nodded.

Courtney watched him, then glanced over at Amelia, who was organizing her spice cupboard, and her heart swelled. She felt so fortunate to have these people who loved her, these people who looked out for her and took care of her and came running anytime she needed something. She was about to speak her thoughts aloud when her doorbell rang. She was so unfamiliar with the sound that she just stared at Amelia for several seconds.

"Hello? There's somebody at your door," Amelia said, shooing her out of the kitchen by waving a dish towel at her.

Courtney laughed as she crossed the living room to the front door, which was open. Through the screen door, she could see a very tall silhouette standing on her porch and she faltered, suddenly wishing she was wearing something nicer than old gym shorts and a beat-up T-shirt.

Rachel Hart was dressed more casually than Courtney had ever seen her and yet she was still stunning. Her cargo shorts were navy blue and her mile-long legs were surprisingly tanned beneath them.

She had simple brown sandals on her feet, her toenails polished a deep purple. Her scoop-neck T-shirt was bright white and hugged her body as if it was tailored for her—which Courtney had to admit, it might have been—and tortoiseshell sunglasses completed the look. Her hair was loose and fluffy and looked impossibly soft, glimmering in the sun. Her hands were full and she looked the tiniest bit…unnerved.

"Rachel," Courtney said as she reached for the door. "Hi. It's nice to see you." And it was. Courtney had to admit that, too. Rachel handed a bottle of wine to Courtney, then pushed her sunglasses up onto her head. Courtney felt the need to stifle a gasp when the crystal blue of her eyes was revealed.

"I was in the neighborhood," Rachel said with a shrug, surprising Courtney with what seemed to be a touch of shyness.

"You say that a lot," Courtney said, grinning at her. "Come in. Please." She stepped back.

Rachel held out the other hand, which grasped a wooden and pewter bird feeder. "This is for your new yard."

Courtney blinked at her, enormously touched. "Rachel. This is so sweet of you. It's beautiful. You didn't have to do this."

"I wanted to." Rachel looked at the floor, and it seemed like now that her hands were empty, she didn't know what to do with them. She tugged at her earring and then glanced up at the living room…and blinked in shock. "Wow. You did all this in two days?" There wasn't a box to be seen and the room looked like it had been arranged this way for months.

Courtney's laugh filled the air. "School starts on Wednesday but I need to go in on Tuesday, so I wanted to have tomorrow to get myself ready for it. Besides, I didn't really have much. And the cable's not hooked up yet, much to my dismay, so there wasn't the ever-present possibility of plopping down to watch TV. But it looks pretty good. It's coming along."

Rachel was interrupted by Amelia, who entered from the kitchen, her keys jingling in one hand. "Baby, I've got to go," she said, rubbing Courtney's arm.

"Oh," Courtney said. "Okay. Um, Rachel Hart, this is my best friend, Amelia Tyler. Amelia, my realtor, Rachel."

Amelia stuck out her hand, and Courtney could see her trying to be discreet about sizing Rachel up. "Nice to meet you, Ms. Hart. My husband, Carl, is a mortgage broker and works over at the Citibank in Pittsford. I believe you've worked with him on occasion."

Rachel's face lit in recognition as they shook hands. "Yes. Oh, Carl's great. Very easy to work with. Please tell him I said hello."

"Will do." Amelia kissed Courtney on the cheek. "Call you later, honey."

"Okay," Courtney said as Amelia took her leave. She and Rachel stood somewhat awkwardly in the middle of the living room until a loud crash sounded from the kitchen.

"I'm okay," Mark called out and made Courtney grin.

"My brother-in-law," she said by way of explanation to Rachel, pointing toward the kitchen with a jerk of her head. "He was checking out the furnace and stuff. Hooking up the washer and dryer." Turning to the kitchen, she said, "Mark, can you come in here? I'd like you to meet somebody."

Mark's handsome features were tinted a gentle pink when he entered the living room, toolbox in hand and a smudge of peanut butter at the corner of his mouth. Courtney reached up and wiped it away with a chuckle before making the introductions.

"Heading out?" Courtney asked.

Mark nodded, his eyes darting all over the room. "Yeah. Yeah, I am. We still on for tomorrow night?"

"As long as I can get my school stuff all set, I'll be over for at least the first half."

"Cool. I'll see you then." He turned to Rachel and did his best to look her in the eye. "Nice to meet you, Ms. Hart."

"Rachel. Please. It was nice to meet you, too."

He blushed some more and practically ran out the door.

Courtney waited until she heard the engine of his pickup turn over before she burst into laughter. "Oh my God. Poor Markie. I think you made him nervous."

"How so?" Rachel asked, smiling at Courtney.

Courtney cocked her head at Rachel, still chuckling. "Did you look in the mirror this morning?"

A small circle of red suddenly blossomed on each of Rachel's cheeks and she cleared her throat. "Well, he's very cute. It's too bad I don't play for his team or I'd seriously think about asking him out." She then blinked at Courtney, almost as if she'd just realized what she'd said.

Courtney abruptly stopped laughing altogether.

Did she just come out to me? With the entry of that thought into her brain, Courtney realized that she hadn't even wondered. She'd just assumed Rachel was a gay-friendly straight woman who'd found a niche customer base in the queer market. She found herself weirdly excited to learn otherwise, like she'd just discovered her team had a ringer. Part of her wanted to dance a little jig of happiness, but she managed to maintain her composure.

Looking down at her hands, she was thankful they were full or she was certain they'd be jittery. For some reason, today Rachel was making her a little jumpy, and she suddenly sympathized with Mark. Taking a glance at her right hand, she did a double take and remarked, "This is a really nice bottle of wine, Rachel. Wow."

"I'm glad you like it."

"I know it's only early afternoon, but I was going to have a glass anyway." Leaning in, she lowered her voice conspiratorially. "Back-to-school time. It's when all us teachers take up drinking again. Care to join me?"

Rachel smiled, a real, genuine smile, despite the fact that she seemed a bit nervous. Courtney was taken aback by the way it completely altered her face, how it went from cool and composed to friendly and gentle. "No. Thank you, though. I have to get going."

Courtney's disappointment deflated her somewhat. "Oh. Okay."

"But I do appreciate the invite. Another time, maybe?"

"Definitely. Thank you for stopping by." She held up her hands. "With presents. For future reference, anybody bearing gifts is automatically moved to the head of the entry line. The bouncers have instructions."

"I'll keep that in mind." Moving toward the door, Rachel turned back to her. "The house looks great, Courtney."

"Thanks. Come back again when you have more time. I'll give you the tour and you can see it actually furnished." Courtney had trouble keeping her eyes from roaming over Rachel's backside as she headed down the walk to her car parked on the street. *Nice.* Her brain was already busy moving Rachel's ranking from Icy Cold to Mildly Cool. And just a tad insecure, which Courtney found intriguing. *If I could just get her closer to Almost Warm, that'd be a start,* she thought with a giggle. *I might be able to work with that.* Then she stopped, realizing exactly the route her train of thought had gone. What surprised her, though, wasn't that she'd actually been thinking somewhat sexual thoughts about a woman other than Theresa.

What surprised her was that she'd enjoyed it.

She chewed on that thought as she stood in the doorway and watched Rachel drive away down the quiet street.

Courtney busied herself for another hour, throwing a load of laundry in just to test Mark's washer-hooking-up abilities. She organized the upstairs linen closet, piling the towels in a neat, geometric stack. She smiled when she thought how Theresa would have made a snide comment about her anal-retentiveness.

It was the opening day of football season, and she was almost glad she didn't have the cable hooked up yet. Much as she'd enjoy watching the games, it was a beautiful day and she so wanted to test out her new porch and observe her new neighborhood. The bottle of wine Rachel brought was staring at her from the kitchen counter. She picked it up and studied it, debating. It was a very good bottle of wine. Courtney wasn't a connoisseur by any means, but she enjoyed wine and was learning what she could little by little. This was a scarlet red merlot that she'd seen in her favorite wine store several weeks before. The description made it sound sumptuous, but on her teacher's salary she balked at the $34 price tag, thinking she'd wait for some kind of celebration before she made a splurge like that. The fact that Rachel brought it to her was a strange, but not unwelcome coincidence.

"A new house seems like celebration enough," she said aloud as she dug her corkscrew out of the drawer and went to work.

Courtney's mother had given her and Theresa matching wicker rockers when they'd moved into their house. Now they occupied Courtney's new open front porch and looked like they belonged there. The house was a comforting beige color that bordered on almost-yellow. The trim was cream and the accent was the deep forest green of a Christmas tree. The brown wicker rockers looked as if they were designed specifically for that particular porch, their dark green cushions matching the accent color of the house almost exactly.

Courtney dropped into the far chair and propped her feet up on the ridge of the porch, pushing slowly to rock, enjoying the openness of the design. She sipped the wine and her eyes closed almost immediately as she let the flavors and body of it roll around her tongue.

"Good God," she whispered. It wasn't often that sipping wine was akin to an almost sexual experience, but this was so good and so sensual as she swallowed and felt it flow into her body like some magic elixir. It was the best wine she'd ever tasted.

"Howdy, neighbor!"

The unexpected voice was frighteningly close and so loud that it made Courtney literally flinch in her seat. Her wine sloshed, dripping onto her bare thigh, and she pressed her hand to her chest in a vain attempt to calm her racing heart. She turned to her right and saw the tall, lanky man standing in the driveway next door. He had unkempt dark hair and Coke bottle glasses that were too big for his gaunt face, but he was dressed neatly in jeans, a tucked-in blue T-shirt, and work boots. Courtney put him in his mid- to late forties.

When she thought she could speak without squeaking, she said, "My God, you scared the crap out of me."

The man chuckled, a weird, stilted sound that made Courtney furrow her brows at him. "Sorry about that. My mom always said I move like a cat." He moved closer to her house and stuck his hand over the ridge of the porch. "Bob Ross."

Courtney shook his hand. "Courtney McAllister." She had to tug a bit to get him to release her.

"Nice to meet you, Courtney. You all settled in?"

"Yeah, I think I am."

"Good for you. Good for you. You from around here?"

She nodded. "Been here all my life."

"Me, too," he said, matching the pace of her nod. "You work nearby?"

"I teach high school English." If he noticed she left off the location, he didn't show it. "You?"

"I'm the head groundskeeper over at Wood and Russell."

"Yeah?" She had to admit to being impressed. Wood and Russell was a nationally known marketing company housed in an old mansion estate on East Avenue. The outside was positively pristine with thick, lush grass, lilac trees, and several varieties of flowers that appeared as bursts of radiant color on the property. You couldn't drive by without remarking on its beauty. "You do a great job. That place is gorgeous." Glancing over Bob's head, she could see that he worked as hard on his own property. It was maniacally neat and she immediately felt the pressure to keep up.

He looked down at his feet, seemingly embarrassed by the compliment. "Yeah. Thanks. I've got a great garden in the back. Lots of vegetables. You like vegetables?"

"Sure. Yeah, I like them."

"You like zucchini and tomatoes? I've got a ton of them now that the season's coming to an end."

Courtney nodded, taking a too-large gulp of her wine.

"I'll bring some over for you. I've got way too many to eat."

She had the sudden vision of Bob showing up at her door at all hours, his arms overflowing with zucchini, an expectant smile on his face. "That's nice of you," she said, hoping she was keeping the dread from being obvious. After all, maybe he was just a nice guy and she was jumping to conclusions.

He looked down at his feet. "It's nothing. I like to share is all." Looking back up at her through his thick lenses, he asked the inevitable. "You married?"

Courtney swallowed, not willing to give away too much to this total stranger, but hating the idea of lying. "No, not right now." She could have sworn she saw his eyes light up.

"Maybe we could have a drink sometime. Or something."

Wow, you don't waste any time, do you, Bob? "You know, I'm just recently out of a relationship." The lie slipped out so easily,

Courtney was ashamed of herself. Theresa would have been so disappointed. "Bad breakup." She punctuated the story with a you-know-how-it-is expression tossed his way, which caused him to nod sympathetically. Inside, she cringed. Theresa would have just blurted out the facts, told him in no uncertain terms how things were and she and Bob probably would have ended up being buddies. She had been proud as well as no-nonsense that way, always standing up for herself, and people respected her for it. But now, without Theresa's strength bolstering her, Courtney floundered, stumbling a bit, and she was embarrassed by her lack of conviction. If Bob noticed, he didn't comment. "You seem like a really nice guy, but I'm just not ready to jump back in, you know?"

Before he could respond, her phone rang. *Saved by the bell!* She sent up a silent prayer of thanks. "That's me," she said, jerking a thumb over her shoulder. "I should probably get that."

He stepped back from her porch. "Sure. I'll see you later, then."

"It was nice to meet you, Bob."

"You hang in there, Courtney. It'll get better," he reassured her as she took her wine and fled to safety.

Amelia was on the other end of the line. She sounded a little muffled and the background noise almost drowned her out completely.

"Where are you?" Courtney asked, sticking her finger in her other ear in the hopes of hearing better.

"I'm in the damn mall," came the irritated response. "I swear to God, if my children live to see their senior years, it'll be a goddamn miracle." There was some static and some shuffling, then, "Are you out of your mind? Those shoes are a hundred and seventy-five dollars. What the hell do you need one hundred and seventy-five dollar shoes for? Are your feet that important?" There was a garbled response that Courtney couldn't quite make out, then Amelia's irritated voice again. "Do I look like I'm made of money to you?" Courtney stifled a laugh and waited patiently for her friend to return to their conversation. "C.? You there?"

"Still here."

"Sorry about that. Do yourself a favor. Don't ever have kids.

If you decide against your better judgment that you want them, I'll give you mine."

"So noted," Courtney said, knowing that the truth of the matter was, Amelia's kids were her world, her heart, and her loves. She'd do anything and everything for them and usually did. They were good boys who would grow up to respect their significant others because of the values Amelia and Carl instilled in them. If Courtney were ever to become a mom, she could only hope to be as good at it as Amelia.

"I wanted to see what was up with the visit from Ms. Icy Cool." As if the idea had only occurred to her, she quickly added, "She's not still there, is she?"

"No, she's not. She only stayed a minute."

"You weren't kidding about her looks. Damn, that girl is *hot*. I'll bet she's crushed a few men's hearts in her time. I think she turned *me* on."

"Poor Mark practically fell all over himself."

Amelia laughed, remembering his faltering after seeing Rachel from the kitchen. "I told him he should ask her out. She'd turn him down, of course, but it would be good practice for the boy."

Courtney dug her fingertips into the back of her shoulders, kneading the knot that had formed there from all the lifting and moving she'd done over the past three days. "Well, she'd turn him down anyway, because—as she informed me—she doesn't play for his team."

Only the sounds of frantic shoppers could be heard on the other end of the phone for several seconds. Courtney could almost hear the whirring of Amelia's brain as she processed the information. "Wait. She *told* you that? Just…told you? Out of the blue?"

"Completely out of the blue."

"Wow. Now I *know* she's crushed some male hearts. You're going to jump on this, right?"

Courtney frowned. "Jump on what? What do you mean?"

"What do you mean, what do I mean?" Amelia's eye roll was almost audible. "You don't just blurt out that kind of information unless there's a reason."

"I'm not following you."

"Of course you're not, because you're *out of practice*. Mark shouldn't be asking that girl out. You should."

"What? Are you crazy?"

"No, I'm not, but you are if you think she didn't just give you a personal invitation to ask her out. Come on, C. Open your eyes."

Courtney was certain that Amelia was reading into things way too intently. "That's just nuts. The woman doesn't even like me that much."

"Excuse me, but didn't she show up at your house today? *With gifts?*"

"She probably does that for all her clients. It's good business."

"Good business, my ass. I'm telling you, the girl has opened the door for you. All you have to do is step through."

Courtney's heart was pounding at the prospect. "I don't know, Meel."

"At least think about it. Okay?"

"Yeah. All right." She knew she'd think about nothing else now. Wanting desperately to change the subject, she told Amelia about New Neighbor Bob. She tried hard not to make her description of their conversation come across as creepy.

"Is he creepy?" Amelia asked, not missing a beat. "He sounds kind of creepy."

"I think that remains to be seen. I'm going to wait to pass judgment until I know for sure. I mean, the guy offered me vegetables. I thought that was nice."

"He offered you zucchini and then asked you out. It's creepy is what it is."

Courtney laughed at Amelia's tone and promised to be careful with the information she gave out to strangers. She was still chuckling when they hung up, but her thoughts went traitorously zipping back to the gorgeous realtor who had visited a couple hours ago.

"Good business, my ass. I'm telling you, the girl has opened the door for you. All you have to do is step through."

Was Amelia right? Courtney knew she and Rachel hadn't exactly started things on a positive note. Even during their business transactions, the realtor had been professionally detached, not venturing very far into personal conversation. Oh, she wasn't mean or standoffish. She was simply…coolly professional. Today, however, she'd seemed a bit out of her element, a description Courtney would bet money wasn't one that was applied to Rachel Hart, Million Dollar Producer, very often. She wondered what that had been about.

She wandered into the kitchen and refilled her glass, wanting very much to go back out onto her porch, but grimacing when she peered out the window and saw Bob working in his front yard. Instead, she got a folding lawn chair from the basement and took it out into the driveway, putting her house between her and her neighbor. She felt guilty doing it but just wasn't in the mood for small talk at that moment. She wanted to think about what Amelia had said.

❖

What the hell?

Rachel entered her top-floor apartment and tossed her keys onto the small mahogany table along the wall. She fell back against the closed door and blew out a breath, trying unsuccessfully to clear her mind.

She felt like a pod person from *Invasion of the Body Snatchers*, barely recognizing herself. What the hell had she been thinking today? She never personally visited a client after the sale. Never. When it was done, it was done. End of story. Sure, she always sent something…a fruit basket or a bottle of champagne or whatever…to say thanks and to ensure that the new owners would pass Rachel's name around to friends and family looking to buy or sell. It was a smart thing to do, good business. But she never just popped in like she had today at Courtney's. Her clients were her clients, not her friends. But she'd felt…compelled. It was the weirdest thing and she had no explanation for it. She thought of Courtney, setting up house in a new place, and she just…wanted to see her. And she'd taken gifts, for Christ's sake. *Personal* gifts. A handcrafted bird feeder? Seriously?

She pressed her fingertips harshly into her eyelids and wondered in disbelief as she recalled the mother horror of all horrors: by outing herself, she'd practically thrown herself at Courtney. Thrown herself! Like a schoolgirl! She might as well have shown up in a T-shirt emblazoned with I Like Girls across the front. What the hell had she been thinking? Once she realized what she'd done, she couldn't get out of there fast enough. It was all she could do to keep from having a full-fledged panic attack right there in Courtney's new living room. She was barely able to stop her hands from shaking and she was still surprised she hadn't sprinted to her car once she'd cleared the front door. Courtney must think she was a complete whack job, not to mention pathetic and prone to oversharing.

"God, could I have been more obvious?" she chastised herself aloud.

She flopped onto her leather couch, thoroughly disgusted with herself. Her client's face invaded her mind unbidden. Courtney had looked so cute in her shorts and ratty T-shirt, all settled in and ready for a glass of wine. She seemed so much better than when she'd signed the papers for the sale or when Rachel had picked up the keys. Today, she'd been relaxed, happy even. It was a nice change.

Rachel stood up and crossed the large, open living room to the French doors on the outside wall. They led to a roomy balcony that overlooked the intersection of Goodman and Park from four stories up, and it was her favorite spot in the world to sit and watch the world go by. This balcony was a large part of the reason she'd not only purchased the building, but decided to renovate the top floor for her own living space, taking two midsized apartments and remodeling them into one big one that she lovingly referred to as "the penthouse." The three floors below housed her six tenants.

Sundays were usually very busy for her, but today being the day before a holiday, she had no appointments or open houses scheduled and was blissfully happy to have the day to herself. She pulled the doors open and let the warm late-summer air flow into the room, inhaling deeply in the hopes of grounding herself, of shaking off the inexplicable weirdness that had caused her uncharacteristic behavior today. A soft breeze lifted her hair and rearranged it before setting it back down against her head, and she relished the feeling, gentle and pure.

A glass of iced tea and a good book seemed to be the perfect order for the day and a good way to get her mind off the questions poking at her to which she had no answers. The lounge chair on the balcony might as well have been calling her name, its pull was so strong. She headed for the kitchen to get herself the iced tea, passing her answering machine on the way and noting the blinking red light that indicated a message.

Knowing instinctively who it was because everybody else called her cell, she punched the Play button as she walked by. Her little sister's voice filled the room.

"Hey, Raich," Emily said, in her always cheerful tone that would forever sound little-girlish to Rachel, despite the fact that Emily was now married and seven months pregnant. "Just calling to say hi, see what you're up to. I saw a Sold sign on that gigantic house in Pittsford the other day. Congratulations. Anyway, give me a call when you get a free minute so we can catch up. Oh, and I talked to Dad earlier in the week. He said to say hi."

That last bit was added quickly, like somebody turned up the speed on Emily's speech and made her talk faster. Rachel rolled her eyes as she poured her iced tea. Rachel barely spoke to her father. More accurately, she tolerated him and she had every intention of keeping it that way. Emily was always trying to get them to talk in-depth, to visit, to have dinner. She was never successful, but she kept at it. And once she became pregnant after years of trying, their father was around even more often. She was now expecting baby number two, so Rachel knew their father would become an even more common presence in Emily's life, especially now that his second wife was gone. Rachel mentally shrugged. He could say hi all he wanted; Rachel didn't care.

On her way back through the living room, she picked up the remote and clicked on the plasma television that adorned one wall. It was football day, and though she loved to watch the games, it didn't yet feel like fall to her and the draw of the balcony was just too great. She turned the volume up so she could hear the play-by-play, then went outside and stretched her legs out on the lounge. She sipped her tea, listened to John Madden comment on the plays, and tried her best not to think about Courtney McAllister.

CHAPTER FIVE

Mark Benetti's small Cape Cod house was surprisingly well decorated, considering it was inhabited by a single, straight male. His furniture was tasteful and comfortable, with modest pieces purchased from Pier One and Eddie Bauer. His artwork was colorful and interesting, and blended well with the overall look of the place, and he had several lush plants scattered about the living room. Not surprising were the flat-screen television that was a bit larger than necessary and the theater-quality surround sound that was wired throughout the entire first floor.

Mark was a handsome man in a little-boy way. His hair always looked tousled, even after he spent time taming it. He stood just under six feet tall, with a lean, solid build and broad shoulders. His face was soft and gentle, and his eyes so reminded Courtney of Theresa's that she often caught her breath in surprise. His smile was huge as he waved Courtney and Lisa into the living room. He kissed Courtney on the cheek and his gaze settled on Lisa.

"Mark, this is Lisa Whitney. I invited her to tag along today. Don't worry, she's a Bills fan. Lisa, my brother-in-law, Mark Benetti."

The two shook hands a bit longer than necessary and Courtney suppressed a smug grin. She snapped her fingers in front of Mark.

"Hey. Beer?"

Mark blinked. "Oh. Sorry. Sure. Lisa? Beer?"

"That would be great," Lisa answered and Mark, clad in a Bruce Smith football jersey that had seen better days, disappeared into the kitchen. Kickoff had already taken place and she took a seat on the well-worn, comfortable couch next to Courtney. "He's cute," she whispered in Courtney's ear.

Courtney nodded, boosted by Lisa's exuberance. She was glad her new friend had chosen to tag along. Lisa had called earlier that day, knowing Courtney had her first day of school the next morning, and asked if she wanted to go out for her last evening of summer vacation. Since Courtney had already made plans to watch the game with Mark, she invited Lisa to come with her, knowing Mark wouldn't mind. Now she was really glad she had, unexpectedly pleased with the obvious chemistry between the two.

Mark returned with their drinks and the three of them made small talk throughout most of the first quarter of the game as the Buffalo Bills started surprisingly strong. Lisa pointed at the new quarterback.

"You know, he's young, but he's got great potential. Another season or two and he'll be reading the defense like a pro. I hope we give him that long."

Mark blinked at her, then shifted his attention to Courtney as a sad grin split his face. Courtney squinted at him, trying to put a finger on what his expression meant. "I think so, too," he responded. "And he can move."

"Scrambling's a plus," Lisa confirmed with a smile. "We haven't had a scrambler in quite a while. He could be good for us. Now all he needs is some protection and we'll be in good shape. Last year's offensive line was a joke."

Mark beamed in Courtney's direction as Lisa was focused on the television screen and Courtney almost laughed out loud. She knew they'd get along, but had no idea about Lisa's football knowledge. Nothing turned Mark on more than a woman who knew her sports.

She purposely withdrew a bit to let the two of them get to know each other better. As she tried to focus on the game, she was startled to find her thoughts taking her back to the previous day's visit from her realtor. What was it about Rachel Hart that kept her in the forefront of Courtney's thoughts? It certainly wasn't that she was open and approachable; she was quite the opposite. And she was about as warm as a chunk of ice, so it wasn't that. Courtney's brows knitted together as she struggled to come up with a suitable explanation for why she couldn't get this woman off her mind.

As if reading her thoughts, Mark pulled her out of her own head. "Hey, Courtney, any more hot realtors come to visit you recently?"

Lisa turned her smiling face in Courtney's direction, a clear expression of "what's this?" written all over it. Courtney felt her face warm.

"Not since yesterday, smart-ass, no."

"Okay," Lisa said. "Somebody fill me in."

Mark took up the story before any sound left Courtney's mouth, telling Lisa about the beautiful woman who had simply shown up on Courtney's doorstep unannounced and offering presents.

Lisa's gaze met Courtney's and she tossed her a mock-scolding glare. "I can't believe you didn't tell me this story."

"It was no big deal," Courtney said, brushing the incident off. "Besides, the real entertainment came when Mr. Benetti here tried to be suave and cavalier with peanut butter on his face. Very funny stuff."

Mark shook his head and took a swig of his beer to cover his embarrassment.

"Didn't work, huh?" Lisa asked him teasingly.

Mark gave a self-deprecating chuckle. "No. Not even a little. Smooth I am not."

"Wouldn't have mattered," Courtney added smugly. "She plays for my team."

Mark's head whipped around and he blinked at her. "Seriously?"

Always up for teasing, especially when it came to Mark, Courtney cocked her head to one side. "Why do you say that? She doesn't fit the stereotype so she can't be gay?"

"What? No!" he sputtered. "No, of course not. I just—"

"She's hot and feminine so you wouldn't expect she'd be a lesbian, right?"

Mark pursed his lips as Lisa's head followed the conversation as if the words were a tennis ball being batted back and forth. "Cut it out, Court," he said quietly. "You know I don't think like that."

She let him off the hook. "I know. I'm just teasing. But yes, Rachel is gay."

Mark snorted. "Amelia told me to ask her out."

"She told me the same thing," Courtney replied. She stared for several seconds at her beer, feeling two pairs of eyes focused on her, before muttering, "God, I can't believe I just said that out loud."

"Courtney, you should *totally* ask her out," Lisa said with jubilance, then reined herself in. "I mean, do you want to? She sounds attractive. Do you have anything in common with her?"

Courtney looked up at her. "I have no idea," she answered honestly.

"Welcome to the wonderful world of dating," Mark said, leaning across the carpet to touch his beer bottle to hers with a clink. "Enjoy."

"Coffee's a safe bet," Lisa suggested gently. "It's not too constricting. It can last for hours if things are going well or just a few minutes if they're not."

Courtney nodded, knowing Lisa was right and wondering if this was possibly the dumbest idea she'd ever had. *I don't even know why I want to put myself through this. What is it about Rachel that has me even considering it?* She tried to shake the blue eyes and wavy blond hair from her thoughts, hardly successful. She forced herself to focus on the television screen, trying her best not to dwell. That's when she realized a blue-jerseyed player was streaking down the field untouched and her attention returned to the game. "Go! Go!"

To their credit, both Lisa and Mark seemed to understand the uncertainty of Courtney's situation and knew it was better to leave it alone for the time being. Soon it didn't matter, because all three of them were cheering the Bills' touchdown.

❖

Keep ringing…keep ringing…voice mail would be really, really good here. Courtney kept her fingers crossed and held her breath as Rachel's cell phone rang for the third time. *One more and I'm home free.* She chose not to analyze why the idea of Rachel actually answering the phone terrified her so much, opting instead to pour all her energy into superstition, crossing her toes as well.

"Rachel Hart." The voice was crisp and professional, and for a split second, Courtney thought maybe she did actually have voice mail. Until Rachel spoke again. "Hello?"

Well aware that beginning a conversation with the clearing of your throat was less than classy, Courtney did it anyway. "Um, hi. Rachel? It's Courtney. Courtney McAllister."

"Oh, hi, Courtney. How are you?"

"Good. I'm good. You?" God, did she always sound this much like a fifth grader?

"I'm good."

"Good." The thump of Courtney's shoe as she kicked at the doorjamb seemed inordinately loud in the quiet of her house.

"Did…you need something?" Rachel prodded after several seconds of silence went by, and Courtney squeezed her eyes shut, unable to focus on anything other than what a bad idea this had been.

"Well, I was just wondering…if…" She cleared her throat once more, then sucked in a huge lungful of air. "If maybe you'd be interested in getting some coffee with me sometime. Or something. Sometime." A phone to the forehead seemed in order, so Courtney rapped herself once. Twice.

"That would be nice," Rachel replied, and Courtney speculated whether or not she'd just imagined the hesitation. "Can I get back to you? I don't have my schedule handy, but I'll take a look at it and let you know when I've got some free time. Is that all right?"

"Sure. That'd be great. You have my number, so I'll wait to hear back from you."

"Perfect. Thanks for calling."

"Thanks for answering."

They both laughed and hung up. *In the history of date proposals, that was pretty much a disaster,* Courtney thought, shaking her head in self-deprecation. *"Let me check my schedule and get back to you" doesn't seem to be filled with promise. God, I'm out of practice.*

Fully expecting never to hear from Rachel again, she was surprised by the disappointment that settled over her, and for the first time, she realized that she really would like to see the realtor again. Blowing out a resigned sigh, she flopped down on the couch and reached for the remote.

❖

The mouthwatering smell of garlic wafted down the first-floor hallway as Rachel opened the foyer door on Tuesday evening. She inhaled deeply while fishing in her shoulder bag for her keys. She knew immediately that Jeff was cooking, and her stomach overtook any other order-giving organ in her body, forcing her feet away from the elevator and instead down the hall to the first apartment on the left. She tapped lightly on the heavy wooden door.

"Jeff?"

The door was opened in mere seconds, the warmth and comfort of home cooking washing over Rachel in a wave.

"Well, what do you know?" Jeff said with a smile that crinkled the corners of his hazel eyes. "It's that skinny beggar-girl from the top floor looking for food again."

"Ha ha."

"Come on in, gorgeous."

Jeff Porter was quite attractive in a rugged, ordinary-guy kind of way. His sandy hair was buzzed into an almost-crew cut and he had the most interesting eyes Rachel had ever seen on a man... sort of a light brown with flecks of green and gold. He'd moved into apartment 1A after his seven-year marriage had disintegrated. Rachel had owned the building for just about a year then and they'd hit it off right away. There was something about him that drew her...safety? Kindness? She wasn't ever able to put a finger on it. She just knew Jeff was like the big brother she never had. He was the closest thing to a best friend in Rachel's life and she often wondered if he knew that.

"I'm trying something new with my sauce," he said as he led the way into the galley kitchen. "I could use some fresh taste buds."

Rachel smiled at his white, stain-spotted Kiss the Cook apron she'd given him for Christmas the previous year. "This isn't yet another one of your devious ploys to win me over to your side, is it?"

"It might be."

"How many times do I have to tell you? Lose that thing between your legs and the scratchy whisker face and I'll think about it."

"Tease."

He held out a wooden spoon coated with red tomato sauce, cupping his hand under both the spoon and Rachel's chin. She blew gently, then tasted.

"Oh, wow." She nearly swooned as she savored the fresh, warm blend of flavors. "Jesus, Jeff. That's incredible."

"Yeah?" He was very pleased. Rachel never lied about his cooking. If it was awful, she'd tell him. She'd done so in the past.

"Oh, yeah." She took the spoon from his hand and helped herself to another, larger taste. "Oh, my God," she muttered, closing her eyes again.

Jeff smiled. "I call it Orgasm in a Pan."

"You would." She chuckled and wiped the corner of her mouth with a fingertip. "Seriously. Incredible stuff. You're a god in the kitchen."

"Yeah, well…" He blushed and quickly picked up a new wooden spoon, stirring the sauce. "So…tell me about your day. Sell any houses?"

"Two," she said with a smug grin as she dropped her bag on a kitchen chair and helped herself to the open bottle of merlot Jeff had left breathing on the counter.

"Nice!" He touched his glass to hers, the ping zipping around the room like a firefly.

He pulled two boxes down from the cupboard. Holding one in each hand for her to see, he asked, "Ziti or rigatoni?"

She smiled affectionately at him, loving him for taking her in with only a split second's notice. "You already know the answer to that one."

"Rigatoni it is."

They worked in companionable silence, familiar with the ritual of sharing dinner. Jeff continued to prepare the pasta while Rachel set the table, poured more wine, and sliced the bread. It was a routine they'd mastered and enjoyed, and Rachel loved his company, often thinking "Who says men and women can't just be friends?" She knew a lot of people who would argue that it was an impossibility, that while she was busy being proud of their platonic friendship, Jeff was probably wishing she was straight, and that was fine with her. By unspoken agreement, she and Jeff never talked about it. They were simply good for each other, like ten-year-olds, the athlete and the tomboy, best friends until they hit their teens and realize boys and girls don't mesh that way.

"I need your advice," Rachel said once they sat down to eat. She buttered a slice of fresh Italian bread and immediately plunged it into her sauce. She avoided looking up at Jeff. Asking for help was not something she did often, and she was a little uncomfortable even saying the words.

If Jeff was surprised by the request, he didn't show it. He knew better. "Okay. Shoot."

She had filled him in briefly when she first began business dealings with Courtney McAllister—the abrupt end to their first meeting, the apologetic phone call. She hadn't seen him over the long weekend, so she told him about her spontaneous visit on Sunday.

"Classy move," he said, impressed. "That was nice of you."

"It was uncharacteristic of me."

"So what?"

"I also came out to her." Rachel poked the inside of her cheek with her tongue before grabbing her wineglass and taking a healthy sip.

Jeff studied her closely, seeming to know that she was bothered by the admission. "Again, I ask, so what? You said she's gay, right?"

"Yes." She sighed, feeling a tingle of frustration building up inside her. "I just...I don't know *why* I blurted that out. It was so bizarre. And so pathetically obvious. Jesus."

Jeff chuckled as he chewed. "Raich, you need to relax." He

reached across the table and tapped on her forehead. "You spend too much time in here. Stop thinking so much and just…live."

Rachel inhaled deeply and blew it out. "She asked me out."

Jeff's eyebrows lifted in an attempt to meet his hairline. "Seriously?"

"She called me last night." She tried to suppress the grin. "It was cute. She was kind of stuttery and nervous and asked if I'd like to get a cup of coffee sometime."

"This is good." Jeff's eyes on her made her squirm and she worried that he could see too much, that he knew her too well, and that he realized she'd never actually had this reaction before, this uncertainty. "This is very good. You said yes, right?"

"God, this is delicious." Rachel shoveled a forkful of pasta into her mouth with a pleasurable groan.

Jeff smiled at her, his expression telling her that yes, he did notice her avoidance of the question. "Raich?"

"I told her I'd get back to her." Rachel felt heavy with indecision. "I don't know, Jeff. She's got so much…*baggage.*"

Jeff snorted. "And? I've got news for you, babe. We've all got baggage." He waved his hand in the air. "Hello? Heart broken by college sweetheart. Has a hard time trusting anybody." He pointed at her. "Parental issues stemming from childhood divorce. Control freak who worries too much, has trouble getting close, and overanalyzes everything."

Rachel glared. "I am *not* a control freak," she muttered.

Jeff snorted again, his way of telling Rachel she was very nearly the epitome of the phrase. "She's not asking you to marry her. It's *coffee*, for God's sake. Relax. God, reasoning with you is like reasoning with a brick wall."

Rachel made a face at him. "I'll think about it." She sipped her wine.

He rolled his eyes good-naturedly. "You do that."

After several beats of silence, she said, "It could be fun, right?"

"Sure it could. It could be a blast."

Rachel mulled that over as she looked off into space. Then she sighed with feigned weariness. "I don't know. She's probably not prepared for me. I'm a lot of work, you know. There's a lot of crap to chip through." She winked at Jeff and took another bite.

"You never know," he said with a grin and a shrug. "Maybe she's got a good chisel."

CHAPTER SIX

Courtney was reasonably sure her head was about to explode. Any minute now: *Blam!* Brains all over her chalkboard. The poor cleaning woman would have quite a mess to clean up.

It was to be expected, though, and after thirteen years of teaching, Courtney was almost used to it. The first couple weeks of school were always bumpy. New kids, new staff members, often new rules or policies, once in a while there were even new textbooks. It was a lot to take in after more than two months off. She was hauling a lot of stuff home, trying to get lesson plans and classes organized in the middle of the living room at night. By early October, she'd be fine.

It was midafternoon on Friday of the first week of school. The kids had only been there for a three-day week, but they were antsy to get the hell out for the weekend, as were most of the teachers. After the summer break, a three-day week felt like a month. The weather was balmy and Courtney had her classroom windows open, allowing the smell of the impending autumn to permeate the stale air of twenty-five breathing, sweating teenagers.

Andrew Gray, one of the new students, was in the very back of her Shakespeare class and was very obviously text-messaging somebody on his phone. The invention of cell phones and pagers had wreaked havoc on classrooms everywhere, and Courtney had implemented a strict policy in hers. Students were welcome to hold on to them during class, but she expected them to be off. The first time one rang, buzzed, or beeped, she confiscated it until the end of class. If she caught anyone using one, she confiscated it until the end of class. If anyone was text-messaging or taking pictures with it, she confiscated it until the end of class. No ifs, ands, or buts. After three offenses, the student and the phone were excused from class altogether.

As she laid out the assignment for the weekend, she strolled down the aisle casually. Stopping at Andrew's desk, she simply held out her hand for the phone. She continued to talk as she made eye contact with him and he glared back. She was often amazed by how much older the kids could look. Andrew was a senior, so he probably wasn't more than eighteen, but as he stared up at her, all heated glare and five o'clock shadow, she saw a thirty-year-old, very angry man. She had to force herself to continue talking about the homework, refusing to let him see that she found him even a little bit intimidating, as she reached across and snatched the phone from his grasp. He made no move but to narrow his eyes at her. She could feel them boring holes into her back like laser beams as she returned up the aisle. *Occupational hazard*, she could hear Theresa say about the lack of respect kids had for their teachers these days.

And just like that, she felt the now almost-familiar pang of heartache as she dropped the phone into her desk drawer where two others had been relegated, never once missing a beat in her detailing of the essay they were going to write after reading *Hamlet*. She and Theresa used to spend hours talking about their various students, offering one another advice on how to handle each individual problem or issue or subject. It was an aspect of their relationship she had treasured and she missed it immensely.

The subtle shifting of bodies in seats clued Courtney in to the fact that the bell was about to ring, so she wound down her lesson. "All right, that's enough for today. Don't forget the reading assignment over the weekend and the essay due next Thursday." The bell rang, sounding like the most obnoxious of alarm clocks, and the kids sprang from their desks like jacks-in-the-box. Courtney pulled the three cell phones from her desk drawer and held them out as the offenders sheepishly claimed them on their way by. Andrew Gray was last, lumbering slowly up the aisle as if he owned the room.

He was an enormous guy, and Courtney stood as tall as she could in her modest heels, determined to look every inch of 5'6" that she could. She took his glare and sent it right back to him, unwavering in her attempt to not be unsettled by him. *You're the boss*, she heard Theresa say. *Don't let him know he's getting to you.* He said nothing as he approached, just held eye contact as he stepped inappropriately into her personal space. She held her ground, despite the almost panicked instinct to take a step back from him and the pounding of her heart. She was certain he could probably hear it as loudly as a tribal drum, but she didn't move. He was so close she could smell him—sweat, aftershave, and cigarettes—and he stayed there for several seconds, their bodies no more than an inch apart. Finally, he took his cell from her hand, broke eye contact, and moved away, exiting the classroom just as calmly as he had strode up the aisle, no hurry at all. She expelled her breath in a whoosh of relief.

"Jesus Christ," she whispered as she dropped into her chair and rubbed angrily at her forehead, annoyed at the situation as well as the realization that she'd felt completely disheartened by a student.

At thirty-five, she was certainly not an old woman; she was barely middle-aged. But she felt ancient when she thought about the differences between her students thirteen years ago when she was a young substitute teacher and her students now. They had no respect for authority today, not like when she was in school. They had no respect for their elders, either. The thing that amazed her, though, was that this lack of respect generally wasn't a result of them being bad kids. It was more often a result of them not ever being *taught* respect by their parents. She heard kids in the hall every day mouthing off to teachers or aides in ways that made her head spin and sent her flashing back to the whack upside the head she would have gotten from her mother if she'd been caught verbalizing such insolence. Today, the parents seemed not to care. Either that or they didn't have the time to care. Or they were too tired to care. Whatever the reason, it was a sad state of affairs when the idea of being polite simply because it was the right thing to do went flying out the window. She wondered how parents today managed. With all the scheduled events their kids had lined up, all the doodads and gadgets they required to keep up with the Joneses, the Web site access, the cruelty of the media, how was it possible to raise a child to have family values and reverence for the rights of other people?

Only when the noise in the hallway began to dull did Courtney realize she'd been sitting at her desk, lost in her own thoughts, for too long. The appearance of the cleaning woman in her doorway, prepared to give the room its end-of-the-day scouring, only solidified her dawdling.

"Hi, Ms. McAllister," the woman said timidly. "Am I early?"

"No." Courtney smiled at her as she gathered her stuff. "I'm late." Thank God her last class of the day was a study hall. Shaking herself free of the clinging fog of discomfort with which Andrew Gray had shrouded her, she locked her desk, bade the cleaning woman a nice weekend, and hurried out of the classroom toward the large lecture hall that held almost fifty students anxious to be gone for the weekend.

❖

The evenings weren't chilly yet, but they'd definitely become cooler. It was a sure sign that summer was over and autumn was fast approaching. Within two months, temperatures would be down into the forties and it was even possible that a light blanket of early snow would make an appearance. The idea didn't sit well with Courtney; winter was hard for her.

She sat in group in shorts and a long-sleeve T-shirt and was grateful to not have the air-conditioning blowing on her, causing her arms to break out into gooseflesh. She listened as Richard gave them a shy recounting of his most recent date with Ms. One Floor Down. The exhausted look he'd carried when she first met him seemed to be vanishing slowly in stages and he looked almost content today as he recounted his story. Courtney was envious, but couldn't help smiling along with him as he spoke. Next to her, Lisa seemed just as happy for him.

"He's so sweet," she whispered as she leaned closer to Courtney. "He reminds me of my grandpa."

Courtney nodded, thinking suddenly how strange it was that

two people so far apart in age could be going through the exact same type of grief and be pulling for one another to break through to the other side.

After a few moments of silence, the balding man named Ted spoke up. "I don't like the winter. I dread it."

Nods and murmurs of agreement rolled around the room.

"Tell us why, Ted." Constance's face was the picture of gentle expectation.

"It's the time of year when I miss my wife the most." He sighed, studying his own lap. "At least in the summer, I can find things to do to occupy my mind. I'll do yard work or go to a baseball game. But I'm a homebody at heart and winter makes me want to stay home, warm and cozy in the living room, by the fire. I haven't felt like I could just do that since she's been gone. It makes me feel so alone to sit there without her." He rubbed at his chest as though he felt a physical pain there. Courtney wondered if maybe he did.

What Ted said was almost a carbon copy of the way she felt about the icy season. The picture he painted of sitting in front of a fire made her ache with desire for that coziness she'd been unable to thoroughly embrace and enjoy since Theresa's death.

"Please tell us that goes away," Courtney said just above a whisper. She squinted at her hands folded in her lap as she gathered her thoughts. *It's not going to do me any good if I'm not honest at these sessions.* "My partner's been gone for two and a half years, and the thought of winter makes me want to run away screaming." She met Ted's gaze across the circle. "I totally get it."

"It fades," Edith offered up, her papery thin voice cracking. "It does fade, but it doesn't go away. Not really."

The group absorbed the words in silence.

"Courtney?" Constance Mays's words cut through her thoughts, causing her to blink rapidly. "How've you been doing otherwise? The move okay? The new house?"

Happy for the change in subject, sort of, Courtney wet her lips and felt the attention of six people focused on her. She cleared her throat. "Yeah, otherwise, I'm good. I'm doing all right. The closing was hard. Giving up the keys to our house was harder." She heard the sympathetic, bitter chuckles as they filled the room. "But I made it through. I actually feel a lot better now that I'm in my own space. Every room doesn't call up some painful memory, you know?" In her peripheral vision, she saw Lisa nodding. "And…" She took a deep breath. "I asked somebody out."

Lisa's head snapped around and she felt her stare. "You did?"

Courtney inclined her head once in affirmation. "I did."

"That's fantastic," Constance praised her. "That's a big step, Courtney. You should be proud of yourself."

"Yeah, well, I haven't heard back from her, and I almost don't expect to, so it may have been for nothing." She was conscious of the pronoun she dropped, but there really wasn't much reaction from anyone. She was equal parts surprised and relieved. "But I'm glad I did it anyway. I feel like I took a step."

"How did it feel?" Constance asked, her expression kind.

"Scary as hell."

The room rumbled with understanding chuckles of agreement.

Thinking back to the bumbling and stuttering she'd done when she spoke to Rachel, Courtney wished she could call and simply reclaim her words. *Please disregard that last call. Unfortunate lapse in judgment. My bad.* But that hadn't been an option; she'd been stuck knowing Rachel had heard every stumble, every uncertainty and hesitation, and was probably still rolling her eyes at Courtney's feeble tone. It had been almost a week and she hadn't heard a thing. No return call, no message about her schedule. Courtney supposed it was probably better this way anyhow.

"I can't believe you didn't tell me," Lisa teased good-naturedly, nudging her with an elbow.

Courtney lifted one shoulder in a half-shrug. "I didn't want anybody to know. I was embarrassed."

Lisa squeezed her arm. "Well, I'm proud of you anyway."

CHAPTER SEVEN

H i, Courtney. This is Rachel Hart. Listen, I know it's been a while since your call and I'm really sorry it's taken me this long to get back to you. Life has been a little chaotic recently. Anyway, I was just wondering...are you familiar with Happy Acres? It's the animal shelter out on the east end of the city, near the thruway? They're having their annual thank-you shindig for the volunteers and I'm invited. It's very informal and casual...just drinks and hors d'oeuvres, that kind of thing, but it's usually a pretty good time. I was wondering if you'd be interested in accompanying me. It's Friday evening at seven. Please don't feel obligated, but if it's something that you think might interest you, I'd love for you to come with me."

Courtney blinked at the answering machine in disbelief as Rachel rattled off her number and the message ended with a click. She'd played it twice but still didn't quite register the facts, so she punched the Play button one more time, hunkering down with her elbows on the counter and her face practically pressed against the plastic as the husky voice filled the kitchen air for a third time.

When a knock sounded on the screen door, Courtney was still staring at the machine. She called out, "Come on in, Markie."

Mark entered the kitchen, dressed in khaki slacks and a green short-sleeve button-up shirt. He looked casually handsome and Courtney felt her heart skip a beat the way it did every time she looked at his face. For a split second, she could see Theresa, and it threw her just like always. She often wondered if that feeling would ever fade away. She supposed it would and found herself torn over whether or not she wanted it to.

"Ready?" he asked. It was Sunday morning and they had a standing date once a month to have brunch together. They'd spend an hour or two eating, catching up on life, talking about Mark's family, and in the fall, they'd watch football together, just as they'd done when Theresa was alive. Mark would often bring whatever woman he happened to be dating at the time. Once Theresa was gone, they'd vowed to not break the routine. It was out of respect for her and it was a way for them to hold on to some semblance of normal life in her absence.

Courtney debated for only a second before pointing at the machine and ordering, "Listen to this." She played the message for him while he fidgeted.

"I'm starving," he prodded. "Can we go?"

Sighing with impatience, Courtney pointed at the machine. "Did you listen?"

"I did." He grinned. "She just asked you out."

Courtney nodded. "I think you're right."

"That's great, Court. You've been waiting for her to call back."

She knew that was the truth, but she was sure the expression on her face told Mark she was less than enthusiastic.

"What's up?" he asked, thoughts of breakfast apparently shelved for the moment. "This is good. Isn't it?"

Courtney rubbed at the corner of her eye, then turned to look at him. "Do you think she's out of my league?"

Incredulity settled across his face. "*What?* Are you serious?"

Gesturing at the answering machine with a defiant chin, Courtney snorted. "She didn't even stutter."

"So what?"

"God, you should have heard me talking to her, trying to ask her on a date. I sounded like a twelve-year-old boy asking out his crush." She groaned, wishing she'd taken the original route she'd entertained and sent an e-mail instead. "She's so...put together, you know? Everything in its place—hair, clothes, makeup—smooth speech, impeccable posture. Nothing rattles her. I'll be awkward and clumsy next to her. I'll probably embarrass her."

"Sweetheart, look at me." Mark took her by the shoulders and turned her to face him. "It's not a marriage proposal. It's an evening out." He brushed her hair sweetly out of her face. "And if anything, *you're* out of *her* league."

"You think?" Courtney's voice was small as she looked up at him uncertainly, hesitant to allow herself to feel reassured.

"Yeah, I think." He kissed her forehead. "Can we eat now? I'm starving."

Not for the first time, Courtney found herself wishing she was a straight woman, for no other reason than she and Mark could be together and it would be almost like being with Theresa again. She sighed internally, knowing that was a silly assumption to make, but the thought didn't go away just because it was dumb.

At Binky's Diner, they got a table with a minimal wait—unusual for a Sunday morning there—and sat down without looking at a menu, knowing from habit what they wanted. They placed their orders with the waitress, who joked with them familiarly, and then sipped coffee as they chatted.

"How was the first full week of school?" Mark asked as he added more sugar to his cup.

"Not bad," Courtney replied, scanning the restaurant and the faces of the patrons. "I made it through yet again. Tomorrow, it will start to feel more routine."

"Good kids this year?"

"For the most part, I think, aside from one difficult one." Courtney relayed the story of her run-in with Andrew Gray the previous week.

Mark focused on her face. "You be careful, okay? Kids today, especially the boys, don't think twice about defying authority figures."

"Yes, Dad," she teased, feeling silly about the whole thing, but loving Mark for his concern.

An errant thought tickled her mind, telling her Rachel Hart, Million Dollar Producer, would probably put Mr. Gray right in his place, just like Theresa would. She felt the corners of her mouth hitch up the smallest bit at the idea of her not only taking him on, but winning.

As their food arrived, she promised Mark she'd be extra careful and then changed the subject. "So, what about you? How's work? What's new?"

They rambled on as they ate, back and forth in a comfortable friendship that was difficult to find between a straight man and a gay woman. Courtney had often wondered why that was such an uncommon pairing. Gay men and straight women got along famously; you could find them on television all the time. But it was rare to find the lesbian/straight man combination, and she didn't understand it. Didn't straight men and lesbians have a lot of things in common? In general, stereotypical terms: women, sports, cars, construction. Not that Courtney had the first clue about engine mechanics or building a house, but she loved sports and she never failed to notice a beautiful woman. Her friends were often surprised by how much time she spent with Mark. She knew a big reason for that was their biggest, most important common bond: Theresa. But still, Mark was a great guy, interesting and funny, and Courtney often felt that if she'd met him under some other circumstances, if she *hadn't* spent ten years of her life with his sister, they still would have ended up as close friends.

The waitress cleared their plates and topped off their coffee cups. Mark stared into his, suddenly quiet.

"What's up?" Courtney asked.

"Nothing." He cleared his throat.

His uncharacteristic lack of eye contact made her squint at him. "You think I don't know you better than that?" She grinned to take any sting away.

"I'm just being mushy. Feeling a bit lonely lately." He tried to steer away from the subject, and Courtney knew he worried about reminding her that she was also alone.

She simply nodded in understanding. "Me, too, honey. What about that girl you met last month when you were out with the guys? Ever call her?"

Waving the memory off, he replied, "I waited too long on that one. She's seeing my buddy."

"Ow."

"Yeah. My fault for dragging my feet, though."

"You know…" She hesitated, wondering if she should even think about heading down the path in front of her, lest she overstep her bounds. Making a decision, she continued. "You and my friend Lisa seemed to get along great that night at your house. She's single." She sipped her coffee and watched his face. "And she thinks you're cute."

He blinked at her, a look of confusion crossing over his features. "She's…?"

Courtney waited for him to continue, tried to help him along. "She's…what? Hot? Not your type? Female?"

"Straight?"

It was Courtney's turn to be speechless for the moment. When she found her voice, she began to laugh softly, with realization. "You thought she was gay?"

"Why wouldn't I?" Mark said, sitting back in his chair, his face scribbled all over with "duh." "You brought her. She's your new friend. I guess I just…assumed."

It made perfect sense, Courtney had to admit it, and it explained his strange mood of excitement and sadness during the football game. It had never occurred to her that he thought Lisa was off-limits. Shaking her head at their lack of communication even after knowing one another for so long, she said, "Yes, she's straight. And you should definitely give her a call." Studying his face, seeing the anticipation, the possibility, the desire for her approval, Courtney loved him even more than she thought possible.

"You wouldn't mind?"

She smiled widely and covered his hand with her own. "I wouldn't mind at all." She pulled out her cell phone, pushed a couple buttons, and rattled the number off for Mark to jot down on a napkin. "I'll give her a heads-up that I shared her number with you."

He didn't revert back to his teenage years, as most people would have. He didn't ask her any more about what Lisa thought of him, or if Courtney thought Lisa would say yes. He simply nodded once, said thanks, and sipped his coffee.

Courtney continued to grin and tried not to think about what a great couple they'd make. "So," she said after a minute or two of silence. "Predictions for today's game?"

He groaned like a man in pain. "We're going to get our asses kicked." Into his cup, he grumbled, "I hate the fucking Patriots."

❖

Bandero was an upscale restaurant that specialized in pretentious Southwestern cuisine and overpriced drinks, but it was her mother's favorite, so Rachel didn't have a lot of say in the matter of where they'd meet for lunch on Tuesday. She was right on time, as always, and wasn't surprised that her mother had arrived first, as always. Alice Sullivan was already occupying her favorite table in the corner by the back window and she was already sipping on one of the restaurant's enormous signature margaritas that, in Rachel's opinion, were long on the sour mix and short on everything else. Rachel took a deep breath and steeled herself for the next hour and a half, vowing to not let her mother bait her and to not pick a fight of her own.

"Yeah, good luck with that," she muttered under her breath as she zigzagged through the crowded and noisy tables toward the back corner.

Alice was dressed in her usually impeccable style of designer pantsuit and too much jewelry. Today's choice was a deep eggplant color with an ivory silk blouse underneath and a bright, multicolored silk scarf knotted loosely around her neck. Her bottle-blond hair had been tinted recently and looked very modern, easily taking ten years off her appearance. Hair color was where the similarities between mother and daughter stopped, though. Where Rachel had crystal blue eyes, Alice's were hazel. Rachel was tall and lean, Alice was rather short and a bit on the plump side, despite her penchant for whatever fad diet was in the news at the time. She carried herself well, though, and had a confidence level that caused heads to turn when she walked through a room.

Alice looked away from the window and watched her daughter's approach.

"Hi, Mom." Rachel bent and kissed Alice's cheek.

"Don't you eat?" Alice asked by way of greeting. "You're too thin."

"I'm not too thin, Mom." Rachel took a seat across the table from her and unfolded her napkin. "How are you?"

Alice sipped her drink and waved a hand dismissively in the air as she began to unload about her lazy husband, her stupid clients, her annoying coworkers, and her irritating neighbors.

Rachel ordered a glass of chardonnay in preparation for the lunch, and felt her eyes glaze over as she listened to her mother's usual negative diatribe. She tried to will her mind back in time, back twenty-five years or more, when she remembered her mother as happy, smiling, and loving. It was before her father left, and Rachel was eleven or twelve. Emily was five years younger. The older Rachel got, the harder it was to remember the details, but she always tried to put herself back there in an attempt to drown out the depressing droning on of what Alice had become. Rachel could be seemingly focused on Alice's face, apparently paying rapt attention to whatever was being complained about at the moment, but in reality, she was back in time. She was fondly recalling the smell of home-baked chocolate chip cookies waiting for her after a long day at school. She was remembering Alice trying to teach her how to crochet and young Rachel not quite able to twist her long, gangly fingers in the right directions. She could almost smell the fresh flowers that always adorned the interior of the house and the laundry on the line, flapping in the gentle breeze and soaking up the incomparable scent of the outdoors.

Alice had launched into how appalled she'd been by the uncleanliness of a house she'd recently been asked to sell when she was cut off by the blessed appearance of the waiter.

"Would you care to hear our specials?" he asked cordially.

"Absolutely," Rachel replied, before Alice could dismiss him. She wanted to keep him at the table as long as possible. He went on for several minutes, describing each special in mouthwatering detail. Rachel didn't really listen—she'd already decided on the chicken Caesar salad—but she let him ramble on as she nodded politely after each selection.

Once the waiter had taken their orders, Alice dove right back in. "I see you sold the place out on Wayworth. What did you get for it?"

"Three-eighty," Rachel replied, knowing so instinctively where this was going that she almost mouthed her mother's response with her.

"Oh, Rachel, you could have gotten another twenty thou for that house." Her expression showed a sliver of disgust at her daughter's incompetence.

"Well, the seller was perfectly happy with the offer and was ready to move on."

"You're right. Who needs another twelve hundred dollars in commission?"

"I do just fine, thank you." Rachel tried not to give her answer through clenched teeth, but failed miserably.

"I've been telling you for years, dear, you need to work on that killer instinct. You'd make a lot more money."

Rachel nodded and finished off her wine, signaling the waiter by holding up her empty glass and pointing to it. Desperate to change the subject, she asked, "Have you talked with Emily lately?"

Alice scoffed. "I called her on Saturday, but *he* was there, so I didn't talk long."

He was Rachel and Emily's father. According to the Book of Alice, he was the sole reason for any and all difficulty in Alice's life and she rarely used his name. "Bitter" wasn't a strong enough word to describe Alice's feelings about her husband leaving her a quarter of a century ago, and don't get her started on "that slut" he'd married less than a year after their divorce. Her death a few years earlier had served him right, according to Alice. Finally, punishment from above or some such justification, the warped logic of which made Rachel's head spin.

"Oh." Rachel found it strange that the only time she ever felt an inkling of protection for her father was when her mother disparaged him. In those instances, did Rachel feel a little too much like her mother? The thought made her enormously uncomfortable and, as usual, she steered the conversation in another direction. "Well, she's feeling great. No more headaches, but the cravings won't go away."

For a split second, Rachel was sure she saw the Alice of thirty years ago in the glow that zipped across her face. "She mentioned that earlier in the week when we talked. It was salt and vinegar potato chips at that point."

Rachel grinned. "It's saltines with peanut butter now."

"Ugh." Alice shook her head with fondness. "I remember those days."

"You do?"

"Oh, yes. With you, I was traditional. Chocolate ice cream all the way. For months. With Emily? Baked potatoes. With bacon bits…remember those things in the jar?"

"The fake bacon you sprinkled on salads?"

"Exactly. I must have gone through twenty jars of those damn things during my pregnancy with her."

"I didn't know that."

"Oh, yes."

The waiter arrived with their lunches, and unfortunately for Rachel, that was the end of Alice's fond reminiscing. She was immediately on to less pleasant things, as if she realized she'd ventured into the wrong arena and quickly backpedaled. Rachel sighed internally as Alice began complaining about the newest realtor in her office.

Over the years, Rachel had perfected the art of pretending to listen. It had served her well growing up in a house filled with the depression and bitterness of her mother, and she'd discovered fairly recently that it actually helped her in her job, too. Not that she always tuned people out, but just like a bartender, people seemed to want to unload on their realtor, tell her all the reasons why they were selling or why they bought or what was so great—or so awful—about the house. Most of the time, this information was very useful. But on occasion, she'd ended up with a client who just liked to talk. On and on and on. Her talent for appearing as though she was paying rapt attention had become a gift and she used it well.

Now, as Alice droned on about the audacity of the new guy,

Rachel found her thoughts drifting to the voice-mail message she'd received Sunday night from Courtney. It was a complete fluke that she hadn't answered; nine times out of ten, she had her cell phone clipped to her waistband even when she was puttering around her apartment. Sunday night, however, she'd left it on the dresser on vibrate and had wandered into the kitchen in a robe to get something to drink. She hadn't heard the buzzing sound and hadn't bothered to look at the phone again until Monday morning as she got ready for work. She was actually surprised by her own surprise at finding the message from Courtney thanking her for the invitation to the volunteer happy hour on Friday. She was also taken off guard by the giddiness that seeped in at Courtney's acceptance. *I'd love to go with you,* were her exact words. Rachel could still hear them replay in her head, Courtney's exact inflections and tone of voice intact. It embarrassed her no end that she'd saved the message and had listened to it more than once during the day.

Who the hell am *I?* she wondered, not for the first time since she'd met Courtney McAllister.

The salad was quite good, she noted as she quickly checked back into the one-sided conversation taking place before her. Alice was still rambling, her scowl accentuating the deep crevice that had taken up residence between her eyebrows. Rachel nodded and made a sound that conveyed her attention. Then she returned to the more pleasant thoughts of Courtney. What the hell was it about the woman that drew Rachel so strongly? She couldn't seem to put a finger on any one thing. Courtney was extremely attractive in the physical sense, for sure, so there was definitely that. Those green eyes of hers... Rachel mentally shook her head. *God, those eyes.* Rachel had never understood what it meant to be lost in somebody's eyes until Courtney had looked directly at her. In addition to the beauty of her face, she had a trim, athletic body, the kind Rachel had always found most attractive—though she suspected beneath the jeans, sweats, or shorts lay some very feminine curves...

Okay, okay, Rachel's brain snapped, stopping her in midthought. *She's fun to look at; we've established that. Big deal. What* is *it that's pulling you?*

It was her face, something in her face that Rachel found… magnetic. The kindness in her face? The gentleness in her tone? The obvious intelligence? There wasn't much that was sexier than a smart woman. Or was it that little bit of sadness that made people want to take care of her, protect her? Maybe a combination of all of it?

Rachel Hart was not easily drawn to people. It just didn't happen. She had dated. Of course she had dated. She'd even had a couple of somewhat-long-term relationships, but nothing, nobody, ever stuck. She was a loner, she was set in her ways, and she liked it that way. As Jeff's voice interrupted her thoughts to tease her with "control freak" comments, she tried hard to block it out. She didn't need anybody, nor did she really want anybody. She liked her life the way it was, her routine the way she planned it, and things were fine. There was a little part of her that cringed inside, worried about somebody like Courtney coming in and messing everything up, disturbing the order and causing unpredictability.

But those eyes…

Rachel gave her head a quick shake and focused across the table.

"Are you listening to me, Rachel?" Alice asked, annoyance etched clearly on her face.

"Yes. I am. Of course I am." Rachel shoved a forkful of salad into her mouth as Alice took up right where she'd left off, unable to understand how the manager of her office could possibly put up with the shenanigans going on with this new guy. Rachel nodded, willing her mind to concentrate on the words dropping uninterestingly from her mother's mouth and not to take her back into the territory of thoughts and theories of which she was unsure and couldn't compartmentalize.

Those eyes…

CHAPTER EIGHT

Very informal' is such a relative term." Courtney sighed as she roughly yanked the blouse off and grabbed another from a hanger in the closet. "Very informal to me and very informal to her could be two very different things."

Amelia chuckled with amusement. "Sweetie, you need to relax a little bit or you're going to frighten the poor girl away." She reached around Courtney and grabbed a deep green blouse with three-quarter-length sleeves out of the closet. "Put this on with your khaki slacks, the low-waisted ones, and tuck it in. Brown belt. Those shoes." She pointed to a pair of simple, comfortable brown leather shoes with a modest heel.

Courtney dressed obediently, never questioning Amelia's suggestions. Since college, she knew without a doubt that Amelia had an inherent sense of fashion and she'd never steered Courtney wrong. Courtney had learned that if she shut up and wore whatever Amelia told her to, she'd be fine.

"I'll be downstairs getting my stuff ready." Amelia stopped and studied Courtney. "Just pull a little of your hair back. Use that funky gold clip you bought a couple weeks ago."

"Yes, ma'am," Courtney responded with a grin. She heard Amelia's sneakers as she descended the hardwood stairs and headed for the dining room, in which she was mounting a border for Courtney. She was very good at such things, Courtney was very bad at them, and it gave Amelia an opportunity to spend the evening away from the chaos of her own household.

Standing in the bathroom, Courtney finished applying some light makeup, then styled her hair the way Amelia had ordered. The addition of some simple gold earrings completed the ensemble and she studied herself in the full-length mirror on the back of the door. *Not bad,* she thought, her gaze starting at her shoes and sliding critically up her body, taking in the fit of the pants, the curve of her own hips, the snugness of the blouse, ending at her face where she made eye contact with herself. *Not bad at all. I think.* She freed a couple strands of hair so they hung in corkscrew curls near her ears.

She thought about her date and found herself suddenly self-conscious about looking good enough to be standing next to somebody who looked as good as Rachel. "Nope. No pressure there," she muttered to her reflection and rolled her eyes. "No pressure at all."

Deciding this was as good as it was going to get, she spritzed on a lightly scented perfume and headed downstairs. She stopped short as she turned the corner and heard conversation coming from the dining room. Steeling herself, she continued on her path and was surprised to see Rachel and Amelia discussing the border Amelia was going to mount.

"Hi," Courtney said. "I didn't hear the bell." She hoped her swallow wasn't audible as she tried not to gawk at the sight of the woman before her. Rachel wasn't dressed any more fancily than Courtney—she wore a nice pair of jeans and a simple black top— but she was stunning nonetheless. Her wavy hair was loose, her legs—as always—went on forever, and for the first time, Courtney was treated to a full-on, close-up view of her ass, snugly held in denim and begging for a caress.

Amelia jumped in. "I saw her pull up, so I let her in before she could ring the doorbell." She gestured to the rolled-up wallpaper border and tools spread out on the dining-room table. "We were just talking about my project. Did you know Rachel owns her apartment building?"

Courtney blinked. "Um, no. I didn't know that."

"She does. And she's put up wallpaper, borders, she's painted, she's stenciled. She's a gay man trapped in a woman's body."

At that, Rachel burst into laughter. Courtney watched her, absorbing the sound, musical and husky at the same time, and was shocked to feel a tingle low in her belly. When Rachel turned and looked at Courtney, her eyes dancing, Courtney felt her breath catch.

"You look terrific," Rachel said, her gaze skimming quickly but thoroughly over Courtney's frame. "I'm really glad you decided to go. Are you ready?"

Courtney nodded quickly, words seemingly impossible. *What the hell is wrong with me?*

Rachel turned toward Amelia and waved as she followed Courtney to the door. "It was nice to see you again."

"Same here," Amelia replied. "Her curfew is eleven, by the way," she added with a wink.

"I'll see what I can do." Rachel winked back and Courtney shot a glare in Amelia's direction as she closed the door.

"Have fun!" Amelia called.

Once settled comfortably into the BMW, Rachel turned to glance at Courtney "So," she said. "How are you? How's the house?"

"It's great," Courtney replied with a smile, grateful for the banter. If she could keep on jabbering, she wouldn't have a chance to focus on her nervousness. She talked about her plans for the different rooms, colors she'd chosen for painting, how many more trips to Home Depot she had in her future. Rachel contributed succinct comments here and there and they both laughed often. The twenty-five-minute ride was over in no time.

Happy Acres consisted of a large one-story brown building that sprawled wide and flat across the land. Courtney had been there more than once, but it had been a while—several years at least—and many renovations had been made since her last visit.

"Wow," she said as Rachel slid the BMW into a parking spot in the busy lot. "They've really done a lot to this place."

"Been a while since you've been here?"

"Theresa and I adopted our beagle, Polo, from here way, way back. Then we came again a few years ago when we knew Polo was getting up there in years, but we couldn't bring ourselves to pick another dog." She grimaced. "It felt too much like we were trying to replace him before he was even gone, you know?"

"Sure. Losing a pet must be very hard." Rachel waited for Courtney to reach her side before walking toward the building.

"You told me you don't have a dog because you're in an apartment, but now I know you own the building." Courtney bumped Rachel with her shoulder as they strolled. "So...since you're the landlady, why don't you have one?"

Rachel pursed her lips in thought, as though trying to find the best explanation. Before she could speak, though, she was interrupted by a heavyset, rather loud woman who called from across the yard.

"Rachel Hart!" She bustled up to them and threw her arms around an obviously unexpectant Rachel. Courtney pressed her fingertips to her lips to keep from bursting out in laughter at the expression on Rachel's face, which was a mix of *here we go again* and *God, help me*, as she met Courtney's eyes over the woman's shoulder. "It's so good to see you!" The woman held Rachel at arm's length, and everything she said sounded like it should have an exclamation point after it. "It seems like every time you're here, I'm not!"

Courtney didn't need more than the quick glance Rachel shot her to know that missing the woman was intentional on Rachel's part. She bit her lip to keep her smile to a minimum.

"Betsy, this is my friend, Courtney McAllister." Rachel turned Betsy by her shoulder so she faced Courtney. "Courtney, this is the head of volunteer coordination here at Happy Acres, Betsy Crawford."

"It's a pleasure to meet you, Betsy." Courtney shook the meaty hand held out to her.

"Same here!" Betsy said, smiling widely and pumping Courtney's hand with enthusiasm. To Rachel, she added, "Are you bringing me another volunteer?" Facing back to Courtney, she gushed, "Rachel practically lives here! And we wouldn't have the new wing if it weren't for her!"

Absorbing this new information, Courtney looked with surprise to Rachel, who hurriedly grabbed her hand and pulled her in the direction of the building. Over her shoulder, she said to Betsy, "I want to introduce Courtney to some of the others, so we'll catch you inside, okay?"

If she was put off by their abrupt exit, Betsy didn't show it. Within seconds, she was shouting out somebody else's name and heading into the parking lot, presumably to squeeze the air from their lungs.

"Sorry about that," Rachel chuckled. "Betsy can be… exuberant."

Courtney didn't mention that Rachel still had a hold of her hand. Instead, she tried her best to soak up the warmth of it, to note how well her own hand fit inside Rachel's, how comforting and sensual it was to be led by a beautiful woman. "So…they wouldn't have the new wing if it weren't for you?"

Rachel blushed a pale pink that Courtney found charming. "I donate money when I can," she stated simply.

"Enough money for a *wing*?" Courtney asked. "I'm impressed."

"I sell expensive houses," Rachel said with a shrug. "And I love animals."

"That's the best reason." Courtney let the subject drop, not wanting to make Rachel any more uncomfortable than she already had. Besides, there were many far less admirable ways to spend your money. That Rachel used hers to help homeless animals made her seem more…human than Rachel Hart, Million Dollar Producer, came across sometimes.

The next hour was a whirlwind of activity for Courtney. It seemed like every two or three steps, they ran into somebody else who knew and wanted to chat with Rachel. After the fourth person, Courtney realized she'd never remember all the names and she gave up trying, which actually allowed her to relax a little bit and just take it all in. Rachel's popularity was impressive and something Courtney hadn't expected. If asked to describe Rachel's personality, Courtney would have had to mention the phrases "a little cool" and "somewhat standoffish," but at Happy Acres, she was warm, well liked, and extremely knowledgeable.

Inside the building, the first thing Courtney set her gaze on was a giant wall of glass cubicles to her left, each one occupied by a cat.

"Oh, my God," she whispered, awed.

"People tend to forget to spay or neuter their cats." Rachel's voice was colored with disapproval.

Courtney had always been indifferent toward felines. She knew people loved them as pets, but they really didn't do anything for her. Not like a dog. At that moment, however, she wanted to take each and every one of them home with her. Many people stood peering into the glass, talking with Happy Acres staff and asking questions. Courtney's gaze stayed on them even as she followed Rachel through the lobby to the far corner where a large table was set up with wine and hors d'oeuvres. "Will they get adopted?" she asked.

Rachel watched her as Courtney's eyes traveled over each and every square of glass, taking in each cat. "The younger ones will. The older ones...they'll be here for a while. We have some volunteers who will end up taking them home if they don't get adopted. Don't worry. They're well taken care of here."

Courtney nodded, understanding but not totally convinced.

"We have volunteers who come in every day and play with them or sit with them in their laps or just spend time near them."

Swallowing down unexpected emotion at the sheer scope of abandoned animals, Courtney nodded again, trying hard to let Rachel's gentle reassurances make her feel better about the cruelty of the world.

"Hey. Red or white?" Rachel asked softly, pulling Courtney's gaze to meet hers.

"Oh. Um, red. Merlot. Please."

Taking the glass offered to her, Courtney pounced on the opportunity to chat with Rachel before anybody else showed up to steal her attention. "This place is enormous," she commented. "I don't think I realized it."

"More than fifteen thousand animals are taken in each year. It has to be big."

"Wow." The overwhelming number of abandoned animals made Courtney blink in shock. "What made you start volunteering?"

Rachel shrugged, popping a grape into her mouth, and chewed thoughtfully. "I started donating first. I got one of those sappy letters in the mail with the emaciated puppy on the front." She made a face that made Courtney laugh.

"Yeah, I've gotten those, too."

"Then I was on my way to see a client who lived out here and I decided to stop in and visit, just for the hell of it. I wanted to see where my dollars were going and I was completely blown away. All the people here, helping out just because of the kindness of their hearts, walking the dogs, cleaning the kennels, helping with paperwork, it just astounded me. I decided maybe I could give more than money."

"It must be hard," Courtney grimaced, "seeing all the strays and animals people have abandoned."

"It is. It can be horrific. Believe me, there are times when I just want to beat the crap out of some people. But Happy Acres has a no-kill policy, which is very unusual, so if nothing else, I don't worry that these animals here have time limits. You know?"

"That is a relief, isn't it?"

"It's a huge part of why this place means so much to so many people. Just look around."

Courtney did, and for the first time, took in the utter volume of attendees. The lobby was full and people spilled out the doors into the front lawn area of the building, the fall air still mild enough to be comfortable in the evening. There had to be close to 250 volunteers present. "I'm impressed."

Rachel smiled widely, the dimples Courtney had imagined suddenly appearing on her flushed cheeks, the white flash of her teeth surprising Courtney in its appearance. She vowed right then to make Rachel smile as often as possible; it lit up her entire face.

"I'm glad you think so," Rachel said proudly. Before any more could be said, a handsome man in his sixties appeared to shake her hand and chat with the two women about the state of Happy Acres.

At the end of the night, riding home in the car, Courtney reflected on the previous few hours. If there was one thing she regretted about the evening, it was that she didn't get nearly enough time one-on-one with Rachel. The snippets she'd had, though few and far between, were fun and enlightening, and every time somebody stole Rachel's attention, Courtney felt cheated out of the additional tidbits that might have been forthcoming had the interruption not occurred. At the same time, she was a little bit relieved because she knew they'd have things to talk about on their next date.

Next date?

She didn't let herself dwell too long on that phrase as the blur of lights in the distance flew by out the car window. She forced herself to focus on the present as they sped down the expressway, heading back into the city and toward Courtney's house.

"Did you have an okay time?" Rachel asked, her voice quiet and soothing in the dark interior of the BMW.

"I did." Courtney smiled widely, hoping Rachel could see. "I had a terrific time. Thank you so much for bringing me. I may have to start volunteering now myself."

"Well, I certainly didn't drag you there to trick you into joining the staff."

"No?" Courtney's teasing lilt assuaged any worry Rachel might have had.

"No."

"So...now it's my turn to drag you somewhere, isn't it?"

Rachel's eyes didn't leave the road, but the corner of her mouth quirked up just a little. "Yeah, I believe it is."

"Hmm..." Courtney tapped her forefinger playfully against her lips. "What to do? What to do?"

"Should I be worried?" Rachel said with a grin.

"Oh, yes."

"Uh-oh."

Courtney laughed and reached across to pat Rachel's thigh. She tried hard to ignore the warm firmness of the muscle that flexed beneath the denim. "I'll go easy on you at first, keep it simple. How about you come over and I'll cook you dinner?"

"You'll cook me dinner?"

"I'm a fantastic cook."

"Well, I'm not, so this may work out well for me."

"There you go. What night is good for you?"

"Hmm. Let me think." Rachel caught her bottom lip between her teeth as she did so.

The soft orange light from the dashboard shone on Rachel's face just enough for Courtney to see her features, notice the sexiness of the gesture, and to feel an interesting pang low in her belly. It was a feeling she hadn't had in a very long time and it surprised her in its insistence. She cleared her throat and looked away.

"I know next week is out. I'm booked every night. But the following week should work. I'll have to double-check and make sure, but I think I'm free Wednesday and Friday," Rachel said finally. "I have to show houses the rest of the nights, though I'm usually done with that by eight."

Courtney nodded, hoping her faint blush wasn't apparent in the dark interior of the car. "Great. Give me a call when you've decided which night works best, and we'll plan on it. Is there anything you're allergic to or don't like?"

Rachel pursed her lips and squinted in thought and again, Courtney had to look away. "Nope. I think I'm good. No allergies." She added with a smirk, "I'm not really a fan of Brussels sprouts, but I'll eat them."

"I'm making a mental note. No Brussels sprouts. Got it."

They made a right-hand turn and came to a stop. Courtney was surprised to note they were in her driveway. Her Jetta sat alone; Amelia's car was nowhere to be seen, her project probably long completed.

"Home sweet home," Rachel said.

"So it is."

Noting the darkness of the windows, Rachel commented, "You know, you should put a light on a timer so it looks like somebody's home. For safety."

Courtney turned to look her in the eyes, and the pale blue color of them was shockingly apparent even in the faint light available. "You're right. I'll do that," she said softly. She wet her lips and added, "I really had a great time tonight, Rachel. Thank you."

Rachel shifted in the driver's seat so she faced Courtney. "I'm glad you enjoyed yourself. So did I. Thanks for indulging me."

The air in the car seemed suddenly thick, heavy, and warm, almost intoxicating. They looked at one another for several long seconds before Rachel leaned forward and placed her lips gently on Courtney's. The kiss wasn't demanding or controlling at all, which surprised Courtney for some reason. Instead, it was soft, gentle, promising, and it took her completely by surprise. She sank into it, wanting to let Rachel set the pace, but there was a sudden blossoming in her core, a wanting she hadn't felt in what seemed like decades. She reached up and placed her hand on the side of Rachel's face, the skin there soft as velvet. She threaded her fingers into the hair at the base of Rachel's neck and tightened her hold, parting her lips just enough to allow the tip of her tongue to dart out, testing the waters. She heard a sharp intake of breath and then Rachel's tongue touched hers, the warm wet of it so delicious Courtney almost cried out.

She pulled back then, suddenly, and released her hold. Rachel withdrew as well, her chest heaving as deeply as Courtney's, apparently as startled as she was at the turn of events. Courtney brought her fingers to her own lips and blinked at Rachel in astonished surprise.

"Um…" Rachel managed only one word, seemingly unable to form a coherent thought.

"Yeah," Courtney responded with a vigorous nod, additional words eluding her. After several more seconds, she reached for the door handle, feeling the overwhelming urge to get out of the car before whatever was going on between them consumed her completely. "You'll call me? With your schedule?"

Rachel stared at her, as if trying to catch up. "Oh. Oh, yeah. Yeah. Tomorrow."

"Great." Courtney stepped out of the car, then turned back and leaned down. "I really did have a wonderful time."

Rachel smiled, relief flooding over every other emotion. "Good. Me, too."

"I'll talk to you soon."

"Okay."

❖

Rachel remained in the driveway, watching Courtney walk to the side door of her house and wondering how she could look so beautiful in the unflattering outside light that cast weird shadows over her frame. Courtney got the door unlocked, then turned and waved to Rachel before entering the house. Rachel waved back, slid her gearshift into reverse, and backed out of the driveway, realizing she had been pleasantly surprised by the direction the evening had taken. She wasn't sure what exactly she'd expected, but it certainly hadn't been making out in her car while sitting in Courtney's driveway. She hadn't even intended to kiss her. And when she had, it was just going to be a quick peck, a chaste I-had-a-good-time sort of thing. The participation of tongues was something she hadn't counted on.

Baggage or no baggage, that woman certainly can kiss. Wow.

She drove home unsure, a bit shaken, and with a silly grin plastered on her face.

CHAPTER NINE

*O*h, baby. God damn, you're so wet."
    "Please..."
    "I'm still shocked sometimes, you know? After all these years I still can't wait to get my hands on you."
    "Please. Honey, please?"
    "I was watching you tonight, across the room. You were so damn sexy, just standing there talking to that guy. He wanted you. You know that, don't you? Don't you?"
    "Yes."
    "You were standing close to him, laughing at his jokes. You did that on purpose, didn't you?"
    "Yes. Theresa, please...touch me?"
    "You knew he wanted you and you used that to make me jealous, didn't you?"
    "Yes."
    "He wanted to touch these breasts...wanted them in his big, meaty hands...wanted his mouth on them just like this."
    "Oh, God."
    "I could tell. You were talking and he was watching your chest."
    "Honey...please? Please..."
    "And all I kept thinking was, 'Go ahead, dude. Look all you want. Fantasize all you want. You'll never have her. She's going home with me. You know why? Because she's mine. Not yours. Mine.'"

"Theresa..."
"You're mine, Courtney."
"Yes...please...touch me..."
"You're mine..."

Courtney's eyes popped open. She lay in her bed and stared at the ceiling in the darkness. Breathing in ragged gasps, she tried hard to calm her racing heart, her entire body radiating heat. Like an electric blanket, her skin emanated even warmth. Theresa's words still echoed through her subconscious.

"You're mine..."

She remembered that night more vividly than almost any other memories she had of her lost wife. It was the last time they'd made love and it was by far one of the most passionate. They'd been at a holiday party with a bunch of local educators and Courtney had been cornered by a fellow teacher—she couldn't even recall his name now—and had feigned polite interest. She'd realized two things at once: the man was more interested in her breasts than her words, and Theresa was watching from across the room. She could still feel the whoosh of eroticism when she understood the power she suddenly held. Inching closer to the man, she didn't flinch away when he leaned closer and said something supposedly funny in her ear. She laughed at his lame attempt at a joke and casually put her hand on his arm as she spoke to him. Peripherally, she watched her wife and saw the subtle shift in her stance. Theresa, too, was having a conversation with somebody, but Courtney could tell she was paying more attention to what was going on across the room than to the words her companion was saying to her.

Upon their return home late that night, they'd barely made it through the front door before Theresa was on her, kissing her possessively, nipping at her skin, pulling at her clothes. They left a telltale trail of fabric from the foyer up the stairs—a blouse here, a pair of panties there—until Theresa had slammed her onto her back on their bed. She'd remained on her back well into the wee hours of the morning, Theresa laying claim to her, body and soul, over and over again, until she'd begged...for everything. She'd begged to be touched. She'd begged for release. She'd begged for sleep when Theresa had whispered "again" seductively and demandingly in her ear.

Now, in the darkness and solitude of her new bedroom, Courtney rolled over onto her side and tucked her legs up so she was as small as a child. The hot burning between her thighs pounded, trying to get her attention, trying to coax her fingers there to relieve the pressure, but she was too freaked out by the timing to allow herself the pleasure.

She had kissed Rachel. Well, technically, Rachel had kissed her. But Courtney had kissed her back, and more importantly, she'd *wanted* her. And then she'd had a sex dream about Theresa. It was a little too coincidental to be a coincidence.

The throbbing between her legs refused to let up. She squeezed her thighs together tightly and balled the pillow in her fist.

Yes, she'd been with another woman since Theresa's death, but it was a disaster, something that never should have happened. Courtney had had too much to drink, she'd forced herself to do something she thought she *should* do, but had realized much too late that she wasn't ready to do. She'd hurt not only herself, but the other woman as well.

She rolled over onto her other side, feeling suddenly wide-awake and still uncomfortably turned on, steadfast in her refusal to grant herself any relief. She knew it was a ridiculous form of punishment for what had happened between her and Rachel, but somewhere deep in her subconscious was the little voice that would forever accuse her of cheating on Theresa whenever she so much as thought about another woman. As she recalled the very first time she'd masturbated after Theresa's death, her eyes welled. She'd cried all through that orgasm, certain she'd done something horribly disrespectful to Theresa's memory. It didn't matter that she'd masturbated plenty of times when Theresa was alive. Her anguish was irrational and she knew it, and she still couldn't hold back the tide of emotion that had washed over her. She'd stayed in bed for more than two days afterward. Amelia had to bodily pull her from the sheets and force her into the shower.

Her emotions were sitting too close to the surface now. She couldn't allow herself to think about Rachel, to think about how good it felt to be next to her, to kiss her, to *want* her. Courtney knew at that moment that if she dwelled on what it all meant, she'd dissolve into heart-wrenching sobs and she just couldn't bring herself to go there. The bright red numbers on the bedside clock said 3:57 and she knew instinctively she'd be getting no more sleep.

In the kitchen, she put the teakettle on the stove to heat up some water and puttered around in the dim yellow of the night-light Amelia had plugged in for her. It seemed less disturbing than turning the overhead light on, and she made tea often enough that she could probably do it in her sleep anyway.

Hot mug in hand, she wandered through the dining room in her bathrobe, the smell of wallpaper paste still tickling her nostrils. Amelia had done a beautiful job, and Courtney had the sudden urge to call her and tell her so again until she remembered the ungodly hour.

The yellow hue from the streetlights outside shone in just enough to help Courtney revisualize the subtle grapevine design of the border that ran along the wall against the ceiling. She'd decided to decorate the dining room in a slight and understated wine theme, with grapevines and old wine labels as part of the décor. She had her eye on a nice wood and wrought-iron wine rack that she planned to buy soon, stain to match the gumwood trim of the house, and place right against the wall centered beneath the high leaded-glass windows that were on the...

Her breath caught in her throat as she glanced up at one of the windows and focused on the silhouette outlined in the window of Bob's house next door, seemingly looking right at her. With her heart hammering in her chest, Courtney moved quickly out of the line of sight, pressing her back against the dining room wall as if she were some sleuth in a mystery novel, about to be caught by the villain. Her tea sloshed over her hand and she gritted her teeth against the heat of it, but she was too panicked to move and set it down. She gave herself a few seconds to catch her breath, her palm to her chest like an elderly woman as she looked around and tried to think clearly. The dining room was dark. The streetlights peeking in dimly didn't do much to lighten it, and she almost chuckled when she realized Bob probably couldn't see inside at all—if that's what he was even doing. Despite the pounding of her heart and the overexcited rushing of her blood, she rolled her eyes at herself.

"Jesus, Courtney, paranoid much?" she muttered aloud. Just because Bob was up at four in the morning and happened to be standing in his window, it didn't mean he was trying to look in her house or at her.

She continued to reason it out. How would he even know she was up? She hadn't turned on any lights. He couldn't possibly predict she'd be standing in her dining room at four a.m., exactly the time he looked out his window.

She shook her head at the ridiculousness of it all, but found herself just a little too freaked out to fully stand back in her earlier position. Instead, she turned very slightly so she could peek just enough to see without standing in full view. Bob's upstairs light was on and his curtains were open. She could see the white wall of the room and the corner of what was probably a frame of something mounted on the wall. Bob was nowhere to be seen and in a few more seconds, the light went off. Courtney expelled her breath in a loud whoosh. Scrubbing hard at her forehead, she went into the kitchen and cleaned off her hand and mug.

The anger began to settle in then, as it always did when she realized how utterly alone she often felt without Theresa. If she were alive, Courtney would have run back upstairs and woken her up. Theresa would have "gotten her butch on," as she liked to joke, and come downstairs to make sure everything was as it should be. She would have teased Courtney for her overactive imagination and tendency toward paranoia, they would have laughed over the whole thing, and—most importantly—Courtney would now feel safe. She missed that. And when the missing started, the anger subsided and the sadness took its place, filling her, the weight of it pressing down on her. She missed feeling safe and protected, relieved to have another person in the house, in the bed with her. That feeling hadn't been detectable in a long, long time.

As her eyes pooled with the inevitable tears, she took her tea into the living room and flopped down onto the couch. The sudden exhaustion was nearly overwhelming.

❖

"No, no. Sit down. I'll get it." Forestalling her sister's attempt to rise from her chair with a firm hand on her shoulder, Rachel waited for her to sink back into the La-Z-Boy recliner. "How are you feeling?" she called to Emily from the kitchen as she poured a glass of ice water for her sister and grabbed a can of Coke for herself.

"Like a beached whale." Emily grimaced at Rachel as she took the water, looking every bit as uncomfortable as Rachel thought she must have felt. Despite sitting in the most comfortable of chairs, she still looked awkward and irritated. Her legs stuck straight out in front of her, and her swollen belly was enormous and in the way of everything. "I'm so glad this is almost over. I'm huge. Everything is bloated or swollen or puffy. I had to take my wedding rings off. I haven't seen below my waist since last month. Are my slippers on the right feet?"

"They are," Rachel said with a grin, not wanting to laugh at Emily's discomfort, but finding her unarguably beautiful just the same. "Nine months is a long time, huh?"

"You're damn right, it is."

Rachel continued to grin as she sipped from her soda and watched her little sister try unsuccessfully to find a relaxed position. "Can I help?"

"No. Just try to keep that smirk to yourself."

Rachel's grin widened. "I'm sorry, honey. But you are glowing. You know that, right?"

"That's probably just the sweat I've worked up trying to shift in my seat."

Rachel wasn't fooled by Emily's faux crankiness. Her sister was born to be a mother and was at her happiest when pregnant, the anticipation of a new child enough to make her giddy. She was an incredible parent, showing patience, guidance, and determination that Rachel never knew she had. Watching her now, Rachel felt herself fill with pride.

They didn't look a lot alike. Most people were surprised to know they were sisters. Rachel favored their father heavily, the light hair, the pale eyes, the long, lean frame. Emily was more their mother, a bit shorter, not heavy, but not as long and lean as Rachel, her hair more reddish than blond, her eyes a much deeper blue. Despite the lack of resemblance, though, they couldn't be closer. They didn't have a lot in common and their personalities were quite different, but they meant the world to one another. Rachel credited their parents' divorce for that. She had taken it upon herself at a very young age to be the Grand Protector of her little sister, often to Emily's dismay.

"What does the doctor say?" she asked, snapping back into the present. "Is everything okay?"

"Well, that's why I asked you to swing by."

Arching an eyebrow, Rachel braced herself. "What's wrong?"

"Nothing's wrong." Emily waved her hand dismissively, her fingers sausage-like and swollen. "Relax. I wanted to let you know that I decided to have another C-section."

"You did? How come?" Rachel knew that once a woman had a C-section, as Emily had with her firstborn, the option was there to have another with the next child. She was surprised, though, because she'd been sure Emily would opt for natural childbirth. It was what she'd wanted with Jake before unforeseen medical emergencies involving the umbilical cord and his neck.

"Greg and I got talking to the doctor about it, and it just seems like it's better all the way around. I won't have to go through labor, which means no screaming." She winked. "I already have a scar, so that'll be nothing new. Plus, the baby will come out all round instead of with a cone head and it's less traumatic than squeezing it through a teeny, tiny little hole." The ice cubes in her glass clinked as she lifted the water to her lips and took a healthy gulp. "Not to mention, there won't be any of that messy ripping-Mommy-open-down-there nonsense."

"That's reason enough for me right there," Rachel agreed.

"And I've arranged it so you can be in the room."

Rachel blinked at her. "What?"

"If you want to," Emily added quickly. "I know you were supposed to help me give birth to Jake and nobody knew he had other plans, so...I wanted you to have another opportunity. No pressure, though. It's completely up to you."

"Are you kidding?" Hiding her grin was not an option; she beamed. "I'm so there."

"Good." Emily smiled back at her, obviously pleased by her sister's enthusiasm.

"When?"

"I'll know in the next couple of weeks. As soon as the doctor schedules me, I'll give you a call."

"Thanks, Em." Rachel felt a little silly with the goofy grin plastered across her face, but she couldn't seem to make it dim even a small amount.

❖

"Okay, that would have scared me, too." Amelia took a sip of her coffee and studied Courtney carefully as they sat at the Tyler's kitchen table. Courtney had dropped by to thank Amelia in person for the beautiful job she did on the dining room the previous night and ended up telling her of the early morning scare she'd had.

Courtney waved a dismissive hand. "Please. It was me being paranoid because I had very little sleep and weird dreams."

"What kind of dreams?"

Courtney almost kicked herself for even bringing them up. "Nothing important. Just weird stuff that didn't make any sense." She felt Amelia's gaze on her as she took a bite of the brownie she snagged from the plate in the middle of the table.

"Uh-huh." Amelia's tone said she didn't believe a word of it, but she was letting it go for now. "So? How was the date?"

"The date." Courtney tried to hide the smile that forced the corners of her mouth up. "The date was good."

"Apparently," Amelia said with a chuckle. "I can tell by looking at you." She reached across the table and playfully slapped at Courtney's arm. "Details, girl!"

Courtney recounted the entire evening, from start to finish, sharing the size of the crowd, the number of people she met, Rachel's popularity and passion for the organization, and how impressed she'd been with all of it.

"Sounds like you had fun with Ms. Icy Cool."

"I did."

"Kiss her good night?"

The twinkle in Amelia's dark eyes made Courtney blush, which completely gave her away.

"You *did* kiss her, didn't you?" Amelia cackled with glee.

"If you must know, *she* kissed *me*," Courtney corrected, feeling a smile blossom on her own face.

"And?"

"She kissed me *very* well."

Amelia smiled. "That's so great, C. Are you going to see her again?"

"Yeah, I'm going to cook her dinner."

"That's fantastic. Once she tastes your cooking, you'll never get rid of her."

"We'll see." Courtney became gradually quiet until she was studying the brownie as if it were some sort of new species.

"C? What's wrong?"

Courtney knew better than to try to hide things from her best friend. Amelia was always aware when something was bothering her, and she wouldn't let her rest until she gave it up. It was less aggravating to just let her win from the beginning because they both knew she'd end up winning anyway. Courtney met her gaze. "Do you…" She furrowed her brow and concentrated on finding the right words, then tried again. "Do you think it's weird that I kissed Rachel and then had a sex dream about Theresa that same night?"

"Oh, honey." Amelia waved a hand glibly at her. "I've kissed Carl and then had a sex dream about The Rock. Is *that* weird?"

Courtney wrinkled her nose. "Um, a little. Yeah."

"Hey!" Amelia tossed her napkin at Courtney, making her laugh. When their giggling eased up, Amelia scrutinized Courtney's face closely. "Do you like this girl?"

Courtney inhaled deeply and blew it out. "It's kind of early on… but, yeah. I think I do. I'd really like to get to know her better."

Approval showed on Amelia's face. When she spoke, her tone was gentle. "Theresa would be okay with that. She wouldn't want you to be alone. You know that, right?"

"I do know that. I do. Deep down inside, I do. But there's still that little voice that won't shut up, you know? It's always there."

"The one that says you're cheating on her?"

"That's the one."

"You've got to ignore it, C. It doesn't mean anything. You've got to tune it out."

"Easy to say."

"I know."

Amelia's twelve-year-old son, Kyle, chose that moment to interrupt and for that, Courtney was grateful. He kissed her cheek as he walked by, his body all gangly limbs and enormous feet, his face a carbon copy of his mother's.

"Hey, Aunt Courtney."

"Hi, Kyle. What's new?"

"Me and the guys are gonna shoot some hoops down at Mike's." As an afterthought, he looked to Amelia. "That okay, Ma?"

"Be back here by four," she said sternly.

"'Kay."

"God, he's getting big," Courtney said as she watched him bolt from the room.

"You have no idea." Amelia sounded wistful. "Sometimes, I feel like I placed this little baby gently in his crib and when I came back in the next morning, he was practically a teenager." Looking back at Courtney, she said, "When is she coming for dinner? And what are you going to make her?"

"No idea. On both counts. It won't be this week; she's busy. But she said next week was a definite. She's supposed to call me to confirm her schedule." Inside, Courtney hoped it would be sooner rather than later. She also wondered if she'd survive the wait, but she wasn't yet ready to admit either fact aloud.

❖

"Hello?"

"Courtney? It's Rachel."

"Hey. Hi. How are you?"

Warmth spread through Rachel's body as she listened to Courtney's voice, certain she sounded glad to hear from her. "I'm good. I didn't expect to get you. Aren't you in school?"

"It's my lunch hour. Do you want me to hang up and then you can call back and I'll let my voice mail pick up?"

Rachel could hear the teasing note and she laughed with self-deprecation. "No. I'm good. Thanks, though."

"What's up? Are you calling to give me your dinner night preference?"

"As a matter of fact, I am."

"And?"

"How's next Wednesday?"

"Next Wednesday's perfect. Does six work for you?"

"Six would be great. What can I bring?"

"Just your smiling face. Think you can manage that?" Courtney's teasing had taken a tiny detour into enticing and Rachel couldn't remember the last time she'd participated in a little innocent flirting. She had to admit, she liked it.

"I think so. Will yours be there as well?"

"Oh, it definitely will."

"Good. I'm looking forward to it."

"Me, too."

Rachel hung up the phone, feeling both nervous and elated, like a high school kid asking somebody out. She'd been right; when checking her schedule, she found she had both Wednesday and Friday free. To her surprise, she also found she'd rather see Courtney again sooner than later. That gave her a case of the jitters.

Chiding herself for being ridiculous and refusing to analyze it any further, she pulled out the paperwork on a house she was going to show that afternoon and tried to concentrate. These clients were difficult. Nothing ever seemed to be quite right; there was always some small issue with each house that negated every positive aspect, and Rachel was beginning to lose patience with them. But these were also the kind of clients that were her bread and butter. If she could find these overly particular, hard-to-please people a house that they loved, they'd pass her name on to everybody they knew and she'd get more business out of them as payment for her hard work and fortitude. More business meant more money. More money was never a bad thing. Trying to focus, however, proved more difficult than she'd expected as her mind kept drifting back to her date with Courtney, bringing an inadvertent smile to her lips.

Friday evening had gone *way* better than she'd ever expected. Courtney had been charming and fun and seemed really impressed with Happy Acres and its staff—not that impressing her had been the point. But the animal shelter meant a lot to Rachel and she found herself inexplicably pleased that Courtney had understood that immediately.

Her gaze slipping from the paperwork in front of her to an unspecific spot in the living-room air, Rachel touched her fingertips to her lips. Kissing Courtney had *not* been in her plans. She was not one to move that quickly. Truth be told, she normally moved much slower than was deemed necessary by most normal people. She thought things out, planned each step with painstaking precision, mapped out her life from beginning to end. Spontaneity was not a common word in her vocabulary. But Rachel couldn't help herself; that kiss had been truly unexpected, totally spontaneous.

And hot. God.

Rachel was almost positive her lips were still warm to the touch.

She was nervous. Just a little bit. Moving too quickly always had that effect on her. Being impulsive meant that more than likely, something would bite you in the ass later, when you weren't expecting it. If there was one thing Rachel Hart despised more than anything else in the world, it was being caught off guard.

Her brain tossed her the image of Courtney from Friday night, sitting in Rachel's car, the soft yellow of the streetlights casting streaks in her hair, those big green eyes looking at her, into her. Who wouldn't have kissed Courtney McAllister at that moment? How could she possibly have been expected not to?

She touched her own lips once more. And damn if that kiss hadn't been worth it. Jesus. She forced herself to concentrate on her clients and the house she was going to show, trying her best to push Courtney and the previous night from her mind for the time being. She was only partially successful.

CHAPTER TEN

There was a chill in the air that was uncharacteristic for very early October, even in upstate New York. Courtney had a love/hate relationship with autumn. She loved the beauty of it, the changing leaves painting the trees in bright oranges, reds, and yellows, turning the horizon into a canvas of color. She loved the idea of pulling out her warm, cozy sweaters after weeks and weeks of heat that could often become uncomfortably humid. She loved the smell of a wood-burning fire crackling in the fireplace and the crisp taste of the cooler air. At the same time, autumn meant the impending winter, which she despised. She hated being cold. She hated maneuvering her car on slick, icy roadways, something that had made her almost unreasonably anxious since Theresa's accident. She hated the chore of shoveling the driveway and brushing endless piles of snow off her car. Most of all, she hated that winter where she lived could last almost six months.

The room in the community center had been too chilly during group. Pulling the sleeves of her sweatshirt down past her wrists, she stood up and gathered her windbreaker, wishing she'd worn something a tiny bit heavier.

"Want to grab a drink?" Lisa asked, smiling as she slung her purse over her shoulder.

"On a Tuesday?"

"What, is there some rule I don't know about that says no alcohol consumption is allowed on Tuesdays?"

"I don't know," Courtney hedged as they spilled out of the

room and into the hall. "I've got some papers that need grading. I should be a good girl."

"Screw being a good girl. Good girls never have any fun. Just one drink. Come on."

Courtney couldn't help but smile at her friend's insistence. She wondered if Lisa wanted to talk a little bit about Mark. "All right. But just one."

"Take my car?"

"Sure."

The bar they chose was dark, cozy, and practically empty. Just the way Courtney liked it.

"So, is group helping you?" Lisa asked once they were seated and each had a glass of wine in front of them.

"I think it is," Courtney replied with honesty. "I mean, even if I don't participate much, just hearing that other people are going through the same stuff as me is a big help."

"Even if they're all old enough to be our parents?"

"Or grandparents?" Her feet propped on the rails of the bar stool, Courtney shifted to get a better view of her friend. "We're kind of in our own little tragic party, aren't we?"

Her mouth pressing into a firm, straight line, Lisa agreed. "It's hard. I feel like we don't really belong with the rest of the group because we're so much younger, but it doesn't mean we're not going through the same pain, the same confusion, the same worries." She sipped her wine, then perked up just a bit. "I like that Ted guy."

"He seems really nice, not as far removed as the others. Maybe we should invite him to have a drink with us sometime."

"We should."

"Definitely. I bet he'd come. He likes us. On the other hand, I think Joanne hates us."

"I think Joanne hates everybody. That is one bitter woman."

"Don't ever let me get that way. Promise me."

"I promise," Lisa reassured her, patting her arm. "I'll slap you or something."

"Slap me hard."

Lisa arched a teasing eyebrow. "Interesting request. But, hey, if that's what you want…"

Feeling the heat of her own blushing, Courtney poked at the inside of her cheek with her tongue and gave a self-deprecating chuckle. "Yeah, so not into that. But thanks."

"What are friends for?"

They sat in silence, each with a small grin on her face. Courtney couldn't remember the last time she'd felt so comfortable with somebody so new in her life, and even if group didn't work the way it was supposed to, she'd always be grateful that it introduced her to Lisa.

"I like Mark," Lisa said, totally out of the blue. She shot an apprehensive expression Courtney's way.

"That's great," Courtney replied. "I'm glad. He's a good guy." She was afraid to ask too much. While she wanted to know how it was going, she also didn't want to make either of her friends uncomfortable by seeming nosy or opinionated.

"He is."

Courtney waited for more, but none came. Deciding Lisa was testing the waters, she chose not to push. When Lisa—or Mark, for that matter—was ready to talk to her, she would. She hoped.

❖

Wednesday had been crazy. Courtney felt pulled in sixteen different directions throughout the day and began to wonder if the clock would ever reach three. The kids were talkative and distracted and she had to fight the urge to give them a pop quiz simply so she wouldn't have to deal with them for half an hour.

She was also reaching the limits of her patience with Andrew Gray. He seemed to be very fond of invading her personal space, like a youngster who hasn't yet learned the concept of boundaries. He never touched her. He just sauntered up the aisle at the end of the class like he hadn't a care in the world. His eyes never left her face and he never said a word. He simply inched up so close that she had to force herself not to give in and step back. Mark was right, it was pure intimidation, and she refused to be baited or to let him win. Her rational teacher's brain told her she needed to go talk to her boss and have something done. But her female pride sneered, *And tell him what? "Andrew Gray stands too close to me"?* She was frustrated and it made her snippy and she hated it. And she so wished she could talk to Theresa about it. She'd have the right advice, just like always.

The deep red, smooth-tasting merlot went a long way in helping Courtney to calm down and relax. It was a new brand from Washington she hadn't tried before and she was pleased with its warmth and fullness. She studied the color, momentarily hypnotized by its ruby depths. Letting a sip roll around on her tongue, she closed her eyes and willed her stress to seep from her body. This was supposed to be a fun, enchanting evening and she didn't want something as insignificant as the proximity of a student more than two hours ago to color the ambience she was trying to create. Scraps and empty packages were strewn around the kitchen like litter on a highway and she sipped her wine, looking at it with disdain. *I could really use a self-cleaning kitchen.* Shaking her head with a grin at the ridiculous prospect, she began a quick tidy, sweeping garbage into the wastebasket and lining dishes in the dishwasher. Rachel would arrive within a half hour and she didn't want any part of the house looking like a cyclone had gone through.

The dining room looked terrific. She'd toyed with the idea of candles, but worried that they might seem too forward. Not that the idea of a romantic dinner with Rachel was unpleasant. More to the point, Courtney didn't want to scare her away on the second date. The place settings were neat and orderly, her rich, plum-colored place mats pulling the same shade out of the border Amelia had mounted. The dishes had the same color in their pattern and Courtney found herself actually impressed with her own decorating skills...not something she'd have said she was good at. But with the soft light from the chandelier bouncing off the crystal water glasses, the room looked warm and inviting and she was proud.

Back in the kitchen, she double-checked all the food. The pork tenderloin was seasoned and ready to go into the broiler. It had been Theresa's favorite cut of meat, but that's not why Courtney had chosen it. She knew she could do a good job on it; that was her reasoning, but a tiny twinge of guilt hit her right between the eyes just the same, and she did her best to shake it away. Green beans from her parents' garden were sitting in a pot. The next burner over held a matching pot of potatoes that was boiling gently. The chocolate cream pie for dessert was in the refrigerator, and though Courtney had really wanted to make something homemade, time just hadn't been generous with her, so it was store-bought.

Deciding a last-minute checkup was in order, she bolted upstairs to the bathroom and gave her reflection one last look. Her hair was pulled back in a gentle twist and she'd applied just a tad of mascara, which Amelia said always brought surprised attention to her eyes. Not wanting to be too presumptuous by overdressing, she'd opted for a casual outfit: jeans and a deep green lightweight sweater. Knowing there wasn't much more she could do and she was out of time anyway, she ran a quick hand over herself—straightening her top, tucking a strand of escaped hair behind an ear, reclasping her earrings. Just as her foot hit the top step, the doorbell rang and sent her heart into her throat.

"Oh, Christ," she muttered, suddenly shaky.

It was hard to accept how nervous she was. Unsure what to do with the confusion, she swallowed it down and reached for the doorknob, smiling as she took in the sight before her. Rachel stood on the front steps, a bottle of wine in one hand, a small bouquet of yellow lilies in the other, and a grin on her face. She was dressed as simply as Courtney in hip-hugging jeans and a snug white shirt with several enticingly unfastened buttons. Her hair was wavy and loose and Courtney had to fight the urge to reach out and rub it between her fingers.

"Hi," Rachel said and held out the flowers.

"Hi," Courtney responded, taking them, allowing their fingers to brush casually and enjoying the feel of it. "These are beautiful." She stood aside to allow Rachel to enter, the vague hint of her perfume causing Courtney's head to lift slightly as she walked by, like a dog catching the scent of a bone.

"I hope red is okay," Rachel said, indicating the wine. "I wasn't sure what you were making for dinner."

Courtney examined the bottle, once again impressed with the quality of the brand. "Red is great. And for somebody who doesn't know much about wine, you do an awfully good job picking it out."

"Thanks," Rachel said as she followed her into the kitchen.

As Courtney stretched to reach a wineglass off the top shelf of the cupboard, she was certain she could feel Rachel's eyes roaming over her, causing both arousal and nervousness to battle within her. "So. How was your day?" She concentrated on operating the corkscrew, hoping the tremble of her hands went unnoticed by her dinner companion. Why the hell was she so nervous?

With a sly grin, Rachel stepped forward and took the bottle and corkscrew from her. "Here, let me." She went to work on the bottle, talking as she poured. "My day was okay. I had mostly research to do. No showings today, but I set a couple up that I think will be successful."

After rinsing out her own glass and setting it close, Courtney leaned the small of her back against the edge of the counter and watched Rachel's hands as she decanted the deep crimson wine into the clear glasses. To her, there was something mesmerizing about red wine—its color, its depth, its aroma—almost as if each individual bottle had a story to tell. This time, however, the combination of the wine and Rachel's beautiful hands was, for lack of a less predictable word, intoxicating, and she felt suddenly light-headed as she watched Rachel work and listened to her talk. Shaking herself, she tried to focus on the conversation.

"You know," she said as she took the offered glass from Rachel's hand, "I don't think I've ever met anybody who was a full-time realtor. I mean, I know many people are, but I think the common assumption, at least in this area of the state, is that it's a side job."

Rachel nodded. "For a lot of people, it is. My mother is semiretired and she still sells houses."

"Is she your competition?" Courtney asked with a grin.

"I guess she would be if we moved in the same circles. Which we don't." Rachel held up her glass for a toast. "Cheers."

"Cheers." They sipped and Courtney let the liquid coat her tongue and roll around her mouth before swallowing. It was blissfully good, with a hint of fruit, but no sweetness. "Oh, this is wonderful," she commented. "Smooth. That's two excellent bottles of wine you've brought me. I think you should always bring the wine." Realizing the assumption that came with such a statement, she flushed and turned to fuss with the pork.

"Deal," Rachel said softly, leaning against the door frame to watch Courtney work.

An hour later, Rachel sat back heavily in her chair at the dining room table. "Oh my God, I'm full. That was fantastic."

"There's dessert."

Rachel's eyes bugged out. "Dessert? What are you trying to do to me?"

Courtney grinned. "You can certainly take some home if you're too full. I really don't want you exploding all over my newly decorated dining room."

Rachel poured the last of the wine evenly into their glasses. "Tell me about your family."

Courtney picked up her glass and sat back in her chair. "My family. Let's see. My parents are both retired. My dad was a plumber. My mom was a receptionist at a dentist's office."

"Are they still together?"

"Believe it or not, yes. I ended up being a minority in high school because I was one of the few kids whose parents weren't divorced."

A grimace crossed Rachel's face. "Yeah. I was in the majority."

"I'm sorry. How old were you?"

"Thirteen."

"Ugh. That's a tough age. Not that any age isn't tough to have your parents split up, but when you're thirteen…"

"I know. You're old enough to know there's something wrong, but your parents think you're too young to talk to about it."

"Do you have siblings?" Courtney asked.

"A younger sister. Emily. She's pregnant. You?"

"Two older sisters. You're going to be an aunt?"

"Yup. For the second time. I'm going to go into the delivery room this time, too." She shot a smirk at Courtney. "So. You're the baby."

Courtney grinned, aware that Rachel was keeping the focus off herself, but enjoying the banter just the same. She sent a mock-glare back across the table. "That's right. So what?"

"You youngest never know how good you have it." Rachel's tone held a teasing lilt.

"You oldest always say that."

"Because it's true. We pave the way, test the rules, and gauge the punishments. You babies get spoiled rotten and by the time you're teenagers, the parents are too tired to uphold the same rules us oldest had to follow." She shrugged. "It's an age-old imbalance."

"Please." Courtney snorted, smothering a grin. "The oldest got to do everything first. You got to stay up later, stay out longer, never had to wear hand-me-downs. Imbalance is right. In your favor."

They each sat grinning at the other.

"What was your last big splurge?" Courtney blurted out. "Something you bought just for yourself, just because you wanted to be spoiled?" She watched Rachel over the rim of her glass as the thoughts whirred through her mind almost audibly.

"Hmm…" Rachel squinched up her nose and lips in a face of concentration. "I'd have to say…my plasma television."

Courtney sat up in her chair and her jaw dropped open in envy. "You have a plasma television?"

"I couldn't help it. I'm sort of an electronics whore."

Courtney laughed. "Yeah, me, too. Is that a lesbian thing? Straight girls like jewelry and expensive clothes, lesbians like power tools and electronics?"

"Makes sense. What about you?" Rachel's eyes twinkled. "What was your last splurge on yourself?"

"Definitely my pistol."

A gulp of wine went down the wrong pipe and Rachel choked. Regaining her composure, she asked, "You have a gun?"

"Yep. Want to see it?" Courtney started to rise, but Rachel stopped her with an outstretched hand.

"No. No, no. That's okay."

Noticing Rachel trying to hide a grimace, Courtney felt the heat of embarrassment. "You don't like guns, I take it," she ventured.

"No, not really."

"How come?"

"Well...because I think they're dangerous and unnecessary."

"In the wrong hands, sure."

"Guns don't kill people. People kill people, right?" The light note of sarcasm that crept into Rachel's voice poked irritation at Courtney.

"That's right."

"Why did you want one? Why do you have one? What's the draw?" The questions were undeniably accusatory.

The way Rachel's eyes bored into Courtney, she suddenly felt like she was on trial, her head spinning from the weirdly abrupt change in mood. "I like to target shoot," Courtney explained. "My dad belongs to a gun club and we go there to shoot. Theresa and I always talked about getting pistols, but didn't get around to it before..." She trailed off.

"Do you shoot animals?"

"You mean do I hunt?"

"Yes."

"No."

Rachel folded her arms across her chest and sat back in her chair. "Did your father?"

"Yes, but I'm not into that. I could never shoot a living thing." She studied Rachel's face, wondering where this had come from and taking a wild guess. "What about you? Did your dad hunt?"

Rachel inclined her head once in affirmation. "Yeah, he did. I'll never forget the first time I walked into the garage and there was a deer carcass hanging there." The horror of that discovery was written all over her face. "It was appalling. I felt so awful for the poor thing, so degraded, all his dignity gone. They're such majestic creatures and people just...shoot them. I hate it." She looked up at Courtney then, her eyes glittering with moisture. "You know?"

Aware of nothing other than how much she wanted to get up, walk around the table, and hug Rachel until that sad, pained look on her face was gone, Courtney nodded her agreement. "I do."

They sat in silence.

"You okay?" Courtney asked after several long minutes.

Her question seemed to spur Rachel into action. She cleared her throat. "It's getting late. I really should go."

Courtney tried unsuccessfully to hide the disappointment that filled her. Rachel was right. It *was* getting late and they both had to work in the morning. Still, there was part of her that didn't want the evening to end, despite the unpleasant tangent they'd gotten off on. "Yeah. I guess you're right."

They stood at the same time and Rachel began to clear her place setting.

"No, no. Leave it."

"You're sure?"

"Absolutely," Courtney said with sincerity as they moved toward the front door. "I'm glad you came. I really had a great time."

"Me, too. Thanks so much for dinner. It was terrific."

"Oh! Wait." Courtney left Rachel standing in the foyer as she ran back into the kitchen. A couple minutes later, she returned with an enormous slice of chocolate cream pie covered in plastic wrap. "Don't forget your dessert."

Much to Courtney's relief, Rachel allowed a smile to peek through. "Thanks."

"You're welcome."

They held one another's gaze, but before Courtney could make any sort of move, Rachel bent quickly and kissed her cheek. "Good night." With that, she was out the door and down the front stairs to her car.

Courtney waved as the BMW backed out of the driveway and gave a soft toot before heading down the street. She stood framed in the screen door for several long minutes, replaying the evening, weighing the good and the bad, trying to figure out if it could be considered a successful date. While the exact path to their weird conversation about hunting was unclear to her and only served to make Rachel more of a mystery she wanted to solve, she was certain of one thing. She wanted to see Rachel again. She definitely wanted to see her again.

Definitely.

CHAPTER ELEVEN

S eems pretty simple to me." Jeff shoveled a forkful of chocolate cream pie into his mouth and closed his eyes. "God, this is good."

"Don't hog it all," Rachel whined, pulling the plate toward her with her fork. They were sitting at Jeff's small table, sharing the enormous slice of pie Courtney had sent home with Rachel the previous night. "Simple how?"

"You're afraid."

"I'm afraid?" She rolled her eyes. "Okay, Dr. Phil, what am I afraid of?"

"As you said before: her baggage." He pointed his fork across the table at her. "If you can sabotage this now, you won't have to deal with it. Therefore, you started in with the gun talk, which naturally led to the hunting thing. Nothing like starting light and moving on from there, by the way. You see what I'm saying? It can't be easy to take the place of a dead woman. If you screw it up first, there won't be any possibility of you getting hurt down the road."

Rachel's eyes popped open wide. "What? Don't you think you're rushing things a bit? Who said I wanted to take the place of a dead woman? When did I say I wanted that spot?"

Jeff shrugged, obviously not at all deterred by Rachel's increase in volume. He knew her well and could read her like a book, whether she cared to admit it or not. "You haven't been at all interested in anybody in ages. Not a soul. This one? You like her."

The idea of slapping the smirk right off his face held sudden great appeal for Rachel at that moment. She pressed her lips tightly together and glared at him as he chewed another piece of the pie and looked far too satisfied with himself. He was right, God damn him. He was right and she knew it. She *did* like Courtney, more than she was comfortable dwelling on, more than she was ready to deal with. She had no idea if Courtney felt the same way, had no idea where to go from here, and wondered if she'd wrecked everything at dinner with her overkill of disapproval.

When she thought back to the night before, she was mortified by her own behavior, by the way the idea of Courtney's sympathy had embarrassed her. *My God, what the hell was wrong with me?* She had no idea what had set her off, causing her to flay herself open in such a way that Courtney could see everything inside. Dead deer carcasses. *What a charming discussion for our second date.* She'd been utterly disgusted with herself, and the sudden need to get away had been so strong, she was still amazed she hadn't sprinted out of Courtney's house without looking back. She could still see the look on Courtney's face, the compassion in her eyes. It made Rachel feel weak. And worse…vulnerable.

"Have you called her yet?" Jeff asked, snapping her out of her flashback.

Rachel grimaced, hating that she could hide nothing from him.

Jeff sighed. "It's been twenty-four hours. You need to call her."

"I know."

"It's only polite for you to call her."

"I *know*."

He popped the last piece of the pie into his mouth and smiled at her as he chewed.

"I want to punch you right now," she said to him.

"I know," he responded, still smiling.

❖

The next morning, there was a typical October chill in the air. Summer was officially gone and autumn was finally making itself known after taking its good old sweet time arriving. Rachel didn't mind it, though. Upstate New York would surprise many a Southerner with its high humidity in the thick of summer. Those months were beautiful, lush and green, the smells of fresh-cut grass and blooming rosebushes permeating the air. But they could also be very sticky months and Rachel didn't do well at all with sticky. It sapped all her energy and made her cranky. That's why she loved the fall. She loved the way the heaviness of the air eased, the relief it brought. She loved the crisp mornings and the crunch of fallen leaves under her feet. She waited all summer for September to arrive so she could breathe again.

It was Friday, which didn't mean the same thing to realtors as it did to other people. The weekend was their busy time, and Friday was more the beginning of her week than the blessed end of it. She inhaled deeply, loving the scent of the autumn air. Just that smell alone lifted her spirits and made her smile. She felt good. It was a good day, nice weather, and she'd decided she would call Courtney when she got a free moment, maybe see if she was free at all in the next few days. She avoided dwelling on things too much…what Jeff had said, how she actually felt, the color of Courtney's eyes. Instead, she simply inhaled again as she crossed the street to the parking lot designated for her building. Not for the first time, she entertained the questions of what it would cost and would it be practical to have some kind of carport built for her tenants, just enough of a roof to keep the better part of the winter snow off their vehicles.

As she got into her car, she wondered if waiting longer than twenty-four hours to call Courtney was considered an etiquette faux pas. Did people even pay attention to etiquette any more? The kind, gentle face of her paternal grandmother crossed her mind then. Grandma Hart was nothing if not generous and polite. Anything Rachel knew about manners, she'd learned from Grandma Hart growing up. Which side of the plate the fork went on, the simple act of saying "please" and "thank you," holding the door for people, placing your napkin in your lap at meals. Grandma Hart was the sweetest woman Rachel knew. And if she were here right now, she'd not only scold Rachel for neglecting to call and give a proper thank-you to Courtney for dinner, she'd berate her for not going a step beyond.

Without another thought, Rachel picked up her cell and dialed a number she knew from memory.

"Hi, Sandy. It's Rachel Hart. How are you today?" She fit the key into the ignition. "Good. Good. I'm great, thanks. Listen, Sandy, I'd like to place an order. Can you take care of it for me?"

❖

Thank God it's Friday.

It was the only thought going through Courtney's head as she sat at her desk at the front of her classroom and fiddled with a pen. The clock ticked loudly in the silence of the room, the only sound aside from the gentle scratching of pens on paper as her class took a pop quiz. She actually felt a little guilty now about hitting them with it, but they were restless—typical behavior for both a Friday and the proximity to the fast-approaching Homecoming—and she hadn't the patience to deal with them. She'd caught Andrew Gray yet again texting on his phone. She knew he'd reached his limit, that she should toss him out on his ass, send him to the office, but she couldn't bring herself to do it. She just wasn't in the mood for a confrontation with him. She'd confiscated his phone as usual and that was that. Quiz time. Andrew glared at her from the back of the room like always, but she really didn't give a shit.

What she *did* give a shit about was that she hadn't heard from Rachel since their dinner Wednesday night. Hurt, anger, and confusion mixed sourly in her stomach as she tried unsuccessfully not to think about it. Aside from the icky conversation about guns and hunting, hadn't the evening been a pleasant success? She thought so, but maybe she was mistaken. A sudden thought hit and sent her into a momentary panic. Racking her brain, she thought back, trying to remember if she'd mentioned Theresa in any way. She'd been careful about the pork, not saying anything about it being Theresa's favorite…wait. The pistol. She was pretty sure she'd mentioned Theresa during their gun conversation.

Was that a bad thing?

If she thought rationally, didn't it make complete sense that Theresa's name would come up every so often? Would Rachel really expect it not to? That was totally unrealistic, wasn't it? Courtney had spent a decade of her life with the woman; just because she'd passed away didn't mean her time with Courtney was erased. Rachel didn't really expect that, did she?

Or maybe she did.

"She just sounds a little skittish to me," Amelia had said after Courtney filled her in on the evening. *"Give the girl some time. She'll come around."*

Courtney wanted to believe that. Wanted to believe it with every fiber of her being. At the same time, she felt the proverbial phrase constantly appearing in her mind: *I'm too old for this shit.* Why couldn't things be simpler? *You want to date me? Fine. Cool. Let's date.* Why the push/pull? The back-and-forth? It was exhausting and she was beginning to resent having to deal with it at all.

Trying to keep her anguish invisible to her students, she rubbed at her forehead with her fingertips and stifled a sigh of frustration. Before she could analyze further, a light tap on her closed classroom door snatched her attention. It opened and a very large bouquet of flowers in every color of the rainbow entered the room, seemingly with legs of its own since Courtney couldn't see who was carrying it.

"Ms. McAllister?"

Courtney recognized the voice of one of the office aides, Gina.

"Right here." Courtney stood, trying hard to ignore the murmurs, snickers, ooohs, and ahhhs of her class.

"Sorry to bother you, but I didn't have anyplace in the office to put these. I was afraid they'd get knocked over." Gina was a rotund woman in her early seventies. She brushed her graying hair out of her face after she set the vase down on Courtney's desk. Shifting from one foot to the other, she finally pointed at the flowers and whispered, "There's a card."

"I see that," Courtney said with a nod, having no intention of letting Gina or her classroom full of teenagers in on who sent them. She wondered if they were from Rachel and was simultaneously embarrassed and giddy at the thought. "Thanks for bringing them, Gina. I appreciate it."

They stared at one another until Gina sighed and took her leave.

The class was still abuzz with curiosity. Many of the girls looked on with envy and Courtney shook her head, still a little embarrassed, feeling the color that had washed up her neck and across her cheeks. Gina didn't *have* to bring the flowers here. She could have found a way to keep them in the office. She'd done it to cause a stir, which she seemed to enjoy doing whenever the chance arose. Courtney supposed after working at the school for a hundred years like Gina had, you had to create your own excitement. Courtney grabbed the small white envelope off the plastic stand and slipped it into the pocket of her slacks.

"All right. Time's up. Pass your papers forward." Groans filled the air as papers shuffled and Courtney zipped along the front of each row, collecting the quizzes. The bell rang and the class seemed to pop out of their desks simultaneously, like a flock of birds that somehow just knows how to all take off together. "Have a great weekend. I'll see you all on Monday," she said, raising her voice over the din.

She'd only commandeered two phones today, so she withdrew them from her desk drawer and handed the first one off as its owner kept her eyes down. "Sorry, Ms. McAllister," she muttered.

Courtney nodded.

Andrew Gray sauntered up the aisle just as slowly as he always did. Courtney waited for him, steeling herself for his entry into her personal space. He didn't disappoint her and she fought with her own instincts to keep from stepping back. She made direct eye contact with him and never broke it as he took his phone from her hand. They stood like that for what seemed like hours, until Courtney was sure she was going to have to find a chiropractor to help with the kink developing in her neck from looking up for so long. Just when she was ready to scream or give in or both, Andrew grinned and winked at her. She flinched as if he'd poked her and then blinked in surprise.

Did he just wink at me? And—my God—did he actually smile?

"Nice flowers," he said, his voice low, vibrating in the pit of her stomach. Then he and his phone were gone.

Courtney stood, dumbfounded at the strangeness of the scene that had just occurred. Andrew Gray had spoken *and* smiled at her. She whipped herself around in a circle and did a quick, superficial scan of her classroom, half expecting to find cameras and people waiting to jump out and surprise her. Finishing her perusal brought her back to the huge bouquet. She slipped the card from her pocket and opened the envelope.

It read simply: *Dinner was fantastic.*

The grin that spread across her face would not be contained, no matter how hard she tried to control it. With the kids all gone, she took the opportunity to bury her nose in the flowers. There was a white rose, several red and white carnations, half a dozen tulips, and a bunch of other varieties Courtney couldn't name. The arrangement was beautiful and she felt suddenly light. Theresa used to send flowers whenever she found herself in the doghouse, and it never failed to get her out. *This totally makes up for not calling*, she thought. Then, *God, I'm a pushover.*

She didn't care. Rachel sent her flowers. She was flying.

The obnoxious buzz of the bell hit her like a slap and she glanced up at the clock, noting she was going to be late for her study hall. As usual. Grabbing a slip of paper, she jotted a note for the cleaning woman, letting her know she'd be back later to pick up the flowers and take them home. Then she zipped out the door of the classroom, still sporting a half-grin.

What was it about getting flowers that made a woman stupidly happy?

❖

A staff meeting on a Friday afternoon was just about the dumbest idea Courtney had ever heard. Yet her boss insisted on scheduling just such a thing at least twice a school year. Each time, one of the teachers would remind him that maybe it wasn't such a great time for a meeting, to which he'd wholeheartedly agree, and then they'd return to Tuesdays or Wednesdays again…until several months went by and he'd forget about the reminder and schedule another meeting for 4:00 on a Friday.

Courtney coasted into her driveway at 5:13, cursing her principal and thanking her lucky stars above that it was the weekend. The week had seemed to last twice as long as it actually had. Slinging her bag over her shoulder, she went around to the passenger side and bent into the car to gently and carefully retrieve the vase of flowers, which she'd set in a box and packed with newspaper, hoping to keep it from tipping during the ride. She was pleased to note that she'd succeeded.

With great effort, she managed to get everything into the house in one trip, banging against walls and doors all the way in. A breath of relief left her lungs in a puff as she set everything on the kitchen counter and noticed the answering-machine light was blinking. She punched the Play button, then began to tidy up, pulling the vase from the box and arranging the flowers so they were displayed evenly as she listened.

"Hey, it's me." Mark's voice filled the air. "Bills game. Four o'clock on Sunday. Lisa will be here and we'd like you to come. Bring your hot realtor if you want." The mischievous grin was apparent in his tone. "And can you make that taco dip? Pretty please?"

She laughed. Mark loved her taco dip, so much so that the last time she made it, she'd caught him in the kitchen, away from the rest of the guests, eating it with a spoon. *Lisa will be here and we'd like you to come.* "We'd" like you to come? Wow. She made a mental note to call Lisa.

The machine beeped. "Hi, honey. Just calling to remind you about dinner tomorrow night. And don't forget about shopping on Sunday. Around six. Love, Mom." Courtney laughed again. Her mother, for some strange reason, always felt it necessary to sign her answering machine messages. It was simultaneously weird and endearing. She frowned as she realized she wouldn't be able to make Mark's on Sunday because she'd promised to go Christmas shopping with her mother, who loved to get an early jump on the season and who would be finished with her shopping before the beginning of November. Courtney had never quite managed to be that efficient.

"Hi, Courtney. It's Rachel." Courtney stopped what she was doing, listening intently as her heart rate picked up speed. "I'm really sorry I didn't call sooner. That was rude of me. I wanted to say thanks for dinner the other night. It was great and I had a nice time and...I should have said so sooner." There was a pause, as if Rachel were trying to formulate her thoughts before she continued. "I was also wondering if you'd like to do something again sometime. Maybe catch a movie or something? And I'll completely understand if you don't. I wasn't exactly..." She trailed off as if she was suddenly uncertain. "Well, anyway, just give me a call if you want." She left her cell number.

Courtney punched the rewind button and listened to the message again.

And again.

And again.

What was it about Rachel's husky voice that made Courtney feel it in various parts of her body—in a good way? And why did she feel downright giggly that the woman had called at all? Despite Courtney's determination to classify Wednesday night's dinner as a success, the fact remained that during part of it, Rachel had been somewhat rude and very judgmental, almost confrontational. Why wasn't Courtney more annoyed about that? More wary? She wasn't as tough and self-confident as Theresa had been, but she was no Milquetoast either; she wasn't the kind of person to let others run her over with their opinions. And, frankly, the last thing in the world she needed right now—or ever—was to be dating some kind of bipolar psycho. So why did she want nothing more than to see Rachel again? To call her right this very second and take her up on her offer? Rachel had said nothing about the flowers, but it was possible she wasn't sure if they'd been delivered yet and didn't want to ruin the surprise. Courtney should call her to thank her for those, if nothing else. Right? It was the polite thing to do, after all.

After listening to Rachel's message one more time, Courtney leaned back against the counter and sighed, feeling suddenly confused and tired because she had way more questions than answers and no idea what to do about any of them.

CHAPTER TWELVE

It never failed to send a happy shiver through Rachel's body when she showed up at Happy Acres to find that one of her charges had been adopted. Rex, the giant shepherd/Lab mix, had been adopted by a family with two kids and a lot of land. She breathed an involuntary sigh of relief. Dogs that big were hard to place. She was happy for him. And she was thankful.

Small dogs, however, were always the first to go. She clipped a leash onto a small, hyper mix of at least three breeds she could pick out by eye: cocker spaniel, Jack Russell, and poodle. He had been picked up as a stray and the Happy Acres staff had named him Charlie.

"Hi, Charlie. Want to go for a walk this morning?" The dog jumped at her thigh like he was on a pogo stick, and she couldn't help but chuckle at his antics.

"Off," she said sternly and tugged the leash downward until he was in a sit. As soon as she stood back up, Charlie jumped again and Rachel repeated the command and tug. When he sat, she gave him a little piece of a liver treat from her pocket. After five or six times, Charlie was watching her expectantly from his sit, his big brown eyes soft and friendly, a dribble of drool on the side of his mouth as he anticipated the liver. "Good boy," she said, pleased at his quickness and smarts, and rewarded him. "You're not going to last long here, buddy, don't you worry. Some lucky person is going to snap you right up. Come on. Let's get some air."

They strolled the grounds, Charlie stopping every couple of feet to either sniff something, pee on something, or both. Rachel grinned, knowing that was the terrier in him. They continued on their sporadic walk and Rachel let her mind wander to the subjects that were taking up most of her time.

First, Emily had called the previous week, finally. The doctors had given her an exact date for her C-section. November 2, the following Saturday. It was official. Rachel had found it a bit odd that it was on a Saturday, but apparently, there were doctors that actually had weekend hours. *Who knew?* She'd be in the delivery room watching surgeons cut open her sister and pull her niece or nephew into the cold, cruel world. She was simultaneously joyous and terrified.

God, what if I puke?

Not horrendously squeamish by nature, she still found the idea of seeing an actual medical procedure performed before her eyes a bit…unnerving. But she knew Emily had gone through a lot to make sure Rachel could participate, and she didn't want to let her baby sister down. She was deeply touched and prayed to the stars above that she didn't embarrass herself or Emily during the birth by doing something stupid. Like throwing up.

Shaking those thoughts of nervousness out of her head did nothing to make her feel more relaxed as she and Charlie wandered around the Happy Acres property in the chilly autumn air. Once she was no longer dwelling on the possibilities of hospital vomiting, her brain shifted to the other big thing on her mind: Courtney.

The minute she'd hung up from ordering the flowers, Rachel had suffered a mini panic attack. What was she thinking, sending flowers? What kind of message were they giving off? *You don't send a woman flowers unless they mean something.* Of course, the other voice in her head, the quieter, less heard one, replied that they *did* mean something and if Rachel would relax and let herself go just a little bit, she might get a whiff of exactly what that something felt like.

She hated feeling this way. Worried. Uncertain. A little confused. They were emotions she was unfamiliar with, didn't know how exactly to handle, and Rachel Hart was nothing if not sure of herself. Somehow, Courtney McAllister left her feeling…dizzy and off balance. At the same time, all she could think about was the next time they would see each other. Unfortunately, given their ridiculous schedules, it had been a couple of weeks. Rachel had wall-to-wall showings, Courtney had a week and a half of parent-teacher conferences, and they'd laughed about how stupidly hard it was to find a time they both had open. Rachel, though, refused to throw in the towel, and she got the distinct impression that Courtney wanted to see her just as badly.

Charlie tugged at his leash, trying to smell something just out of reach, and Rachel adjusted her hold as they walked. The last time she recalled being this out of sorts was ages ago. Could it have been as far back as the week after her father left? The day she realized that her mother was in trouble and if she didn't pick up the slack left by her parents and do her best to keep things in order, she and Emily might just fade away? Of course, she understood now, as an adult, that children don't just fade away. At the time, though, she was terrified. She'd spent an entire night wide-awake and staring at her bedroom ceiling, wondering what on earth she should do. Scared, confused, and uncertain, she'd cried silently for hours, worrying about her future, about Emily's future, about her mother's inability to get out of bed. By the next morning, tired of endless weeping and realizing nobody was going to come to her rescue, she'd made a pact with herself. She'd take care of anything she possibly could, and eventually, she was sure her mother would pull herself together.

That's when little Rachel Hart took control of her life; it was her defining moment. She cleaned, she did laundry, and she bathed her baby sister. She cooked dinner. She made sure her mother was breathing. She did her homework and then helped Emily with hers. At thirteen years old, she ran the household for weeks. It might even have been months before Alice emerged from her bedroom showered and fully dressed, and their new life without Rachel's father began. Somehow, Rachel had never been able to let go of that need for control. She had it to this day. She was rigid, contained, and predictable.

Sending Courtney flowers fell into none of those categories. Neither did counting the days until they'd see each other again.

Blowing out a frustrated breath, she said aloud, "I may be in trouble here, Charlie. I may be in big trouble."

❖

"Hello?" Courtney snatched up the phone on the first ring, making a face at herself for looking so pathetically eager.

"Hi there. It's Rachel."

Like Courtney wouldn't recognize those husky tones anywhere. "All done?"

"Yep. I just want to change out of this monkey suit and I'll be good to go."

"I'll be there in fifteen minutes."

"Great. You remember my address?"

"Uh-huh."

"Top floor."

"Got it."

"See you soon."

Exactly twelve minutes later, Courtney slipped her VW into park and hopped out. The building across the street was huge, solid and beautiful, made of red brick and quite a bit bigger than Courtney had expected. She whistled softly. "Nice piece of real estate."

An ornate set of wood-and-glass double doors opened onto a small vestibule, which led to a matching set that were locked. Courtney peeked through the leaded glass at the marble floors in the foyer and whistled again. Rachel owned this building and the fact was impressive. On the right was an intercom system with seven buttons, a name printed next to each. She pushed number seven, which was labeled "Hart." Rachel answered just as the front doors opened and a rugged-looking man entered the vestibule, a set of keys jingling in his hand.

"Courtney?" Rachel's disembodied voice said.

"Your chariot awaits," Courtney answered, then smiled at the man when she noticed he was smiling at her.

"I'll let her in, Raich," he said to the intercom. "And I'll tell her all your secrets before I send her up."

"Thanks, Jeff," Rachel replied. "Don't listen to a word he says, Courtney. He's a big, fat liar."

They both laughed and Jeff turned his key in the lock, holding the door open for Courtney. Once they were inside the foyer, he held out his hand.

"Jeff Porter."

"Courtney McAllister." His hand was warm, his handshake firm but gentle. The softness of his expression surprised her and she liked him immediately.

"It's nice to finally meet you, Courtney," he said as he motioned for her to follow him down the hall. "I've heard a lot about you."

"You have?" Courtney didn't hide her surprise and it made him chuckle.

"Yep." He punched the call button for the elevator. "Rachel's been a good friend of mine for a few years now and we get together every so often to shoot the shit."

Courtney nodded, not sure what to say, not sure if knowing Rachel talked about her made her feel flattered or uneasy or both. "That's great. Rachel's…she's terrific."

"She is. You two going out today?"

"We're going to my friend's place to watch the Bills game."

"Sounds like fun." The elevator dinged and the doors slid open. "She's on four," he said helpfully. "I live on this floor, so I'll see you around."

"Thanks, Jeff," she said as she stepped onto the elevator. "It was nice meeting you," she added quickly as the doors shut. Inside, she let out a big breath, feeling inexplicable relief. *So…Rachel mentioned me, huh? Interesting.* She let a smile creep onto her face, then bit her lip so she wouldn't look like a silly, grinning schoolgirl.

When the elevator stopped and its doors opened, there was only one other door to head to and it stood ajar. The hallway area itself was gorgeous and sparkling and it took Courtney's breath away. It looked old and new at the same time, with gleaming hardwood and fancy crown molding alongside an obviously new double-hung window that spilled daylight onto the hallway and a small crystal chandelier that was suspended from the ceiling. Courtney turned slowly in a full circle, taking everything in, before approaching the semiopened door. She tapped on it gently.

"Rachel?"

"Come on in, Courtney," Rachel called from deep inside the apartment. "I'll just be a minute."

Rachel's apartment gave off much the same feel as the hallway and foyer did. Old and new blended seamlessly together for a unique, classy and elegant, yet warm and cozy atmosphere that you felt instantly. Walking into the living room, Courtney made a game of picking out as much old versus new that she could find in the first few minutes of looking. The hardwood floor was shiny and well tended, but the thin planks that made it up told Courtney they were probably original to the building. Rachel had throw rugs in burgundies and browns tossed in a seemingly casual manner to protect them. An alarmingly large, flat-screen television was mounted on the far wall and Courtney smiled as she remembered Rachel telling her it was her favorite recent splurge. Small surround-sound speakers were placed surreptitiously around the room and Courtney had to fight the urge to turn everything on, just to hear what she knew would be incredible, movie-theater-quality sound that would probably make her drool with pleasure.

"Help yourself to a drink or whatever you want," Rachel called from down a hallway. "There's stuff in the fridge. Or open a bottle of wine. Whatever you want."

"Okay. Thanks."

The apartment was deceptively huge. Each time Courtney craned her neck, she saw an entry to another room. There was a dining room off the back corner of the living room and she wandered casually toward it, drawn by the large windows along one side of the living room. The view looked out the front of the building and there was a small balcony. Courtney had no trouble picturing Rachel relaxing easily in the summer, on a lounge chair with a glass of wine and a book. She followed the throw rugs into the dining room where a midsized wine rack instantly caught her eye and drew her like it had some sort of gravitational pull.

It was almost full, only three of the twenty-five bottle spaces left open. She slid a bottle out enough to read the label. Then another. Then another. She still wasn't terribly well versed in wine, but she was learning, finding it was something that interested her a great deal. The most common conclusion she could draw about Rachel's wine collection was that it was *pricey*. Most of the wines on her rack were brands and varietals that Courtney hadn't tried yet, simply because she couldn't bring herself to spend that much on one bottle.

"Wow," she mumbled as she looked at another bottle of a merlot from the Napa Valley. "Nice."

"Shall we open one?"

Rachel startled Courtney, making her jump. Shooting a sheepish grin Rachel's way, she took a moment to admire the well-worn, low-slung jeans and long-sleeve black T-shirt that seemed to hug every single, desirable curve of Rachel's body. God, the woman could wear rags and still be sexy. Courtney tried in vain to clear her throat. And her head.

"Sorry about that," Rachel said with a smile. "Didn't mean to scare you."

"No, I'm the one who's sorry. I shouldn't be snooping."

"Is that what you're doing?" Rachel cocked an eyebrow, the twinkle in her eyes taking any sting out of her voice so Courtney knew she was teasing her.

"You have quite an impressive selection here."

"Do I?"

"Yes." Courtney furrowed her brows at the question. "You don't know that?"

"To be honest, probably nine out of ten of these bottles came from clients as thank-yous. I don't really know much about wine at all."

"Seriously?"

"Seriously."

"Rachel, you've got some very expensive wine here."

Rachel lifted one shoulder and grinned. "I sell some very expensive houses."

Courtney squinted at her, remembering she'd used that line once before. She found herself wondering how it was possible for one person to present such an overall puzzle and why it was that she wanted to spend as much time as she could trying to figure her out. "Really? What were you doing selling my modest abode, then?"

Rachel blushed adorably and studied her feet. "I sell some more reasonably priced houses, too."

"I see. But *you* brought *me* wine."

"Yes, I did."

Rachel looked up and their gazes held. "It's good to see you," Courtney said softly, feeling like it had been months rather than a couple of weeks.

"You, too." Rachel gestured to the wine rack with her chin. "Pick one for us to take to Mark's."

"What?" Courtney was hesitant. "Oh, no. This is not football wine. This is fancy dinner wine. We should just drink beer or something. Mark doesn't know a thing about wine. This stuff's too good…"

"Courtney." Rachel placed a warm hand on Courtney's upper arm. Courtney could feel the heat through the sleeve of her jacket and fought to ignore it.

"Hmm?"

"I think it's silly to save good wine for a fancy dinner. Don't you? Wouldn't you rather taste it now?"

Courtney swallowed as she listened to the hypnotic quality of Rachel's low voice as she spoke about tasting. God, the woman was sexy, whether or not she intended to be. She just was. "Okay," Courtney managed to croak.

Shifting her gaze to the bottles, Rachel ordered again, "You pick."

Courtney, too, studied the wine. "Um, okay. Let me see." She pulled each bottle out again, studying its label, its original location, its varietal. "Okay, this one?" It was a California cabernet sauvignon from a Napa Valley winery called Groth. Despite its simple black-and-ivory label, Courtney knew from her explorations at local liquor stores that it was a $50–$60 bottle of wine, easily. She also remembered all the rave reviews she'd read about it. "This is a really, really nice wine and you *have* to save it for a special occasion."

"I think I have two bottles of that."

Courtney did a double take and then checked the other bottles again. Rachel was right. There were two. "Still. It's absolutely Special Occasion Wine. Save it. I insist. All right? Promise me?" She waited expectantly for an answer.

Rachel nodded. "Only because you insisted," she said with a wink that made Courtney feel a sudden and inexplicable anticipation racing through her system.

Jesus, how the hell am I supposed to survive this woman? A mixture of excitement and anxiety churned in her gut as she turned back to the rack and pulled a bottle out with barely a glance. "Okay. This one."

"Perfect. Are you ready?"

Oh, God, am I ever ready. "Yup. Let's go. The game's already started."

❖

"They seemed good, didn't they?" Courtney asked as they drove away from Mark's house and waved to Lisa in the doorway. "Don't you think they were cute?"

"They were *very* cute," Rachel agreed. "Very cozy and comfortable with one another. It hasn't been that long, has it?"

"Only a few weeks." She thought about how at ease Mark and Lisa seemed with each other, touching, laughing, sharing private moments of eye contact. It had made Courtney simultaneously happy for them and a little envious. She made a mental note to try to figure out a way to ask Lisa how it was going…if she was having an easy or a hard time, if she was comparing Mark to Stephen and if so, how she was handling it.

Quiet descended upon the interior of the car as each woman focused on her own thoughts about the evening. It had been terrific. The Bills pulled it out at the last possible second, causing the foursome to jump up from their seats and scream in elation at the television. Between Courtney, Rachel, and Lisa, they'd polished off the absolutely delectable bottle of Shiraz from Rachel's wine rack. Courtney sat in Mark's comfy chair and Rachel spent the evening on the floor between Courtney's feet, her elbows resting on Courtney's knees. Courtney found herself playing with Rachel's hair more than once, threading it through her fingers like golden strands of spun silk. Their position seemed so natural that neither of them moved nor acknowledged it. It just was.

"Hey," Courtney said, breaking the silence as she drove. "Thursday is Halloween."

Rachel smiled at her. "So it is."

"Do you have plans?"

"I don't." Tossing a sudden panicked look in Courtney's direction, she asked, "You're not going to ask me to dress up, are you?"

"Hmm...I wasn't, but now that I think about it, that could be fun. Do I get to pick the costume?"

"Um, no." Both women laughed.

"Party pooper." Courtney stuck out her tongue. As she made a left and headed down Rachel's street, she explained, "I suspect I'm going to get a lot of kids at my new house and I'm not used to that. I'll love it, but I'm not used to it. We lived out in the 'burbs, as you know, and only got the few kids on our street. I think this year will be different."

"I think you're right," Rachel said, nodding in agreement.

"Would you like to come over and answer the door with me? I think there are a bunch of scary movies on that night." Courtney pulled into Rachel's lot and shifted the car into Park. "If you like that kind of thing."

"Trick-or-treaters and scary movies, huh?" Rachel asked.

"I like Halloween," Courtney replied with a shrug, feeling a little sheepish.

"That sounds like fun."

"Yeah?"

"Absolutely. What time?"

"Well, if you're not busy, you should try to come by no later than five thirty. The cutest costumes are the teeny, tiny kids and they start out pretty early."

"Makes sense to me. How 'bout if I pick up some dinner and bring it with me?"

"You don't have to do that."

"Okay. But how 'bout if I pick up some dinner and bring it with me?"

Courtney laughed. "That would be perfect."

"Do you like Thai food?"

"Love it."

"Terrific. I'll be at your house by five thirty on Thursday, dinner in hand."

"I look forward to it."

"Me, too." The engine of Courtney's VW hummed steadily as it sat in the parking lot. There was an almost awkward silence for several seconds before Rachel spoke again. "I had a really nice time tonight, Courtney."

"So did I," Courtney replied. As Rachel studied her own lap, Courtney felt a surge of adrenaline, a sudden peak to the desire that had been steadily building all evening, like a slow-burning fire, getting hotter as time passed. She leaned toward Rachel and placed gentle fingertips beneath her chin, turning her so they were face-to-face. "I really like spending time with you," she whispered as her gaze dropped to Rachel's full lips. Before she had any time at all to analyze what she was doing, she pressed her own lips to Rachel's, reveling in the warmth, the soft sweetness.

She felt rather than heard Rachel's breath catch in her chest, and then the warmth of Rachel's hand settled gently on her thigh. The muscle there tightened involuntarily and the feel of Rachel's fingertips digging in nearly made her swoon as Rachel deepened the kiss. Courtney slipped her tongue, hot and wet, into Rachel's mouth and was rewarded by a hoarse moan from deep within her.

She pulled away a fraction of an inch, just long enough to mutter, "God, I could kiss you for hours." Not allowing for a reply, she fisted her hand in Rachel's hair at the back of her neck and tugged firmly, exposing her long, elegant throat and pulling another groan from her. Rachel grabbed Courtney's head with both hands, holding tightly. Courtney licked up the front of Rachel's throat, nipped at her chin, then focused her attention on Rachel's mouth once more.

The sharp honk of a passing car startled them out of their entanglement, and both women sat back in their seats sporting a look of surprise. Meeting one another's gaze, they suddenly snorted with laughter.

"I don't know why we both act shocked when we end up kissing," Courtney said, shaking her head.

"Me, neither. We're damn good at it. Um…" Rachel gestured around them to the now fogged-up windows. "Think you'll be able to get home?"

Courtney laughed again. "Jesus, I feel like I'm sixteen."

"I know. So do I." Rachel leaned toward Courtney and kissed her softly and sweetly on the mouth. "I'll talk to you soon, okay?"

Courtney could only nod, feeling suddenly mute.

Rachel rubbed her thumb over Courtney's bottom lip, kissed her one more time, and then pulled on the door handle and exited the VW.

Courtney crawled halfway across to the passenger seat and rubbed a circle on the hazy window so she could watch her date walk across the parking lot. Rachel's gently swaying hips caused a zap between Courtney's legs that actually made her groan aloud and drop her forehead against the cool glass with a thump.

❖

"God, I've wanted this so badly." Rachel was almost panting with need as she pushed her body against Courtney's, forcing her back onto the bed.

"Me, too," Courtney said, Rachel's head in her hands. Mouths crashed together, lips, teeth, tongues melding, exploring. Hot and wet, wanting and needing, all else a blur of unimportance. Rachel

kneed Courtney's legs apart and pressed herself against the warmth radiating from beneath the silk panties. She began a subtle shifting, a rhythmic movement, sliding her thigh against Courtney's center.

The combination of solid muscle and smooth skin rubbing against her made Courtney feel light-headed with desire. Being surrounded by Rachel's long body made her delirious with need.

"Please, Rachel...please..." Her grainy whisper dissolved into a moan as Rachel applied more pressure with her leg and fastened her mouth onto the pounding pulse point at the side of Courtney's neck. A soft, ragged cry issued from her throat as Rachel bit down gently, nipping the skin there. "Rachel...please..."

"Oh, you are good. You've got her begging." It took several seconds for Courtney to realize the voice didn't belong to Rachel. "Begging is good. You totally own her now." It was Theresa's. "Take your time. Don't rush it or she'll come too soon."

Courtney blinked in disbelief, unable to sit up due to Rachel's weight pinning her to the bed. "Theresa?" She craned her neck, trying to see around Rachel's body and be able to lay eyes on her long-lost love.

"Pay some attention to her breasts," Theresa instructed. "She likes that."

"Like this?" Rachel cupped a handful of lace-covered flesh with one hand and kneaded gently.

Torn between the confusion of what was happening and the arousal still coursing through her veins, Courtney sucked in a breath at Rachel's touch, feeling her nipple harden and push against the fabric and Rachel's palm. Her eyelids fluttered closed of their own accord as she felt the sensations spread through her body.

"That's great, that works, but..." Courtney's eyes flew open as she felt a cooler hand on her torso, pushing her bra up so her breasts popped free. Theresa looked down at her and smiled, her rich, dark eyes gentle, yet dilated with unmistakable arousal.

"Theresa?" Courtney's plea was small and broke off into a cry when Theresa took an aching nipple between her thumb and forefinger and squeezed.

"Try this," Theresa instructed, cocking her head to look at

Rachel, who nodded as if listening to directions on how to program her cell phone. "Nice and easy. Gentle at first, then increase the pressure."

Rachel took hold of Courtney's other nipple and mimicked Theresa's actions.

"This is not happening," Courtney gritted through clenched teeth as she pushed her head back into the pillow. The sizzle of excitement that shot through her body like an electric current was the only thing keeping her from completely freaking out.

"Oh, yeah," Theresa said, commending Rachel as they worked Courtney into a frenzy. "That's good. See how much she enjoys that? It makes it all last a bit longer if you just explore a little bit, build it up. Right, baby?"

Courtney barely registered the question, nodding absently as her eyelids once again fluttered closed and her system focused solely on the fingers that were touching her and what exactly they were doing. She lifted her pelvis, trying to find Rachel's thigh again, to continue the earlier pressure to win herself some release.

"Very good," Theresa said, patting her charge on the shoulder with a proud smile. "You're a fast learner. Okay, now I'll show you how she likes you to go down on her."

Courtney snapped awake and shot to a sitting position, blinking to try to adjust her sight to the darkness of her bedroom. Waiting for recognition to dawn, she lay perfectly still, trying not to notice her labored breathing, the sweaty sheets, and the soaked condition of the apex of her thighs. When she got her lungs under control, she willed her body to relax one muscle at a time until she began to feel normal and slowly lay back down again.

That's when an image of both Rachel and Theresa bending over her, pulling her underwear from her heated and flushed body, assaulted her memory. The pillow took the brunt as she rolled over and screamed into it.

"Are you *kidding* me with this?" she shouted at the empty room.

CHAPTER THIRTEEN

Courtney was glad group had been moved to Tuesday night instead of Wednesday. She felt like she was going mad and didn't know how to grab hold of her own swirling thoughts. Hoping that simply being in the same room with others who'd dealt with similar situations would help her find solid ground, she slammed her car door and pulled her green jacket tightly around her to ward off the autumn evening chill. *The days are getting shorter,* she thought, noting the early dusk as she saw Lisa's car pull into the parking lot. The idea of the approaching winter did nothing to lift her spirits. If anything, it had the opposite effect...long, cold nights alone, short, cold days being stuck inside layers of clothes... she'd never liked the winter. Today, she found the idea of it more depressing than ever.

"Hey there," Lisa said as she met Courtney on the sidewalk. "How are you?"

"Confused," Courtney said honestly. "Do you have time to grab a cup of coffee or something after group?"

"Love to," Lisa said without hesitation, and for that, Courtney felt herself flooded with affection for her newest friend.

"Thanks."

"Are you all right?" Lisa asked.

"I have no idea."

The rest of the group was already present, Constance Mays smiling her customary, comforting smile as the two women came into the room, shed their outerwear, and joined the circle. Once everybody was settled, Constance clasped her hands together and looked at each group member.

"So," she said. "How are we all? What's new? Anybody have anything they'd like to share today?"

There was the usual shuffling and shifting of a group having trouble getting started. After a few minutes of this, Lisa cleared her throat.

"I'm having a bit of an issue," she said, a statement that surprised Courtney. Lisa always seemed so put together and Courtney often forgot that she was going through the same process of loss as the rest of them. "I've been seeing somebody new for a few weeks now, as I mentioned in the last group." She studied her hands, folded in her lap, and was careful not to look at Courtney as she spoke. "And I really, really like him. He's wonderful and sweet and kind..." She trailed off and then swallowed, seemingly bolstering her courage to continue. "But I'm finding that the closer I get to him, the more guilt I feel, and I'm having a hard time with that."

Courtney was shocked by the parallel paths their lives were currently taking. She reached over and covered Lisa's hands with her own. "I, um...I'm having the same problem," she said, making quick eye contact with Constance.

"Me, too," Ted said from across the circle, shooting the girls a half-smile, half-grimace. "But I've got the added complication of my kids."

Constance spoke with authority, the usual note of diplomacy vanished from her voice. "Let's talk about this, then," she said, turning from Ted on her right to her left to make eye contact with Lisa, then Courtney. "After my husband died, it took me almost three years before I could even think about seeing somebody new. It just felt...wrong. Like I was being unfaithful to Gil."

Courtney and Lisa nodded in tandem, like twin bobblehead dolls, as they listened to their facilitator's words.

"I knew it was just my subconscious. I'd been in bereavement for months. I'd heard all the stories, knew what feelings would most likely hit me and when. But still, it was such a strong thing. Anybody here who was raised Catholic can certainly understand how guilt can affect a Catholic woman."

Edith chuckled knowingly from her place in the circle. "Oh, yes."

"Anyway," Constance continued after tossing a grin in Edith's direction, "I had met this wonderful man. He was gentle and understanding and treated me like gold. We had a lot in common and I really enjoyed spending time with him." She shook her head. "It ended up not working out, but that's not the point. My point is that *we all go through this*. No matter what, we all, at one point or another, have the sense that we're cheating or being unfaithful or being disrespectful or whatever to our deceased partners. It's a perfectly normal reaction."

"Which doesn't make it any easier," Lisa said with a grimace.

"Which doesn't make it any easier. No. But knowing that it's normal and that it will pass helps us to plow through to the other side. Plus," she leveled her gaze in Ted's direction, "I had three children to deal with and they often end up feeling the same way as you do. They understood that their father was gone and never coming back, but it was hard to watch their mother try to date somebody else. They had the same worry about the unfaithfulness, the perceived infidelity."

Ted smiled, his face a gently worn visage. "Well, let me throw another wrench into the gears. I lost my second wife a little over two years ago and my kids hated her. Now I've been seeing somebody new for a month or two and I think it's pretty serious. I'm worried my kids won't give her a chance at all, you know? That they'll just hate her, too."

It was such an honest and sad statement, and Courtney's heart went out to him. "Have you talked to them about her?" she asked quietly.

"I've sort of hinted to my youngest, but that was all I had the courage for." He shook his head, obviously annoyed with himself. "My oldest...she's another story altogether."

Courtney thought about Amelia and Mark, how they wanted nothing more than for her to be happy...to find somebody to love and to be happy, despite how much they loved and missed Theresa. She couldn't imagine them wanting anything less for her. "Maybe you should give it a shot, try having just a little more faith in your kids. I know it's hard, but they love you and maybe if you just talk to them..." She shrugged, her suggestion drifting off into the air, unfinished.

Ted nodded and looked like he was mulling it over.

"Good advice, Courtney," Constance said with a smile and a couple others murmured their agreement. "We tend to forget that, for the most part, our loved ones just want us to be happy. Now, Lisa." She fixed her gaze and asked very seriously, "Do you like this man?"

"Yes," Lisa said, and Courtney realized when Lisa once again avoided looking at her that Lisa was embarrassed to be saying these things in front of her, given how close she was to Mark. "I like him a lot." Courtney squeezed Lisa's hand, hoping to telegraph her support.

"Is he a good man?"

"He's wonderful." Lisa's conviction was solid as granite.

"Then talk to him. Tell him exactly what you're going through and how it feels. He might surprise you."

Lisa nodded, looking the smallest bit relieved.

An hour later, Courtney sat across from her at a table in Starbucks, sipping her caramel macchiato with undisguised glee.

"God, I love these things," she said, foam clinging to her upper lip.

"You'd better. It's the only way you can justify the fact that you just paid four bucks for a cup of coffee." Lisa grinned at her, steam wafting off the creamy surface of her chai latte.

For a while, they were quiet, simply people-watching and enjoying the companionable silence their friendship allowed. Then Courtney spoke up. "I'm glad you brought that stuff up in group."

"Me, too," Lisa said. "I think."

"You don't feel any better?"

"Well...I guess I do. I have to admit that just knowing I'm not the only one dealing with these feelings does help."

"Every time I kiss Rachel, I have a sex dream about Theresa." Courtney blurted it out before she could stop herself. Relief doused her like a shower. "There. I said it."

"Me, too!" Lisa's excitement was obvious. "Oh, thank God. I

didn't want to get that personal in group, but that's happened to me, too."

"You've been kissing Rachel and dreaming about Theresa?" Courtney winked.

"Hardy har har. You know what I mean."

"I do." She sipped again and looked around the shop at the other patrons. After a few seconds of silence, she focused on Lisa. "It's happened twice now. I have a great time with Rachel, we end up making out, and late that night, I dream I'm having sex with Theresa and she's being all possessive. Which I usually find sexy, by the way. But now? It just makes me feel guilty for being at all physical with Rachel. And last time?" She remembered what she now referred to as the Threesome Dream and was hit with the familiar mix of excitement and weirdness and suddenly felt very self-conscious about sharing. She shook the flashback away. "Don't get me started on last time. It's just so hard, you know? I want to know when it's going to stop." She grimaced at her own words because the thought of losing what little connection she still had to Theresa—even if it was only in her dreams—terrified her. "Is that bad?"

Lisa cocked her head in sympathy. "How can it be bad? We can't be expected to grieve forever, can we? We need to be able to move on. Right?"

"Right."

"I want to sleep with Mark, damn it." Lisa grinned even as her pale face flushed a pretty pink. "Without underlying issues."

Courtney grinned back. "You're both very lucky people. You make a great couple. I couldn't be happier for either of you."

Lisa sighed. "He's amazing." After a beat, she asked, "Do you want to sleep with Rachel?"

"God, yes." Courtney blew out a breath of frustration.

Lisa laughed outright. "Yeah, she's a damn knockout. I know women who would sell their own children for a chance to look like her." She cocked her head and said, "I like her. She's a little tough to get to know, but I like her."

"She's pretty private, that's for sure. It's not easy to get her to open up, but I'm working on it."

"Good kisser?" Waggling eyebrows were visible over the rim of Lisa's cup.

Dropping her head into her hands, Courtney whined, "Jesus, you have no idea."

❖

"You certainly seem chipper today." Danny Boyle smiled at Rachel while she whistled as she checked her e-mail.

"Are you saying that I'm not usually chipper?" Rachel winked at him.

"Well…" He hesitated for a split second, then laughed. "Yes. That's exactly what I'm saying. You're usually more…intense when you're working." He squinted at her for a minute longer before blurting out, "Are you getting laid?"

"Danny!" Rachel couldn't help but burst into laughter.

Rachel smiled and continued to peruse the computer monitor, well aware of the fact that she was being studied like an insect under a microscope by her officemate. What she didn't tell Danny was that she'd been on the same page for nearly twenty minutes and had no clue what was listed. She'd been thinking about Courtney. More specifically, about kissing Courtney and how today was Halloween and she'd be spending the evening with Courtney. Reflecting on the way they'd made out in the car like two teenagers, wrinkling one another's clothes and fogging up the windows, Rachel unconsciously squeezed her thighs together, trying to alleviate the light throbbing there. Not the kind of woman who normally felt anything even remotely resembling giddiness, Rachel wasn't sure what to do with the growing excitement in her belly.

It had been a long time since she felt this way about another woman. Her last girlfriend left her over three years ago, claiming "emotional distance." To this day, Rachel wasn't entirely sure what that meant, but the fact that she'd adjusted to single life very quickly and easily told her all she needed to know about that particular relationship. Sure, she'd dated on and off since then, had a few one-night stands. She never had trouble finding a woman who was interested *in* her. What she did have trouble finding was a woman who *interested her*. What was it about Courtney that drew her so strongly? She couldn't stay away. She didn't want to.

Like a moth to a flame, but hopefully with less fatal results, she thought humorously.

Another fifteen minutes of staring went by before she gave up on any form of concentration. Pushing her chair back from her desk, she stood.

"I'm going to go for a drive, check my signs, see what's around," she said to Danny, who smirked knowingly.

"Have fun daydreaming," he replied.

The day was cool, but the sky was clear and the sun bathed the world in a warm, cheerful light. Rachel loved to drive in the sunshine; it always helped her to clear her mind and lighten her mood. There was no need for "checking her signs" and both she and Danny knew it. It was their code phrase for "I need to get the hell out of the office for a while before I go insane."

She'd parked in a sunny spot and her car was toasty warm. She shed her light trench coat and tossed it in the backseat, her pants and suit jacket more than enough to keep her comfortable as she drove. She donned a pair of black-rimmed sunglasses and was on her way, no particular destination in mind.

The kids should have a nice night for trick-or-treating, she thought as she slid the cover for the sunroof back and allowed the rays of warmth to stream into the interior of the car. She smiled as she thought about the evening ahead, of spending it with costumed children, scary movies, and Courtney McAllister. She wondered when and if they should talk about Courtney's ex.

Wait, should she be referred to as an ex if she didn't actually leave Courtney, but died instead? The political correctness was suddenly baffling for Rachel, which then made her laugh as she remembered that she'd actually referred to the poor, deceased woman as "baggage" at one point. She frowned in self-deprecation and didn't like not knowing the correct manner with which to proceed. Shaking the confusion from her head, she went back to her original thought. They should talk. Shouldn't they? At some point? She wasn't sure if Courtney had any kind of hesitation or boundaries or whatever when it came to dating, and she didn't want to trample anything she didn't know was there. Courtney hadn't mentioned Theresa very often and Rachel wondered if that was for her benefit or for Courtney's.

She vowed that tonight, she was going to test those waters.

❖

Across the city at the high school where Courtney worked, she was as excited about the evening as Rachel was. She spent more time glancing at the clock than she did actually teaching lessons to her students. More than once, she caught herself humming a little tune as she walked the halls, corrected papers, got a Coke from the machine in the teachers' lounge. The previous night, she'd hollowed out two pumpkins and was looking forward to roasting the seeds as she and Rachel answered the door and doled out candy to the children of the neighborhood, bloodcurdling screams issuing from the horror movie on the television. The perfect Halloween.

For the umpteenth time today, her thoughts drifted to the previous Sunday. When was the last time she'd seriously made out in a car? When she was first dating Theresa, maybe? God… She brought her fingertips to her lips and swore she could still feel the pressure of Rachel's mouth on hers, the warm wetness of Rachel's tongue exploring, sliding along her flesh. That, of course, led to reminiscing about the feel of two sets of fingers fondling her breasts, two pairs of eyes watching her let her guard down, two sets of hands tugging at her drenched panties…

"Ms. McAllister?" The girl's voice was small, uncertain.

Courtney's head jerked, as though she'd been pulled from a dream. She cleared her throat, noticing the room was fairly quiet, that Suzanne Carlyle had finished the chapter she was reading aloud to the class.

Thank God they'd reached the end of the session. She was able to cover her embarrassment by closing her book and shuffling papers on her desk as she spoke. "All right, that's enough for today. Tomorrow, we'll continue with the story. Feel free to read ahead tonight if you want, though I suspect most of you will be out causing trouble." A ripple of laughter went through the room as the students packed up their paraphernalia. The bell rang and they sprang to freedom. "Be careful tonight," she added, infusing her voice with a serious note. Withdrawing three cell phones from her desk, she stood and handed them to their chagrined owners as they exited the room.

Andrew Gray, as usual, was the last one. He moseyed up the aisle, lumbering slowly like he always did and stepped directly into Courtney's space, just like every other day when he picked up his phone.

Today, however, was different.

Courtney was too excited about the upcoming evening, too keyed up, not to mention confused, because she couldn't get Rachel Hart out of her head, and sick to death of being treated without respect by this young man. Today, when Andrew Gray stepped into her breathing space, she planted her hand firmly on his chest and pushed him, forcing him to take a step back.

"You better knock that shit off, buddy," she snarled, glaring directly up into his face. "Right now. This is your last chance. I catch you using that phone one more time, you're out of here. And I don't give a shit whether or not you graduate." She wondered if she actually growled at him.

Andrew seemed almost stunned by her sudden courage. He stood and blinked at her, disbelief clearly etched on his face as a small red circle blossomed on each of his cheeks. He snatched his cell phone out of Courtney's hand and bolted for the door like he was being chased by a horror movie villain, nearly knocking the cleaning woman over in his haste to exit.

"There a fire in here?" she asked as her gaze followed him out the door.

"Actually, I think I may have finally doused one," Courtney replied, her smile huge. Theresa would be proud of her, she was sure of it.

One more class to go and it's time for my Halloween date.

Courtney couldn't keep the grin off her face as she gathered up her stuff and hurried out of the room.

CHAPTER FOURTEEN

I'm glad you're here," Courtney said.

"Me, too."

Courtney handed Rachel a refilled glass of wine and sat next to her on the couch, brushing Rachel's hair behind her ear with warm fingertips in a move that seemed perfectly natural.

Rachel made a show of sniffing the air. "Hey, are those pumpkin seeds I smell?"

"Why, yes, they are. I hope they're not burning." Courtney headed off to the kitchen, calling over her shoulder, "Think you have room after all that dinner? The leftovers are going to supply us with lunch for a week."

The doorbell rang before Rachel could reply, and she stood to answer it.

A tiny little body stood in the doorway. He was barely as high as Rachel's knees and couldn't have been more than four years old. He was dressed in a familiar red and blue costume. She smiled down at him. "Hi there."

He held out a plastic pumpkin pail. "Trick or treat?"

"Hey, Courtney, come in here. Spider-Man is at the door."

Courtney entered the foyer just as the tiny little superhero looked carefully to his left, then to his right. Seemingly satisfied that nobody was nearby to overhear him, he leaned forward conspiratorially. Rachel and Courtney leaned down in order to hear him better. In a hushed whisper, he informed them, "I'm really Scott."

Rachel bit her bottom lip to contain the laughter that threatened to burst forth.

Courtney grinned at him and kept her voice low. "Don't you worry, Scott. We promise not to reveal the true identity of Spider-Man. We can keep a secret." With that, she shoveled an enormous handful of candy from her bowl into Scott's pail. Glancing down the walk at the young couple waiting for him, she said loudly, "You have a good night, Spider-Man. It was so good of you to stop by and check on things."

"Thanks!" He skipped down the steps as his parents waved to the women.

Courtney waved back at them, then closed the door and turned to Rachel. "How freakin' cute was that?"

"Oh, my God, I think I'm in love."

"I hope we don't get too many more that cute or I'm going to run out of candy in ten minutes."

They continued to watch television, munch pumpkin seeds, and share door duties, alternating unless a particularly adorable visitor needed to be seen by both. That happened more than once, and by eight thirty, the street had pretty much cleared of trick-or-treaters.

"Let's give it a little more time," Courtney suggested after pulling her head back in from a glance outside. "There might be a few more."

Rachel loved the childlike exuberance that Courtney seemed to have for the holiday, found it refreshing. She lifted her arm as Courtney joined her on the couch and cuddled close, her head against Rachel's shoulder. They continued to watch *Scream* on the television.

"I can't believe you've never seen this," Courtney said, poking Rachel in the ribs. "It's classic horror, but with intelligent writing."

"I didn't know there was such a thing."

"Well, now you do."

Rachel looked sheepish. "I can't watch scary movies by myself."

Courtney grinned. "I'll protect you."

Rachel hesitated for a split second before asking, "Did Theresa like scary movies?"

Faltering for only a brief moment, Courtney replied evenly, "Not really."

"What kind of movies did she like?"

"Romantic comedies, mostly."

"I like those, too." Rachel turned to look at Courtney, who was suddenly very focused on the TV screen. She felt intrusive, asking about Theresa; it made her uncomfortable, like she was prying. *So much for that idea.* She was disappointed with her own reluctance to push a little harder, but Courtney all of a sudden seemed... vulnerable. Rachel wanted nothing more than to shelter her from whatever Big Bad might come at her in life.

Courtney cleared her throat and they both tried to focus on the movie.

Neve Campbell was sprinting through her house, trying to escape the knife-wielding, black-robed, masked figure determined to kill her. She ran into her bedroom, slammed the door shut, and then opened the nearby closet door. When the killer tried to thrust through the bedroom door, the knob from the closet door locked against the edge of the bedroom door and the killer couldn't get it open enough to enter.

Courtney giggled with glee. "I *love* that! I think it's so creative. I wonder if the guy who wrote this movie had his own bedroom set up like that. How else do you come up with those logistics?" She glanced up at Rachel, who was still looking at her.

"What?" Courtney asked, her voice cracking.

Rachel said nothing. Instead, she cupped Courtney's chin and tilted her face up so their lips could meet. The kiss began as soft, sweet, and gentle, but within minutes became much, much more. Deep. Thorough. Demanding. They sank into each other, the sounds and smells around them fading away. After a short span of time— and not quite sure how she got there—Courtney found herself on her back on the couch, Rachel's body covering hers, Rachel's tongue in her mouth, Rachel's hand under her shirt and caressing her breast through her bra with such determined precision that Courtney felt a rush of wetness between her legs. Eventually, she managed to wrench her mouth away long enough to mutter, "Bed. Raich? I have a bed."

"Maybe we should use it," Rachel husked back at her. "Yes?"
"Absolutely."

They untangled themselves from each other. Rachel clicked off
the television while Courtney stepped outside and peeked up and
down the street one more time, noting no movement other than a
stray tiger cat slinking across the street. She hit the light switch for
the porch, plunging it into darkness, and then locked the front door.
She turned and jumped to find Rachel right behind her.

The thump of her back hitting the door reverberated through
the quiet living room and forced a gasp from Courtney's lungs just
before Rachel's mouth crashed down onto hers. Rachel had several
inches on her height-wise, and Courtney suddenly found herself
thinking what an unfamiliar feeling it was to have to crane her
neck up to kiss somebody. Theresa had been smaller than her and
Courtney had to hunch forward a bit to kiss her. Rachel's hands
were much larger than Theresa's, too; she could feel their warmth
on her waist, when Rachel grasped her shirt and pulled it up and off.
Rachel's voice cut through her thoughts.

"God," she murmured against Courtney's lips. "My God, you
feel good." Rachel slid her hands up the silky soft skin of Courtney's
torso and cupped a breast in each hand, kneading them through the
cotton of her bra, feeling the nipples pushing against the fabric as
she imprisoned Courtney between the door and her own body.

Courtney had a quick flash of her dream, but shook it away,
not wanting the urgency of this moment to end. *Bed.* Combined
with the heat of desire bubbling in her core, Courtney abruptly felt
the burning need to get Rachel to the bedroom, to a place where
they were once again horizontal and the differences between Rachel
and Theresa wouldn't be so obvious to her. Maybe that would help
to tamp down some of the guilt that was springing forth…would
quiet the mantra in the back of her mind that was whispering in a
singsong, "cheater, cheater, cheater," the voice frighteningly similar
to Theresa's.

It wasn't easy, but Courtney managed to free herself from
Rachel's grip, ducking under one arm. "Come on," she said and
hardly recognized her own gravelly voice. She took Rachel's hand
and led her up the stairs to the bedroom. Once there, she barely

had time to turn before Rachel was on her again, Rachel's tongue blazing a fiery trail up the side of Courtney's neck. Courtney tried her hardest to lose herself in the feeling, to drown out the distractions by focusing on the physical, to not hear Theresa directing Rachel on where to touch her and how. It wasn't easy. Theresa's face kept appearing, unbidden, in her mind. If she opened her eyes, she saw Rachel—beautiful, flushed, in control, and so *not* Theresa. If she closed her eyes, she saw Theresa, felt Theresa touching her, kissing her, heard Theresa's voice whispering in her ear.

"You're mine…"

Focus, damn it, she told herself, wanting to push Theresa out of her head, but unable or unwilling to do so and feeling guilty for both things. Her jeans were unfastened and her bra was off and Rachel was lowering her mouth to one erect nipple as her fingers slipped beneath denim.

Concentrate. Concen—oh, my God… An electric jolt of pleasure went searing through Courtney's body and a groan she barely recognized as her own was pulled from her lungs. God, it felt good. Everything Rachel was doing to her felt so good, so incredibly sensual. If she just kept her eyes closed…just kept them closed, maybe she could pretend…

Rachel's teeth raked lightly across Courtney's hardened nipple in her mouth and Courtney gasped at the sensation. She was wet beneath Rachel's fingers, soaked and hot, and each time Rachel moved them, Courtney hummed. Her head back, her eyes closed, she let her body take over and tried not to worry as Rachel kissed her again, slowly, teasingly, using her tongue to give Courtney an idea of what was to come. After several long, luxurious minutes, Rachel pulled slowly away, working down Courtney's neck again. It all felt so good, so…indescribably delicious. Courtney arched up just a little, her head pushing back into the pillow, her eyes still squeezed shut.

"Courtney." Rachel sounded hoarse.

"Hmm?" Courtney hummed dreamily, not opening her eyes. Her fingers moved lightly through Rachel's hair.

"Courtney," Rachel said, a bit more firmly this time. "Courtney, look at me."

Courtney opened her eyes, lifted her head to look at Rachel, and felt a split-second jolt. It was very slight, small, and Courtney did a masterful job of covering, but not masterful enough. It zipped across her brain like a flash of lightning, and she recovered almost as quickly, but she could tell by her expression that Rachel had seen it.

Surprise.

Wetting her suddenly dry lips with her tongue, Rachel pushed herself up on an elbow and withdrew her fingers from inside Courtney's panties. "We don't have to do this. Maybe it's not such a good idea?"

A million thoughts raced through Courtney's head, a million different reasons, a million different false explanations, but she knew deep down that Rachel had seen through her, that Rachel knew what—or more accurately who—Courtney had been thinking about. A phony excuse at this point would just make her even more pathetic.

"I'm sorry." It was all she had to offer.

"It's okay," Rachel said. She reached over Courtney's body and pulled the knitted afghan from the foot of the bed. She covered Courtney's naked torso with it, tucking it around her like she would a child. "I shouldn't have pushed."

"You didn't. You didn't push, Rachel. I..." Being at a total loss wasn't something Courtney was used to and she hated it. "I'm sorry," she said again in defeat.

"Don't be." Rachel stood up and tucked in her shirt, her demeanor completely changed.

"You don't have to go." Courtney braced herself up on her elbows, her legs still dangling off the side of the bed. There was a sad note of begging in her tone that caused her great annoyance and she fought to keep from rolling her eyes.

"Yeah, I think it would be better if I did."

Rachel wanted to run, to sprint far away from this situation. Courtney could see it on her face. And she almost did beg then. Almost. "Okay." Her voice was small, resigned, and sad.

Rachel stepped close, kissed her on the forehead. "I'll talk to you later."

"Okay," Courtney said again, this time in barely a whisper. She managed to hold the tears in check until she heard the front door click closed. "Damn you, Theresa," she whispered to the darkened room, her voice cracking.

When she realized what she'd said, she only cried harder.

❖

"Could we get two more, please?" Amelia waved her hand and gestured to the almost-empty wineglasses on the bar in front of her and Courtney. The bartender lifted his chin in acknowledgement, giving her the universal "I'll be right there" sign as Amelia studied her. "Baby, it's okay. You need to understand that it's okay."

Courtney downed the last of her pinot grigio in one gulp. "I don't know, Meel. I couldn't get her out of my head. Every time I closed my eyes, there she was."

Amelia was trying her best to be gentle; Courtney could feel it and she appreciated it. "Honey, don't you think that's normal?" she asked.

"It's been almost three years. *Three years*. Isn't that long enough?"

"You had the same problem with that phys ed teacher last year, didn't you?"

Courtney sighed and shook her head. "It wasn't the same."

She could almost hear Amelia's mind whirring and she wondered if her friend had ever tried to imagine what it would be like to lose her husband—the only man she'd ever truly loved—and then attempt to make love with somebody new. Wouldn't Carl's face pop into her mind, just as Theresa's popped into Courtney's? It only made sense that it would. How would Amelia handle it? Differently? Better? She wanted to ask Amelia these questions that tumbled around and around in her brain, but she was afraid of giving voice to them, of making them too real, of getting the wrong answers. Was it possible to give your heart fully to more than one person? Did humans have the ability to find true love a second time? They must, right? They must. God, she hoped so. She was too damn young to be alone for the rest of her life. It wasn't fair.

The bartender gave them each a full glass of wine and Amelia pushed a twenty toward him. They sipped in silence for several minutes before Amelia spoke again. "Did you try talking to her about it?"

Courtney grimaced.

"I'll take that as a no."

"How do I broach that subject?" Courtney turned to Amelia. "Tell me. How? 'Gee, Rachel, would you mind if we stopped in the middle of having sex so I can talk to you about the fact that I only see my dead girlfriend's face instead of yours? That won't bother you, will it?'"

Amelia sipped her wine, but she looked a little stung and Courtney felt bad about that. Changing the subject, Amelia asked, "Have you heard from her at all?"

"No."

"Have you called her?"

"No."

"How come?"

Courtney took in a deep breath and blew it out in exhausted frustration. "Because I feel stupid."

"Honey—"

Courtney held up a hand, interrupting Amelia's reassurances. "I know I shouldn't. It doesn't change the fact that I do."

"I know." Amelia watched the sports report being broadcast on the television mounted behind the bar. Without taking her eyes from the screen, she said, "You like this girl, don't you?" She cleared her throat. "I mean, you *like* her."

Amelia always could see right through to the heart of things, and ever since their second semester together in college, she could see right into Courtney's head, read her mind, and Courtney knew it…and sometimes hated it. She had never been able to hide a thing from Amelia, and this moment was no exception.

Also focusing on the TV, she didn't look at Amelia as she answered. "Yeah. Yeah, I do. I have no idea what it is about her. I don't even know her that well. Getting personal information out of her is like pulling teeth." She smiled at that, despite her muddled emotions. "But I like her. I think she's warm and I think she's got a kind heart. I think she's interesting and mysterious. I like her a lot and I'd like to spend more time with her. Get to know her. I think…" Her voice trailed off as the fear of giving voice to the feelings took over. God, it seemed like she was afraid of everything these days.

"You think what?" Amelia prompted gently.

Courtney tried to swallow the apprehension back down.

"You think…it could end up being more than like?" Amelia guessed. Her voice was hesitant, Courtney noted, and she knew exactly what was going on in Amelia's head. Her friend was concerned that Courtney was being too careful, keeping herself closed off emotionally for fear of a meltdown like the one she'd had several weeks after Theresa's death. She understood it, this concern, as Amelia had seen her at the very bottom of despair. It wasn't something they talked about or revisited, but Courtney could see it in Amelia's eyes, hear the worry in her voice even as her mind flashed back to that day more than two years ago…

Two quick raps sounded on the door—Amelia's signature knock—then she let herself in.

"C? You ready?"

She must have heard Courtney's muttered curses and followed them to the kitchen. When she got to the doorway, she stopped in her tracks. Courtney could feel her stare.

"Courtney? What's the matter?"

Courtney was sure that everything about her screamed "frantic." She was hunched over the answering machine on the kitchen counter, anxiously poking at the buttons, panic souring her blood. The machine whirred and then Courtney punched a button again. Static issued from the speaker.

"No," she said, her teeth clenched. "No, no, no…" More punching of buttons ensued.

"Courtney, what's going on? What are you doing?"

Without looking up, she gave an angry explanation. "The stupid car dealer called and left a message that it was time for the Ford to have its oil changed."

Amelia said nothing.

"What, they didn't get the memo?" Courtney's anger built,

simmering almost tangibly just under the surface of her skin. "Don't they know their precious vehicle was cut in half on the thruway by a semi and that my girlfriend was inside? If they want to change the oil, they can go to the fucking junkyard and do it!"

Courtney suspected later that Amelia had been waiting for that moment, knew it would come sooner or later and just stood on the sidelines waiting until it inevitably happened. Courtney had tried her hardest to be so strong, so tough. She'd put on a mask of stoicism, especially in front of Theresa's parents, from the day after the accident, and she'd kept it in place for weeks and weeks. Now, finally, it was slipping and Amelia seemed to know it, seemed almost ready for it. She stood still and silent, waiting as Courtney continued poking at the black plastic.

"And I got so mad at the goddamn idiots that I punched at the buttons on the machine because I couldn't erase the fucking thing fast enough and I..." Her voice cracked, going from fury to anguish in a split second. For the first time since her arrival, she looked up and met Amelia's gaze. "I think I erased Theresa's message by mistake, the outgoing one."

She hadn't been able to bring herself to delete what she felt was one of the last snippets of Theresa's voice she'd ever hear, and this seemed an inexplicably cruel turn of events. To prove her point, Courtney pushed Rewind and then Play one more time. The static filled the room yet again, punctuating her loss with a generic, empty buzz. With a tormented growl, Courtney picked the square black box up, yanking its cord from the outlet, and hurled it at the wall, where it shattered. Her chest rising and falling so rapidly, hyperventilation was a danger, she pressed a hand to her aching heart and looked to Amelia once more, her eyes welling. "Oh, God. Oh, God, Amelia."

Amelia dropped her purse and rushed forward, wrapping her arms around her as Courtney's legs decided to no longer hold her weight. Both women slid to the linoleum floor, the sound of Courtney's keening, pain-filled wail echoing through the entire house as Amelia held her and rocked her gently.

"Oh, God, she's gone. Oh, Meel, my Theresa is gone. She's gone. What am I going to do? Oh, my God, Theresa..."

Courtney had completely fallen apart that day, finally, and it took Amelia and Mark and Courtney's family months to help clean up the fallout. Another collapse was the last thing Courtney needed, and she was reasonably sure Amelia never wanted to see one again.

When Courtney finally turned to look at Amelia now, she wondered if her friend could see the strange combination of excited hope and worried dread that she felt swirling around in her stomach, in her head. Her voice was as small as a frightened child's as she returned to the question Amelia had posed. "Yeah. I think it could be more than like." She blinked several times, no idea what else to say.

"And that scares you?"

"That terrifies me."

CHAPTER FIFTEEN

By Saturday morning, Rachel's mind was a jumbled mess. She wanted nothing more than to spend some time at Happy Acres, quietly walking the dogs, breathing in the crisp fall air, and allowing her brain to clear, but she was due at the hospital by seven and there was no time for meditating. Courtney, clients, her father, her sister about to give birth—it all tumbled in her head like a giant Chex Mix and there was nothing she could do to sort it all out. There was simply no time.

She liked the feel of the scrubs, though. They were like wearing pajamas. Her brother-in-law, Greg, smiled at her from across the small waiting room where they sat and waited to be called in. He wasn't a big man, standing an inch or two shorter than Rachel. His thinning blond hair was covered by the scrub cap, but his goatee was neat and his face was clean-shaven. Rachel was weirdly touched that he'd shaved for the birth of his child. Using one finger, he pushed his wire-rimmed glasses higher on his nose. Echoing her earlier thoughts, he said, "These are cool, huh?" He pulled at the sky blue shirt he sported. "I wonder if we get to keep them."

"I hope so. They'll make a pretty cool souvenir." She watched him as he fidgeted, shifting in his seat. He was nervous, and that only made her affection for him swell.

"I think they're kind of sexy," he confided in a conspiratorial whisper.

Rachel chuckled, recalling all the doctor fantasies she'd

entertained in her life—women in lab coats, women in scrubs of all colors. "So do I," she responded, casually crossing her legs.

"How is it that you're so calm, cool, and collected?" he asked her. "Aren't you nervous at all?"

"Of course I am." The truth was, Rachel felt completely jittery inside, like she had a stomach full of slithering snakes. Her heart was hammering in her chest and adrenaline was rushing through her system as if she'd ingested too much caffeine. She was excited and nervous and thrilled and terrified all at once. Her exterior, however, showed none of these things. It was a skill she'd perfected over the years. *Never let 'em see you sweat.* Unlike Greg, her hands were steady and her knee was not bouncing up and down. As she sat calmly in the orange plastic chair in her scrubs, matching booties covering her shoes, anybody walking by would simply assume she was a doctor chatting with an anxiously expectant father in the waiting room of the maternity ward.

Greg scanned her. "Yeah, well, you suck," he said, but the affection in his tone took any sting from the words.

Before she could make any reassurances, a nurse caught their attention. "Mr. Shipman? Ms. Hart? We're ready for you."

"Oh, God," slipped out before Rachel could catch it.

Greg glanced at her, and the wash of relief was plainly obvious in his features. "Come on, Aunt Rachel," he said, putting an arm around her. "Let's go witness the birth of our own flesh and blood."

The operating room was sterile in every sense of the word…the color, the smell, the sounds. All of it cold, white, and clean. They followed the nurse around the stretcher in the center of the room to the head, where Emily lay sprawled out like a crucified prisoner. IV lines pierced her arms, which were strapped down, but her face was beaming and only brightened as her husband and sister came into view to stand near the head of the gurney.

"Hi, guys," she said, her voice a cheerful whisper. "I'm so glad you're here." Her hair was tousled and her shoulders were bare, but she looked radiant. Greg leaned forward and kissed her softly on the lips.

Rachel took her place on the opposite side of Emily's head from Greg, slightly shell-shocked by the endlessly beeping equipment piled in neat stacks. She scanned over the anesthesiologist, deciding he looked capable and older than twenty-five, unlike Emily's OB/GYN, whose boyishly good looks made him seem as if he'd just graduated from college.

Small stools had been placed on the floor on either side of Emily's head for the spectators. A screen made of the same blue material as the scrubs was erected at her chest so that if Rachel sat on the stool, she couldn't see the procedure. Deciding that was exactly what it was for, she took a seat and smiled at her sister's glowing face.

"Nervous?" Emily knew her sister well and her smile said as much.

"No. No, of course not." Rachel smirked at the lie. "Okay. A little. You?"

"Not at all."

"Good." She looked from one person to another in the room, making mental notes on each of them.

"Stop it," Emily reprimanded her playfully.

"Stop what?"

"Sizing up the crew to decide if they're good enough to operate on me."

Rachel felt properly chastised as Greg chuckled. She had been the protector of her little sister for more than thirty years. She wasn't about to stop now.

"Emily?" Only the doctor's eyes were visible—a bright, festive green framed by dark eyebrows and thick lashes that instantly reminded Rachel of Courtney's—as he got his patient's attention. "We're ready to begin. How're you doing?"

It didn't seem possible, but Emily's smile grew bigger. "I'm ready to have this baby, Doc."

"Good. Then let's get started." With a curt nod, he turned his attention back to the other doctor across the table. There were also two nurses in addition to the anesthesiologist who was standing behind Emily's head and carefully monitoring the beeping equipment.

Greg had one hand holding Emily's and his other hand at the top of her head, stroking her forehead with his thumb. They looked so sweet and in love that Rachel felt a lump form in her throat, much to her own surprise, simultaneously happy for them and sad for herself. Not for the first time, she wished Courtney were there with her.

Shaking what she deemed selfish thoughts from her head, she turned to the blue fabric screen. After a moment or two of deliberation, she pushed herself up a couple inches off the stool. The shining silver scalpel covered in her sister's crimson blood was all she needed to see to drop her butt back onto the seat with a thud. She swallowed hard and met Emily's gaze.

"It's okay, Raich. You don't have to look. It's enough just to have you here."

Rachel nodded, blinking rapidly. Across the bed, Greg seemed to be debating the view as well. He also inched up to peek just a smidge over the top of the screen. Then he sat back down and looked pensive. Rachel smiled at him.

"It's a little daunting," she said, meeting his gaze with a slightly worried expression.

"You know what?" he asked. "This is like being at the Grand Canyon, but not ever getting close enough to look over the edge. When will we have this chance again? Probably never, right?"

His words seeped into Rachel's brain, into her heart, and she knew he was right. A life was beginning today, a life that carried her own blood in its veins, and she was here, in the front row, to witness the birth, something she might never have the chance to do again.

"You're absolutely right." With a quick nod, she stood up, as did Greg, as if they'd done a silent count to three.

Rachel wondered how she would have reacted if she hadn't been able to actually see the baby right then. Not all of it, but a little arm, a tiny shoulder. If those hadn't been visible, the sight of her sister's torso flayed open and her insides exposed might have sent her collapsing to the ground in a heap of dry heaves. Instead, she was astonished to find herself mesmerized by the sight before her.

"Oh, wow," Greg muttered.

Rachel breathed out a lengthy "Ohhhhh" as she watched the procedure, and she would have been hard-pressed to not call it entrancing. "Oh, my God," she whispered. "Emily..." She grasped her sister's hand as she watched.

"Can you see him? Her?" Emily was quietly excited.

Rachel nodded, watching in enthralled fascination as she leaned forward, the fabric screen now touching her torso. Greg mirrored her position. Before either of them could say a word, the doctor in front of Rachel pulled the baby out of the opening in Emily's midsection and held it up.

It was a girl.

She was shaking like a little leaf and her skin was grayish blue. She was covered in slimy crud with wet chunks and pieces of placenta stuck to her tiny body. She had a shocking mop of black hair that was matted to her little skull and she was in desperate need of a bath.

She was also the most beautiful sight Rachel had ever seen.

Much to her own amazement, tears filled her eyes and a lump threatened to close up her throat. Awe caused her to bring her fingers to her lips as she stood there, staring. The level of emotion she felt astounded her, as it wasn't something she'd felt often in her life. She prided herself on her ability to remain in control, to keep a tight rein on things like sentiment. But this...this touched her in inexplicable ways, and she felt the hot trail of salt water running down her cheeks. "She's beautiful, Emily. My God. She's so beautiful." Her words caught in her throat and she squeezed her sister's hand so tightly, she was surprised Emily didn't complain.

The nurse whisked the baby girl to the corner of the room where she was weighed and measured and cleaned up a little bit while the doctors turned their attention back to the hole before them that was Emily's belly.

As Greg and Emily cuddled and kissed, awash in happiness over their new addition, Rachel's hand was still holding Emily's and she squeezed it tightly, her emotions overflowing.

Less than an hour later it was barely noon, but Rachel was scanning for an exit from the hospital. Emily was tired, as was the baby. Greg was ecstatic but descending rapidly from his high, and there were just more people in the hospital room than Rachel cared to be confined with. She tolerated her mother, was civil to her father, and somehow managed to escape before anybody was able to rope her into a lengthy conversation. Besides, she had too much on her mind to come across as anything other than distracted. She wanted to find a way to relax a bit. She wanted to analyze her thoughts and figure out why witnessing the birth of her niece made her feel so open, so emotional, so completely different, and why she wished nothing more than for Courtney to have been there with her to see it all.

❖

Courtney tried hard to busy herself on Saturday, doing little jobs around the house, going to a movie alone, working diligently to not think about how she might very well have blown it with Rachel. Even now, she didn't quite understand how or why it was that she couldn't get Theresa out of her head Thursday night, why she couldn't set her guilt and memories aside and just enjoy the moment, live in the now. It was frustrating, to say the least.

She'd taken Amelia's advice and called. She'd left two messages on Rachel's cell phone Friday. While dialing for a third time, she decided she was starting to project desperation and hung up before the call went through. Plus, she knew that Rachel almost always had her cell with her, and the fact that she hadn't picked up either of Courtney's first two calls might very well have been a hint that Courtney just didn't want to take.

After the movie, she decided to go for a walk down Park Avenue and do a little window shopping. If she were to be honest, she'd say that she was well aware that it was Rachel's neighborhood and that she almost hoped to run into her, but the chances of that actually happening were slim to none, since she knew Rachel was at the hospital with her sister today. That didn't mean Courtney wasn't disappointed as she entered the nearest Starbucks to get herself a latte. She *was* disappointed and she felt a little…lost.

The clientele was sparse and she took a table near the window to do some people-watching and be alone with her thoughts, despite her attempts to banish them. She was only on her second sip when

Peter, her former therapist, strolled through the door. She watched with a smile as he placed his order. He didn't see her until he'd moved down the counter and was waiting for his drink. He gave a surprised wave and headed her way once his cup was in hand.

"If it isn't one of my favorite clients," he said with a warm grin.

"Care to join me?" Courtney asked, gesturing at the chair across from her. "Or is that a no-no in your line of work?"

"It's only a no-no if I'm currently treating you. Which I'm not." He took a seat. "How are you?"

"I'm doing okay. I love my new house."

"That's great. You made it through the move okay, I take it?"

"It was a difficult day, I won't lie to you. But I survived."

"Survival is good."

Courtney nodded and sipped her latte.

"Did you stay with group?" Peter asked.

Courtney grinned at him. "I wondered if you'd get to that. Yes, I've stayed with it. I met a wonderful woman there who's become a good friend, so going was worth it."

"Fantastic. And are you seeing anybody?"

A laugh burst forth out of Courtney's mouth. "You know, I didn't ask you to sit with me so we could have a session."

Peter had the good sense to blush. He was a friendly looking man with a little more paunch than he was probably comfortable with. His round face tinted pink and he broke eye contact for the first time. He chuckled self-deprecatingly. "I'm sorry. It's a bad habit. I always want to know what's going on with people."

"It's what makes you great at your job," Courtney reassured him, feeling a bit guilty for embarrassing him. "And I am seeing somebody. Sort of."

"Really? Do tell."

In less than fifteen minutes, she'd blurted out the entire story of meeting Rachel, dating Rachel, and attempting to sleep with Rachel. She ended with her inability to get Rachel on the phone, adding that she was kind of relieved because she wasn't sure what she'd say to her anyway.

Peter listened intently, his brown eyes on her the whole time.

He nodded periodically, taking it all in. When she finished, he gazed into his cup for several long minutes and Courtney knew he was formulating his reply to her. She laughed.

"We're not having a session, remember? You don't have to find the right wording so you help me without actually telling me what to do." Her laughter faded away and her voice softened. "Just tell me what to do, Peter. Please?"

"Keep your eyes open."

He said it so matter-of-factly that she just blinked at him. "What?"

"Keep your eyes open." She shot him a look of confusion so he'd elaborate. "You like this woman. It's obvious in the way you talk about her, the way you describe her. Is she very different than Theresa? Absolutely. They're almost polar opposites, but that's what's drawing you...the difference, the change. I don't know Rachel and I've never met her, but from what you've just told me, she sounds like a pretty good match. You have to be up-front with her about everything you're feeling, everything that's giving you pause. You have to in order to give her a fair shot, to level the playing field. She's playing in the dark right now because you're not telling her what's going on in your head. She's having to figure it out on her own, do some guessing, and that can be a really scary prospect for somebody because...what if she's wrong? You have to trust her enough to talk to her." He took a sip of his coffee. "And you have to keep your eyes open. *See* her. See *her*."

Could it really be that simple? Courtney knew that, for the most part, people tended to make life way more complicated than necessary, that things were almost always much simpler than anybody suspected. She chewed on the inside of her lip as she pondered Peter's words.

See her.

Courtney sat at the table for another half hour after Peter left, just thinking about what he'd said, what it meant, what she could possibly do next. Her thoughts were such a jumble, she wanted to scream. Deciding against doing so in a public place, she tossed her trash and headed outside to walk it off, despite the nippiness of the late-autumn air.

She'd always thought of herself as a good communicator. She and Theresa had been one of those couples that others envied because they rarely fought. Courtney chalked that up to their ability to talk, to iron things out before they became irreversibly wrinkled, simply by being honest about their feelings. Realizing now that Peter was right, she wondered why it was that she had such a hard time opening up to Rachel and telling her exactly what thoughts were swirling around in her brain. She was concentrating on this train of thought when she absently heard somebody call her name. She stopped short, and the woman behind her bumped right into her.

"Sorry," she muttered as she went around Courtney.

"Courtney," a male voice called again. "Over here."

Squinting, Courtney could see a hand waving in the air across the street. After a moment, she recognized Ted from group standing on the corner with a woman. As she crossed, she saw that they were eating ice cream.

"Kind of a strange snack choice for this time of year," she said with a grin as she reached the pair.

Ted chuckled. He looked good, Courtney noted. Happy. His cheeks were flushed and his expression was glowing with pride. "We're celebrating," he said. Remembering his manners, he gestured to the woman standing next to him. She was small, maybe in her late forties or early fifties, with chestnut brown hair and kind brown eyes. "This is my girlfriend, Marie. Marie, this is my friend Courtney. From group."

Marie pulled off her light fleece glove and shook hands with Courtney. "It's nice to meet you, Courtney. Ted has told me a lot about you."

"All good, I hope," Courtney said, returning the smile. "What are you celebrating?"

Ted beamed. "I'm a grandfather."

"What?" Ted's face was so proud and smiling that Courtney couldn't help but throw her arms around him and give him a hug. "That's fantastic! Good for you. When did it happen?"

"This morning," Ted said, still grinning as he looked from Marie to Courtney and relayed a little bit of the story. Courtney glanced over his shoulder as he spoke and squinted at the familiar face approaching from down the street.

"Rachel?" Courtney waved, astonished by the relief and happiness that flooded her as Rachel met her eyes. She motioned to her, waving her forward, and when a gentle smile crossed Rachel's face, Courtney's relief loomed even larger. God, it was good to see her.

Ted must have noticed that Courtney's attention was no longer on his face and he turned to follow her gaze.

"I'm sorry, Ted. I don't mean to be rude. I just see somebody I was worried about." Focused on Rachel, she bubbled, "Hi." As Rachel's eyes landed on Ted and her pace inexplicably slowed, Courtney grabbed her arm and pulled her closer, gesturing to him. "I'd like you to meet Ted. He's a friend of mine from my bereavement group."

Rachel seemed unable to form any words. Courtney frowned, puzzled, as she watched the play of emotions that moved across Rachel's face.

"Rachel? Are you okay?" she asked with concern.

"I…I'm sorry. I have to go." Before anybody could say anything more, Rachel turned and darted across the street, ignoring the honking horn of the car that nearly ran her down, walking as fast as possible without actually running.

Courtney stood staring after her, uncertain whether she should chase after her or leave her be. At a complete loss and more than a little embarrassed, she uttered to nobody in particular, "What the hell was that?"

Ted still stood next to her, his gaze staring off in the same direction as Courtney's. "That was my daughter."

❖

Slamming the apartment door behind her, chest heaving as if she'd just outrun some horrific monster that chased her down the hall, Rachel willed her heart rate to slow. She tossed her keys and cell phone onto the nearby stand and took deep, even breaths.

Her attempts to focus on her own living room, her own familiar surroundings, failed.

"What the hell is going on with me?" she asked aloud, pressing her hands to her head, baffled by the discord and turmoil roiling inside her gut. She'd felt completely and utterly confused all day. Out of control. Overly emotional. She couldn't remember the last time she felt so open and vulnerable, like she was walking around made of glass and everybody could peer into her and see exactly what she was thinking and feeling. Actually—scratch that—she *could* remember the last time. It was twenty-five years ago when her father left. She'd never seen it coming, couldn't believe her father didn't want to be with her and Emily anymore, and had no idea what to do about her solid, dependable mother who had instantly become a crumbled, decimated shell of her former self. Thirteen-year-old Rachel found that she'd become the man of the house overnight.

It was as if the birth of her niece had somehow opened a hole in her, exposing the vulnerabilities she'd worked so hard all her life to conceal, and she couldn't for the life of her figure out how to close it back up. When her tears began to flow in the delivery room, she'd had trouble stopping them. They continued to roll down her cheeks even after the nurses had placed the baby in Emily's arms, even after they'd whisked her away to be cleaned up and swaddled, even when she, Em, Greg, and everybody else in the world took turns in the small hospital room waiting to see the baby. With no idea how to stop the sudden horror that she was spilling emotion all over the floor, she'd given in to the alarmingly panicked urge to get the hell out, to get away, to run as fast as possible before somebody saw inside her, saw her as weak, saw her utter lack of control. She thought walking would clear her head, thought the crisp chill to the air would snap her out of it, but instead, she felt worse, felt like she was completely losing her mind.

When she held her hand out in front of her, her fingers shook like leaves in the breeze. *Focus. I need to focus. I need to calm myself, to steady my nerves.*

Moving quickly, she headed for the nearest solution: the dining room and the wine rack. She knew that a drink would probably help to calm her down, and that's what she needed right now. Some calm. She pulled the nearest bottle out, barely registering the label. Then her eyes fell on the Groth that Courtney had pointed out during her visit.

"It's absolutely Special Occasion Wine. Save it."

Rachel grabbed the neck of the bottle and pulled it out of the rack. "I have a new niece, my father is apparently buddies with the woman I'm seeing, and I think I'm very possibly going insane," she said to the wine. "I'd say those are pretty special occasions." She opened a drawer and withdrew a shiny, futuristic-looking corkscrew. Within seconds, the bottle was open and she poured a glass, admiring the crimson color, the earthy, zesty smell. When the liquid reached her lips, she closed her eyes and savored the flavors that burst forth on her tongue. Courtney was right. This was definitely special wine, worth the wait.

Courtney...

Courtney knew Rachel's father. From *bereavement group*. That was definitely not something Rachel had seen coming. Her father was in a bereavement group? What the hell for? A split second later, guilt taunted her, teased her, asked her how cold she could possibly be to not have any sympathy at all for a man who'd lost his wife so young.

To silence the nagging, she took a bigger gulp of wine. Bottle and glass in hand, she made her way into the living room, where she flopped down onto the couch and let herself sink into the cushions. For the first time in more than two decades, she felt that she was dangerously close to falling apart and had no idea what to do about it. Another swallow of wine seemed to be the best solution.

Almost an hour later, she had slid to the floor, her legs straight out in front of her underneath the coffee table, her back against the front of the couch. As she poured the last of the wine into her glass, a knock on the door made her jump and she spilled some onto the oak and glass table.

"Damn it," she grumbled, trying to get her legs out from under the table to find a paper towel.

The knock repeated. "Rachel?" It was Jeff. "You okay?"

Before she could reply, her knee bumped the underside of the table and both the wine and the empty bottle fell over with the loud crash of glass on glass.

"Shit."

"Rachel? I'm coming in." Jeff's concern was evident in his tone. The door swung open and he took in the sight before him. Biting his lip only barely kept him from laughing.

Rachel scowled at him, still sitting on the floor as if being held prisoner by her own coffee table. "Quit your snickering and get me a towel."

"Yes, ma'am." He grabbed the roll of paper towels off its holder in the kitchen and began mopping up what little wine had been left in the bottle to spill. Luckily, the wineglass had only broken into three pieces. As he carefully picked them up, he asked, "A little early to be this indulgent, don't you think?"

"It's five o'clock somewhere." Rachel shrugged as she picked up the bottle and put it to her lips, tipping it completely upside down to get the last drops of wine that still clung to the bottom.

"Give me that." Jeff snatched the bottle from her hand, then took it and the pieces of glass to the kitchen. He came back with a wet cloth and wiped the table down. When he returned from replacing the cloth, he brought with him a large glass of water. "Drink this. Maybe we can stave off the killer headache you're screaming toward."

Rachel obediently chugged down half the contents. Jeff took it from her before she could slam it onto the tabletop and shatter more glass.

After studying her for a long while, he asked, "What's going on, Raich?"

"I'm celebrating."

"Really."

Rachel nodded and then brought a hand to her temple as she realized that probably wasn't the best movement to make in her condition. "Yes."

"What's the occasion?"

"I'm an aunt."

Jeff smiled. "That's great. Boy or girl?"

"Girl. Adrianna Michelle. She's gorgeous."

"Of course she is. Congratulations." He didn't comment on the slight slur in her words. He'd never seen Rachel this drunk before, she was sure of it. A little tipsy? Sure. But this? She would have been embarrassed if she wasn't three sheets to the wind.

The distinct chirp of Rachel's cell phone issued from near the door. They both looked in its direction and when Rachel made no move to get up, Jeff went and took a look.

He rattled off the number that was obviously unfamiliar to him. Rachel closed her eyes and sighed.

"That's Courtney."

"You want it?" He crossed back to her and held the phone out.

She recoiled as if he was handing her a dead fish. "No. No, let it go into voice mail."

She felt him watching her, could almost hear the pieces fall into place as he put the puzzle together. Schooling her expression so he couldn't read it was damn near impossible, so she pouted instead. He maneuvered between the couch and the coffee table and settled himself onto the floor next to her, stretching his legs out parallel to hers.

"What's going on, Rachel?" Jeff said for the second time. His voice was gentle and loving. "Is it Courtney?"

"No." To her horror, Rachel felt tears well in her eyes. "Oh, fuck," she whispered, squeezing them shut to prevent Jeff from seeing.

"Honey, it's okay." He put his arm around her shoulders. "Talk to me."

Rachel leaned her head against him, her world swimming sickeningly. She closed her eyes, wondering exactly how she had come to the conclusion that it had been a good idea to polish off an entire bottle of wine alone on a Saturday afternoon. In an hour.

She didn't want to say a thing. She didn't want to put voice to her thoughts, to the phrases that had been bouncing around in her head for days and days like the silver ball in a pinball machine, looking for the best path of escape. But the wine had loosened her security systems, flattened her defenses, and her precious control was nowhere to be found.

"I think I'm falling for her, Jeff." A small, whining groan escaped her lips immediately after the words were out. "I'm falling hard. I want…I want…" Scrunching up her face, she forced the words from her own lips. "I want her to be mine. Damn it. *Mine*." She punctuated the last word with a loud smack to her own chest.

Jeff hugged her to him tightly. "I think that's great."

"Great? You think that's great? It's *not* great. It's awful. Have you listened to nothing I've told you about her? The girl's a mess."

"*She's* a mess?" Jeff's eyebrows reached up to his hairline in surprised amusement.

Rachel folded her arms and blew out a frustrated breath. "Shut up." He grinned at her, obviously enjoying himself. "How the hell am I ever supposed to live in the shadow of Theresa? I don't know if I can. And she never talks about her. I don't even know what I'm up against because Courtney never tells me."

"And you've asked?"

"Once or twice. Or…once."

"I see."

Rachel tried to glare at him. "You see nothing. This is hard. Plus."

Jeff waited, then finally prodded, "Plus what?"

"Plus, she knows my dad. They're friends." She sneered the last word.

"Really? How did that come about?"

"They're in the same therapy group."

"Therapy for what?"

Rachel swallowed and turned away from him. "People who've lost their spouses."

Jeff nodded.

"If I pursue this," she continued, "if I pursue *her*, I could forever be in the shadow of a dead woman. Who wants that?"

"I see your dilemma," he said.

"Dilemma doesn't begin to describe it."

"Then maybe you should just stop seeing her."

Rachel blinked at him. "What do you mean?"

"I mean stop seeing her. Cut her loose." He gestured to the cell phone sitting silently on the table in front of them. "She'll stop calling. Eventually. You'll be free of her. You can go back to your previous life of…predictability and planning. You won't have to worry about her digging her hooks in any further. You won't have to deal with these pesky feelings and emotions. You won't have to worry about not being able to measure up to her first love."

"I could do that. I could just cut the ties. It's barely been a couple months, really. I mean, it's not like she has much of an effect on me anyway."

"Yeah, I can see that."

The tone of Jeff's voice told Rachel very clearly that she was full of shit and he knew it. And truthfully, so did she. Even in her drunken stupor, it was painfully clear to her that she was in love with Courtney McAllister. It had taken the birth of a baby, of her own flesh and blood, to open her up enough emotionally to actually see this fact, and no amount of expensive wine was going to change it. She pressed the heels of her hands into her eyes until she saw colorful stars dancing on the insides of her eyelids. She let out a mighty sigh, like that of Atlas when he was told he was to carry the entire world on his shoulders, and had only one appropriate response.

"Fuck."

CHAPTER SIXTEEN

Courtney glanced at her watch as the elevator door slid open with a ding. As luck would have it, Jeff had been on his way out as she was ready to enter the building, so he'd held the door for her, smiling and looking at her in an odd way that she couldn't describe. Thank God he'd let her in, though, because she'd had no idea what she would say on the intercom if she'd actually had the nerve to press the button and Rachel answered. It was after eight o'clock on Saturday night and she felt a little trepidation over making an unannounced visit, especially given the weird meeting on the street earlier in the day. Part of her was more irritated than anything else over the fact that Rachel just ran away like she did, but a smaller, softer part was more worried. Rachel's face had been so…strained when she bolted, so emotional, so…uncertain. That was an adjective she'd never use to describe Rachel, and that's what worried her.

Ted had explained things a little bit as best he could, given that he now knew full well Courtney was dating his daughter. She admired his attempts at restraint. He never said one negative thing about Rachel, though Courtney suspected she'd hurt him badly more than once. He seemed to understand, though, that she really wanted to hear things from Rachel and he respected that. She'd gone home with a head full of confusing thoughts and no idea what to do next. She'd spent the better part of an hour just working up the nerve to get out of her car in the parking lot across the street.

Now at Rachel's door, Courtney stopped and stood, unable to will her arm up to knock. They had other things to talk about besides Rachel's tenuous relationship with her father. *Let's get it all out on the table. I need to say a few things and I need to know a few things.* She inhaled a giant breath and let it out slowly. She ran a hand through her hair, then down over her hip, and wondered if she was overstepping her bounds by even being here. Was she becoming a stalker? One of those obsessed suitors who couldn't accept that she was not wanted by her paramour? No, that couldn't be true. Rachel was too…magnetic. There was too strong a connection, an inexplicable pull, for her to brush it aside. She knew that Rachel might not feel the same way, that she might actually toss Courtney right out on her ass in just a few minutes. But Courtney also knew that if she didn't make one more attempt to see if the connection ran both ways, she'd regret it for the rest of her life. Something told her Rachel wanted to explore the possibility of them as a couple, too, but she just needed more coaxing.

Oh, my God, did I really just think that? "If I coax her enough, she'll see things my way?" Courtney rolled her eyes at herself. *Maybe this is just ridiculous and I'm being totally stupid.* She sighed and stared at the leather of her shoes for several long moments. Deciding to give up on such a one-sided quest, she turned away from the door. As she did so, it opened, startling her enough to make her jump.

"Holy Christ," Courtney blurted as she turned back around, a hand pressed to her forehead. "Um, hi."

"Hi there." Rachel stood with her head against the door, a gentle smile on her face. She wore a pair of soft-looking plaid flannel pants and a doctor's scrub shirt and was rumpled enough to make Courtney wonder if she'd been asleep.

"I…I didn't wake you, did I?"

"No. I was heading into the kitchen for something to eat and I thought I heard the elevator bell, so I peeked through the peephole." Rachel arched one eyebrow. "You stood here for a long time. Were you ever going to knock?"

Courtney felt her face flush hotly. The peephole! How had she not thought about the damn peephole? It never occurred to her that Rachel might know she was there before she actually announced her presence. She looked down at her shoes again and scratched at her temple, embarrassment blanketing her. "I, um, hadn't decided."

"Do you want to come in?"

Courtney's gaze met and held Rachel's. "Yeah," she said so quietly, it was almost a whisper. "Yeah, I do."

❖

Rachel stepped aside, opening the door wide enough for Courtney to enter and closing her eyes as she inhaled the scent of Courtney's musky perfume. She wouldn't go so far as to say that Courtney seemed agitated, but something was definitely on her mind. She fidgeted a bit with the car keys in her hand and her eyes darted around the room. She was dressed simply in a worn pair of jeans, a deep green sweatshirt, and a tan jacket. Her hair was loose and wavy and she looked adorable.

The four-hour nap—or more accurately, the four-hour pass-out—had been just what the doctor ordered for Rachel. She barely remembered Jeff helping put her to bed, feeding her a handful of Motrin, but she knew she needed to call him and say thanks. His words, his guidance, and his friendship meant more today than ever. Now she had the remnants of a headache, but the wine haze was gone, and she felt…different somehow. Not emotionally overloaded like earlier, but…different. Relaxed? Open? She couldn't put her finger on it. All she knew was that she felt much, much better and seeing Courtney's face warmed her insides in ways she couldn't describe.

Besides that, she was ravenous.

"Want a grilled cheese sandwich with me?"

Courtney looked relieved and she sighed. "Love one."

Rachel smiled and gestured to the couch. "Take off your jacket and have a seat."

"I'd rather help." She tossed her keys onto the little table near the door and then draped the jacket over the couch before following Rachel into the galley kitchen. "Hey, how did things go this morning? I was thinking about you."

Rachel felt her face light up at the memories of that morning in the hospital. "I'm sure you already know this, but I have a niece and she's beautiful. Ten fingers, ten toes, and a mop of dark hair that none of us have any idea where it came from."

"Wow. I can't even imagine what it must have been like to be there."

"It was the most amazing thing I've ever witnessed, Courtney. Truly amazing. I'm blessed to have been included." She pulled a Calphalon frying pan out of a cupboard and set it on the stove, then lit the burner. "I thought I'd have trouble...maybe get a little queasy, but I didn't."

"Not at all?" Getting the cheese from the fridge, Courtney took it to the counter and hauled herself up so she sat on the Corian next to the stove, her feet swinging gently.

"Not even a little bit. It was too...I don't know. Important?"

"That makes sense."

"Does it?" Rachel chuckled as she buttered bread. "It sounds lame and weird to me."

"No! It's not lame, honey. It's not lame or weird. It's sweet. And touching. I'm so glad you got to see it. I'm jealous."

"I'll never forget it as long as I live." She put the bread in the pan and took the cheese slices Courtney handed her. "I just..." Her voice trailed off and she was discomfited by the tears that welled up.

"What's her name again?"

"Adrianna Michelle. Six pounds, ten ounces."

"That's so pretty. And your sister's doing okay?"

Rachel flipped each sandwich. "Emily's doing great. She's on cloud nine." She smiled at the memory of her baby sister, ridiculously happy and grinning even after being doped up on pain meds.

"Of course she is." Courtney slid off the counter and got plates from the cupboard Rachel pointed out. Their tag-team work in the kitchen felt as natural and normal as could be and Rachel tried hard not to dwell on that fact. After a few moments of silence, Courtney seemed to make a decision and dive forward. "Rachel...I swear I had no idea Ted was your dad. I didn't know his last name. In group, he was just Ted."

"Well, now you know."

"What happened between you two? How come you're so angry at him?"

Remaining focused on the sandwiches, Rachel said, "Didn't he tell you the story?"

Courtney shook her head. "I didn't ask him. I wanted to ask you. And he didn't think it was his place. Will you tell me? Please?"

The innocent tone of Courtney's question made Rachel look at her to see if the expression on her face matched the sweetness of her voice. It did. She flipped the sandwiches onto plates and Courtney sliced them in half on the diagonal, the same way Rachel cut her own, and it made her smile. She took the plate handed to her, along with a tall glass of milk, and they went into the living room to flop down side by side on the couch.

"I've got daddy issues, to say the least," Rachel said after a couple of minutes.

"Not an uncommon thing." Courtney shrugged as she chewed.

"I've never forgiven him for leaving my mom. I've barely talked to him since."

Courtney studied her. "Wow."

"Yeah."

"But…he's around. I mean, he's here in town. He didn't move away or anything."

"He's always been around. He spends a lot of time with Emily and her family. He lives on the same side of town."

"But you don't see him because…you don't want to? Or he doesn't want to?"

Courtney's questions were so gentle, so innocuously phrased, that Rachel didn't feel for a second that she was prying. More than that, she *wanted* to answer. She *wanted* to talk about it. She *wanted* Courtney to understand. *Good God, who am I and what happened to the real Rachel Hart?*

"It's me. It's all my doing. He's tried many times to make contact, to get together. Hell, Emily's even tried to trick us into being in the same place at the same time, like some sort of incestuous blind date scenario." She chuckled. "He wants it, but I always catch on and I've always managed to avoid being alone with him at all costs. I'm civil. I'd never cause a public scene. I've just basically avoided being with him one-on-one for…oh, I don't know. Twenty-five years?"

"Why?" Her sandwich and milk gone, Courtney shifted sideways on the couch and propped her elbow on the back of it, leaning her head onto her hand. "Why don't you want to talk to him one-on-one?"

The sudden lump in Rachel's throat felt stuck and it took her a couple of tries to swallow it down. *All right, maybe emotional overload isn't completely gone after all.* She didn't like that idea, but much to her own surprise, she kept on talking. Something about the kindness on Courtney's face, the look of gentle concern, and the joy of having her so close. Even more surprisingly, she told Courtney the truth. "I'm afraid," she said quietly, studying her own hands.

Courtney laid a warm hand on her shoulder, made soothing circles with her thumb. "Of what?"

"Of sounding like a child."

"Sweetie, you *were* a child when he left. Your anger with him is a child's anger. That's nothing to be ashamed of. You don't see that?" Courtney's tone was laced with a sympathetic sadness and Rachel was sure that if she asked her to, Courtney would do whatever she could to take care of her. The feeling simultaneously terrified her and filled her with a sense of wonder and contentment.

"I guess you're right. I just…" Rachel let the words trail off and she heaved a big sigh. This was a subject she was so used to living with, so used to putting in a box and shelving so she didn't have to examine it closely, but now… She wanted to talk to Courtney about it and the feeling was so foreign, she wasn't sure what to do with it. She turned to gaze at Courtney, and her eyes roamed over the sweet, open face. Courtney's complexion was creamy smooth without the slightest hint of makeup. Her eyes glittered with expectancy, with patience. Rachel noticed for the first time that the green irises were emphasized with a dark black line, making the green stand out even more. "What the hell is it about you? Hmm?"

Courtney smiled. "I'm just interested," she said with a shrug. "I'm interested in you."

The double meaning was not lost on Rachel, who leaned forward and tugged playfully on Courtney's hair.

"Tell me more," Courtney prodded.

Rachel breathed deeply, internally shocked that she was about to tell her deepest secrets to this woman—secrets she'd never told another living soul—but made no attempt to stop herself. It was as if she knew she had no choice and that it would just be better to let it out, that it was suddenly *necessary* to let it out. "I seem to have gotten angrier at my dad as I've gotten older. I guess it's because as an adult, things become a lot clearer than they were when you were a kid." Courtney shifted closer to Rachel and laid a supportive hand on her flannel-clad thigh; the contact bolstered Rachel's confidence. "As I told you before, my dad left my mom when I was thirteen. To this day, I don't really know the details. They kept them from Em and me, I'm sure because they figured we were too young to understand such things. Anyway, my mother was a happy, gentle, and kind woman. She wasn't a terribly solid or strong one...she cried easily, she wasn't great at making decisions without my dad's input, but she was wonderful, the best mom a kid could ask for. Her home and family were her life."

Rachel cleared her throat, surprised by the sudden emotion that welled up as she told the story. Courtney squeezed her leg gently, silently urging her to continue. "When my dad left, it was pretty much out of left field for Emily and me. We never saw it coming. Of course, we were kids, how could we, right? But we were shocked. He just left. He said he and Mom didn't love each other anymore and he just left. Moved out the next day. As an adult, I think it's safe to assume he was having some sort of midlife crisis. He was forty, after all, and I'm damn close to that myself, so I get it. I don't like the way he did it, but I get it. But his leaving wasn't the hardest part. Don't get me wrong, it was hard...it was *very* hard. Worse than that, though, was what became of my mother. The sweet, gentle mom I knew disappeared in the blink of an eye. First, she crumbled. Completely crumbled. She was destroyed. She couldn't keep up the house. She couldn't cook meals for us. She stayed in bed for days on end. I know now that she was depressed, but then? I had no idea what was going on and it was terrifying. I didn't know what to do, so I did what I could. I took care of us. *I* cooked dinner. *I* did the laundry. *I* got Emily up in the morning and ready in time to catch the school bus. This went on for weeks, maybe even months, I lost count.

"When Mom finally snapped out of it and began to get her shit together, she was not the same mother I remembered. She wasn't soft and kind. She didn't smile. Her mouth became this straight, angry slash of a line. Her eyes were hard. She was critical of everyone and everything and thought everybody wanted something from her. She had always been optimistic and the kind of person who looked on the bright side. But after my dad left, she was dark. She thought life was just a hardship and that if she didn't keep vigilant at all times, something or someone would blindside her again. She's still like that to this day. Every once in a while, I'll catch a glimpse of light, but most of the time, she's just hard."

"God, you poor thing," Courtney said, and Rachel was surprised that she sounded a little choked up, emotional.

"I realized a couple years ago why I have such a hard time with my dad." Rachel swallowed hard, having never verbalized her thoughts on the subject to another person, not even Emily. "It's not so much that he left my mother. I'm a big girl now. I know these things happen and they always will, and you know what? Maybe my mom was a bitch and I just didn't realize it. Maybe she was impossible to be with. Maybe she was as much to blame as he was. I don't know." She shrugged. "My parents are just people and people fuck up. I know that. But...he just...left me in charge, you know?" Rachel's eyes shimmered with tears about to spill over as she turned and looked at Courtney. "He destroyed my mother, my home, hammered it into rubble and then left it for me to hold together." Her voice dropped to barely a whisper. "God, I was only thirteen years old. I was a kid. How do you do that to a kid?"

"Oh, sweetheart."

"And then he goes off and finds some other woman and doesn't understand why I don't want anything to do with her."

"Come here." Courtney wrapped her arms around Rachel and pulled her close as a quiet sob escaped Rachel's throat. "What is wrong with adults that they put that much pressure on a child? I don't understand it. You did a terrific job, Rachel. Look at you. You're beautiful and successful and from what you've told me about Emily, it sounds like she turned out all right, too. You did good."

Rachel sat up and ran her fingers over her wet cheeks, embarrassed that she'd broken down, but somehow relieved that it had been Courtney who'd seen it. "You know, at the time, when it was all happening, I never really thought about it being unfair. It never really occurred to me that I was missing out on the most important years of my childhood. I didn't realize any of that until I was all grown up." She rolled her eyes with a grin. "And in therapy."

Courtney chuckled. "Therapy can be a wonderful thing, can't it?"

"You've been there?"

"Oh, God, yes. I was honestly bummed when I was told I didn't need it anymore," she said with a twinkle in her eyes.

"You liked it that much, huh?"

"I liked being able to understand myself, to understand my own reactions to things, you know? I liked being able to make sense of my thoughts and know that, for the most part, they were normal."

"I probably should have stayed a little longer. When my dad's second wife died…I was cold and heartless and I didn't handle that well at all."

"Most people don't."

"I didn't go to the wake or the funeral."

Courtney grimaced. "Ugh. Poor Ted."

"I know." Rachel continued. "I barely acknowledged that she'd existed, let alone that she'd died. I was terrible."

"Everybody handles death differently," Courtney offered.

"I suppose. Still. I think I owe my dad an apology for being such a selfish bitch." She sat with that for a while, surprised at how easily she'd said it and even more surprised by how much she meant it. "Did you go to therapy after Theresa's death?"

A string hanging off the hem of her sweatshirt suddenly became very interesting to Courtney. She swallowed as she toyed with it and inclined her head once in a positive response. "Yeah. Actually, Theresa's death is sort of why I was hanging out in your hallway tonight." She shot Rachel a chagrined grimace. "I thought I owed you an explanation."

"For what?"

"For the other night. For freaking out on you."

"You didn't freak out."

"Oh, but I did." Courtney chuckled. "I just hid it well. Sort of."

Rachel gave a half-grin and nodded, but didn't comment, thinking it was wiser to just let Courtney go on.

Courtney took a deep breath, blew it out, and stared off into the middle distance of the room. "I was having trouble not seeing Theresa even though I was with you. Every time I closed my eyes, I saw her face and I felt like I needed to decide who I wanted to be with more, her or you. Which is a ridiculous choice to force myself to make."

"Damn near impossible, I'd say."

"Right?" Courtney laughed, seeming a bit more at ease than she had just a few seconds ago. "I've realized that you're the only one since she's been gone that I've *really* wanted to be with. And that scared me." The volume of her voice dropping significantly, she looked at her own lap as she said, "I should have talked to you about it. I'm sorry I didn't. See…the people left behind by a spouse who's died? We're always uncertain because we always feel like we're cheating on them."

"That makes perfect sense to me."

"Does it? Because it drives me up the wall. And then when I wish I didn't think that way, when I wish I could just focus on being with you…"

"You feel guilty."

"Exactly."

Gently placing her fingers beneath Courtney's chin, Rachel turned her face up and looked into Courtney's eyes, eyes filled with so much…so much intelligent thought, so much emotion, so much to say. "Tell me about her. Please? I'd like to know. What was she like?"

❖

Feeling a sudden inability to breathe, Courtney grabbed up their dishes and took them to the sink in the kitchen where she stood braced against the counter, hoping to get hold of her bearings. Grateful that Rachel didn't follow, she tried to gather her thoughts, to stop the feeling of imbalance she suddenly felt. Rachel wanted to know about Theresa, and when Courtney thought about the expression on Rachel's face, nonthreatening was the first description that came to her mind. Honest curiosity was another. Under most circumstances, Courtney found it easier to avoid getting into great detail about Theresa, but now…now she was astonished to realize she wanted—needed—to talk about her, especially to Rachel. It was somehow important now. Rachel deserved it, deserved to hear what a wonderful woman Theresa was. And she deserved to hear it from Courtney. Taking a deep breath and making a decision, she returned to the living room and plopped down on the couch next to Rachel, who hadn't moved.

"Theresa was a smart-ass," she began with a grin. "She was witty and fun and loved to bust people's chops. She was always the life of the party."

Rachel hunkered down into the couch more comfortably, her arm around Courtney, and pulled her closer. "What did she do for a living?"

"She was a teacher, just like me, except a better one. Her students loved her." She furrowed her brows as she sorted through her thoughts and memories, trying to find the most important things about her beloved partner, the things she would want everybody to know. "She was Italian, and therefore, family was everything to her. Her parents and her brother were very close to her. We saw them all the time and they welcomed me into their hearts with open arms." Turning her face to look up at Rachel, she said, "You've seen how close I am to Mark. We'll always be like that. That's how her family is. Even though she's gone, I'm still a part of them. It's nice."

"That *is* nice," Rachel said wistfully.

"She was kind," Courtney went on. "She had a big heart and a generous spirit. She had a soft spot for animals. Like you do." She felt Rachel's smile against her hair. "She had a very quick temper. At the drop of a hat, she could be pissed off and you'd have no idea." A deep chuckle rumbled up from Courtney's chest. "It took me a while to get used to that and figure out how to deal."

"I'll bet."

"And she loved me." Surprisingly, Courtney was able to say the words without her eyes filling with tears. "She loved me with all her heart."

"She sounds like a smart woman."

"She was."

They sat in silence for long moments, no sound but the distant traffic outside and the ticking of a clock somewhere in the room. When Rachel finally spoke, her voice was very low, as if she was afraid of disturbing the peace that had settled over them.

"I worry," she said.

"About?"

Taking a deep breath, she plunged in. "Living up to her. Not measuring up to her. Being compared to her. Not being as good for you as she was."

Slowly, Courtney nodded as she absorbed Rachel's words. Peter had said this was probably what Rachel was feeling. "Well…I think that all makes sense and I think it's all normal. I don't know that I can make those worries go away, but I can tell you that I don't expect you to live up to her or measure up. You're not her. You're not Theresa. You're Rachel and you are your own person and I'm drawn to you for different reasons than I was drawn to her." She snuggled closer, pulling Rachel's arm more tightly around her. "I can't say there won't be bumps, but I do promise to try my hardest to be honest with you about them."

"I think that's fair." They were silent again for a while, the muffled sounds of traffic and Saturday-night revelers drifting up from the street below. Rachel's voice sliced softly through the air. "Would she have liked me?"

The question took Courtney completely by surprise and she craned her neck around to look at Rachel's face. What she saw was open and raw honesty. "What?"

"Theresa. Do you think she would have liked me?"

Courtney grinned. "Yeah, she would have. You're the kind of person who would have intrigued her."

"What do you mean?"

"Well…you're a successful businesswoman who's obviously very intelligent, but you don't say much about yourself. She would have spent hours trying to pry information from you, trying to learn about you."

"Really?" Amusement shaded Rachel's face.

"Really." Courtney arched an eyebrow. "And she would have thought you were hot."

"*Really.*" Amusement traded places with surprised satisfaction on Rachel's face.

"Oh, yes."

"Hot?"

"Smokin'."

"Huh." They snuggled more deeply into the couch, Rachel's arm still around Courtney and holding her close. "Then I'd have to say your Theresa had impeccable taste in women."

Courtney smiled and laced her fingers with Rachel's dangling from her shoulder. "That she did."

Comfortable quiet descended upon them and Courtney felt rather than heard Rachel's yawn. Squinting at the cable box across the room, she saw that it was going on ten o'clock.

"I should let you get to bed," she said, not moving. "You've had a pretty exciting day."

Rachel tightened her hold anyway. "No. Stay right where you are. I shouldn't be tired. I took a nap this afternoon. I think I'm just warm and comfortable."

Courtney's insides turned to mush. "Yeah?"

"Yeah."

"Okay." She burrowed into Rachel a bit further so they were very nearly, but not quite, lying on the couch. She kicked off her shoes and tucked her legs up into the cushions.

They were asleep within minutes.

CHAPTER SEVENTEEN

Rachel woke with a start. It took her a few seconds of blinking and clawing through her fog-addled brain before she was able to get her bearings and figure out exactly where she was and what the extra weight lying across her body represented. She smiled when the facts became clear.

She was half sitting, half lying down on the couch with one leg bent at the knee and braced along the back of it and the other dangling off the side to the floor. Courtney lay snugly tucked between Rachel's legs, her face resting on Rachel's chest as if it had always been there, as if that's where she belonged. The room was dark, the living-room light having been clicked off by its timer several hours earlier. Rachel remained still for a long time, drinking in the sight of a sleeping Courtney, caught the twitch as she smiled in slumber, felt the rise and fall of her back under Rachel's hand as she drew breath.

Rachel had no idea how long she watched Courtney. It could have been seconds. It might have been hours. She only knew that she hadn't felt quite so relaxed, so content in the presence of somebody else in a very, very long time.

Almost sensing the gaze focused on her, Courtney awoke, her eyes fluttering open, her lungs expanding with that big waking-up breath the body takes as it pulls out of slumber.

Saying nothing, Courtney finally lifted her head and gazed up into Rachel's eyes. Rachel smiled tenderly down at her. Courtney lifted her right hand and ran her fingertips over Rachel's bottom lip, barely grazing the skin, fluttering like the wings of a butterfly.

Rachel inhaled quietly and suddenly at the touch. She watched as Courtney studied her own hand, traced the same path once again. Rachel was astonished as the contact sizzled all the way down her body to settle in her groin. She slipped her own hands up the flat, muscular planes of Courtney's back and dug her fingers into the thick mass of curls, capturing Courtney's head and holding it still, staring directly into her eyes.

It wasn't clear who moved first, but in a flash, they were kissing. Roughly. The couch seemed to absorb them, pulling them down into the leather as if it had arms, snuggling them into the buttery-soft cushions as their limbs tangled and their breaths became ragged gasps.

"God, I want you." Rachel pulled away just far enough to be able to form the words. "I want you so much."

"Then take me to bed," Courtney replied.

"Are you sure?"

Courtney responded by pushing her tongue back into Rachel's warm mouth, leaving absolutely no doubts.

Rachel shifted beneath Courtney's body and succeeded only in rolling them right off the couch and onto the floor with a thud. Stopping their kissing only long enough to laugh at the tumble, their mouths found one another again, like magnet and steel, unable to stay apart. Each helping the other to her feet, they continued the fervent exploration of lips, teeth, and tongue, while at the same time, leaving a trail of clothing behind them. They somehow managed to stumble through the living room, down the hall, past the bathroom and the office, to the bedroom, without falling or causing damage to any household items. By the time they bumped up against the queen-size mattress and actually pried their mouths apart, Courtney was standing in her white lace bra and matching cotton panties and Rachel was topless, clad only in the flannel bottoms.

Her chest heaving, Courtney reached out her hand and cupped one of Rachel's bare breasts, sliding her thumb over its very erect nipple. Her quick glance up was just in time to see Rachel bite down on her own bottom lip.

"Do you have any idea what you're doing to me?" Rachel said, her voice barely a whisper.

"Do you have any idea how freaking sexy you are?" Courtney countered.

Rachel reached around Courtney's torso and grasped the back of her bra. "This needs to come off. Now."

"Ooh, sexy *and* bossy. Who knew?"

Rachel chuckled. "I'm not sure about the sexy part, but lots of people would agree with you on bossy."

Gooseflesh broke out on Courtney's arms as Rachel slid her bra along them and dropped it on the floor. "Well, *I'm* sure about the sexy part. Not a doubt in my mind about the sexy part…" Her voice trailed off as she pulled Rachel's face toward her and devoured her mouth with her own.

The world faded away for Rachel. There was nothing, nobody other than Courtney. And the fact that Courtney seemed somehow different tonight didn't escape Rachel's attention. She seemed relaxed, more open, more at ease than the last time they'd ended up in a similar position. As she eased Courtney back onto the bed and slowly slid her panties down her thighs, it suddenly occurred to Rachel: there was nowhere in the world she'd rather be and nothing else in the universe she'd rather be doing than what she was involved in right that moment. Courtney was everything. Nothing else mattered. She divested herself of her own pants and then crawled across the bed, pushing her knee between Courtney's legs, feeling the hot wetness coat her skin.

Courtney moaned and pushed her head back into the pillows, a handful of Rachel's hair twisted in her fingers. When Rachel used her teeth to tug at Courtney's swollen nipple, the grip on her hair tightened and Courtney gasped.

The warm and silky wetness that met Rachel's fingers as she slid them between Courtney's legs was simultaneously not surprising and completely shocking. Not surprising because Rachel knew she was just as wet as Courtney, if not more so. Completely shocking because it was hard to believe she was able to cause such arousal in this incredible woman. She was in awe, complete wonder as she looked at Courtney's body beneath her. She was fit, built like an athlete, all the muscle and smooth skin laid bare before her and glowing with excitement. But she was also round, curvy, and feminine, and the combination made Rachel's mouth water. Courtney's head was thrown back, exposing her elegant throat. Her eyes were closed.

Beginning a slow, lazy rhythm with her fingers, Rachel shifted to her knees, so she was braced above Courtney on one hand, her legs keeping Courtney's spread wide. She looked down at Courtney's face as she moved through the slickness covering her fingertips.

"Courtney." She said the name softly, waited. "Courtney. Look at me."

Courtney swallowed as she opened her eyes, her breathing continuing in ragged gasps. Rachel gazed at her as she quickened the pace of her hand.

"Say my name."

If Courtney thought it an odd request, she hid it well. She cocked her head slightly to the right, as if wondering if she'd heard correctly. But the half-grin she tossed at Rachel hovering over her made any trepidation disappear.

"Rachel." She whispered the name, elongating it, stretching it out, making it sound a hundred times sexier than it actually was. Rachel felt a spurt of her own wetness and whimpered.

"Oh, my God. Again. Say it again." Her heart rate, her hips, and the pace of her hand were now one and the same, moving all in the same rhythm.

"Rachel."

"Again. Please."

"Rachel." This time, the pitch of Courtney's voice increased and she inhaled sharply. "Oh...oh, Rachel...oh, please..." She dug the tips of her fingers into Rachel's side as she came, her muscles tensing so hard, her body spasming so roughly, Rachel was surprised she didn't simply snap in half. Murmuring encouragement, Rachel coaxed the climax out of her, adjusting her speed and her touch to make it last as long as possible. A glittering sheen of sweat covered both their bodies as they rocked as one.

It seemed like hours before Courtney reached between them

and grasped Rachel's wrist, stilling her movements and easing her fingers out. Rachel let the hand bracing her slide up so that she slid down to the bed, half on and half off Courtney. Their bodies already beginning to cool, Rachel reached down and grabbed the corner of the black fleece throw that was folded neatly at the foot of the bed. She pulled it up over them, tucking it around Courtney and pulling her closer.

"My God, that was incredible," Courtney said, her voice low and husky.

Rachel grinned. "That was only the beginning," she said, drawing a fingertip down the side of Courtney's face, under her chin, and back again. "I have many, many more acts in my repertoire."

"Really. Many, many?"

"Oh, yes. Many, many."

"And I suppose there's a big finale, too?"

"There is. But it could take months or even years before we get to that. And you'd be lucky if you could even stand up, let alone walk, by then." Rachel winked.

Courtney cleared her throat. "That sounds like quite a time commitment. Are you sure you're up for that?"

Rachel's face became suddenly, deadly serious. "Yes. I am." She swallowed audibly. "I am if you are."

Courtney's eyes never left Rachel's as she nodded slowly in the darkness. "I am, too."

❖

"I should get home."

The sun was shining brightly through Rachel's bedroom window when Courtney said the words for the fourth time. They were naked, spooning, with Rachel behind Courtney, her arm wrapped around and fingers drawing lazy circles on Courtney's bare belly. The bedding was a tangled muddle, the decorative pillows with the expensive Laura Ashley shams were mostly on the floor, and the air in the room was thick with the scent of sex.

"I don't want you to go." Rachel answered with the same

response she'd given the other three times. Courtney could feel the smile against her hair and she couldn't help but grin.

"You're nothing if not predictable."

"No, you're supposed to say, 'maybe you should show me how much you want me to stay,' like you did the last time."

"And the time before that? And the time before that?" Courtney laughed outright and Rachel joined her. "I'm sorry, sweetie, but I don't think I can survive another orgasm. My head will explode." She rolled onto her back so she could look into Rachel's face. She looked tired. Her eyes were bloodshot, her lips were swollen, and her hair was a disaster. But the expression on her face was one of radiance and contentment. Courtney had a sudden flash of that same face, tense with desire, bottom lip caught between teeth, whispered pleading. Throwing off the covers, she gave Rachel a quick, chaste kiss on the mouth and was suddenly up and out of the bed, knowing if she stayed, she'd be there for another hour at least and the threat of an inability to walk would become all too real. She found her clothes scattered about and began to dress.

Rachel sighed dramatically and stretched like a lazy cat in the sunshine. "Okay, she's serious this time."

"Afraid so." Courtney stopped midmotion and her mouth watered at the sight of the lithe body on the bed. It took all her strength to keep from pouncing on her like a cobra on its prey. She glared in accusation. "And stop trying to tempt me."

Rachel gave a smug smile. "Hmm. You're reading me too well already. That's not good."

"You must be out of practice," Courtney teased. "Maybe a little rusty? Hmm?"

Rachel slithered out of the bed and across the room in all her naked glory, and Courtney was unable to pull her eyes away. "Rusty?" She kissed Courtney fully, slowly and thoroughly, possessively. When she pulled away, she held Courtney's bottom lip in her teeth, tugged, then let it go. "I don't think so."

"No," Courtney whispered. "Me, neither. Jesus."

They walked into the living room together—Courtney dressed, Rachel completely naked—holding hands.

"Will I see you again soon?" Rachel asked, sounding almost childlike.

"What?" Courtney blinked and shook her head as if pulled from a trance, then rolled her eyes playfully. "Seriously, how do you expect me to be able to concentrate on words when you're walking around like that? Put something on, for Christ's sake. Aren't you cold?"

Rachel grinned. "I haven't been cold since you walked in that door last night."

Courtney felt her own blush and looked down at her feet. Rachel reached out and stroked her cheek, bringing her face back up.

"Call me later?" Courtney asked.

"Absolutely."

They kissed softly and sweetly. Courtney pulled free before things could get heavier. "Okay. I'm going." She snagged her jacket off the arm of the couch and slipped out the door with a quick wave. "Later, babe."

"Count on it."

When the door clicked shut, Courtney stood in the hallway and brought her fingers to her lips, certain she could still feel heat radiating from them, positive she could still smell Rachel's tangy scent. *Unbelievable, this turn of events.* It was the only accurate description. Last night had been a whirlwind, and totally surprising; she'd never seen it coming. She certainly hadn't shown up with the intention of spending the entire night making mad, passionate love with Rachel, but that's exactly what had happened. And this morning? The surprising thing about this morning was that she actually felt all right about it. No, not all right. Good. She felt good. Happy, even.

Happy? Was that possible? Maybe it was... Of course, she also felt utterly dizzy, as if her life was suddenly tipped sideways and spun around in circles like a child's toy top.

And most surprising of all was how much she was enjoying it.

CHAPTER EIGHTEEN

H i there."
"Hey." Rachel took a seat on the stool at the corner of the mahogany bar and propped her feet up on the brass rail near the bottom. Her right knee immediately started bouncing and she resented it, resented any outward showing of being anxious.

"Getcha a drink?" Ted asked. He didn't look as nervous as Rachel felt, but his eye contact was sporadic and darting.

"Just a Coke would be great."

She studied him as he flagged down the bartender to get her soda. In all of the times she'd run into him—at Emily's, in the hospital when Adrianna was born, or wherever—she'd avoided looking at him too carefully. Realizing recently that it had been a defense mechanism, at the time she didn't want him to think she cared at all, not even enough to rest her eyes on him for longer than a second or two. Now she found herself looking carefully, unable to pull her gaze away. His hair had never been thick, but he was almost completely bald on top now. What remained of his light hair circled his head like a donut and he kept it trimmed neatly around his ears and along his neck. Age was catching up to him. The laugh lines around his mouth and the crow's feet at the corners of his eyes had deepened tremendously since the last time she'd noticed them and despite all her anger, irritation, and pain over the last two decades, she still found herself experiencing a feeling of melancholy. Her father was getting old.

"Thanks for agreeing to meet with me," he said as her Coke arrived.

She fondled the little mixing straw, absently poking at the ice cubes in the glass, and nodded.

"I know it was probably Courtney's prodding that got you here." His tone held enough mirth in it to take out anything that might be construed as accusatory, and she couldn't help but smile.

"She had an opinion, yes."

"I'll bet."

It had only been a month since the day Rachel had run into her father and Courtney conversing on the street, but after their heart-to-heart in Rachel's apartment, there had occurred an almost unspoken pact to reunite Rachel and Ted—or at least get them on speaking terms once again. Rachel suspected Courtney and Marie, Ted's current girlfriend, of conniving to make things happen. She could pretend to be mad about that all she wanted, but the truth was, she found it somewhat heartwarming to know Courtney was taking care of her in this way. Even if it was kind of meddling.

"How about your mom? Does she know you're here?"

A snort escaped Rachel's nose before she could catch it and Ted smiled at the sound. "Uh, no."

"Yeah, I didn't think so." He took a healthy slug from his bottle of Heineken.

The sportscaster calling the golf tournament in a stage whisper was the only sound in the bar for a long time. After all, it was late afternoon on a Thursday and there were only three other patrons this early. Rachel sipped from her Coke and heard Courtney's voice in the back of her mind.

"Just be honest. Say what you feel, what's in your heart. He's going to be just as nervous as you are. Remember that. Just talk to him."

"I'm sorry about Kathy." She said it so quietly that for a moment, she was unsure if she'd actually spoken out loud or had just thought it.

Her father looked at her, his lips pressed together in a straight line. The pale blue of his eyes was identical to Rachel's, and she felt like she saw them for the very first time. "Thank you."

"I was really angry with you then."

He nodded slowly, turning the beer bottle in his hands.

"But that's no excuse. I should have at least paid my respects. I'm sorry I was selfish."

"It's okay. I understand." He cleared his throat. "Thanks for that."

"Sure." She sipped again, feeling like she'd made progress, but uncertain which way to go next.

"I'm sorry, too." Studying his beer, he didn't meet her gaze.

"For?"

"For doing things the way I did. Back then. With your mother."

There it was. *That didn't take long*, she thought with surprise. *Marie must have prepped him as well as Courtney prepped me.* The lump that suddenly blocked her throat was completely unexpected, and Rachel swallowed several times in an attempt to keep control of things. "It was hard," she managed to say.

"I know. And I was young and your mother was young and young people do stupid things. They don't always handle things well."

Rachel listened, feeling almost as if she was in some surreal moment. She'd been waiting for more than twenty years to hear her father apologize, and now that he was doing just that, she had no idea what to say.

"We had problems, me and your mom. Lots of problems. The marriage died because of both of us, not just because of me. It takes two to tango." He swigged, his gaze on the television mounted high behind the bar. "But I didn't handle things well."

Rachel found her voice at the same time she felt her resentment building. Courtney had warned her that this would probably happen and that she should go with it, that it was the only way to clear the air. "I was a kid, Dad. You know that, right?"

"Yeah, I know that."

"You and Mom were so wrapped up in your own shit that neither of you seemed to remember you had two children."

Ted's face reddened at that and Rachel wondered at his embarrassment, wondered if he sensed her anger and whether he thought he deserved it.

"Do you know who kept things together after you ran away like a coward?" she went on. "Who cooked? Who cleaned? Who bathed Emily? Who kept the household running? Me, that's who. Me."

Ted nodded, still unable to look her in the face.

Her voice dropped to a whisper. "I was a child."

"I know. I'm sorry." He did look at her then, and the unshed tears welling in his eyes matched hers. "I'm sorry, baby. I'm so very sorry."

She took a deep breath and used the napkin from under her glass to wipe her nose, both relieved to have finally said the words that she'd kept locked up for so long and embarrassed that she'd shown any emotion at all. What was the matter with her, anyway? Courtney was turning her into a sap. She almost laughed when that thought crossed her mind and she realized that she didn't mind sap status as much as she'd assumed she would.

Ted gestured to the bartender and ordered himself another beer.

"Can I get some rum added to this?" Rachel asked, pointing to her Coke as the bartender grinned at her.

They sat in more silence, sipping their drinks, like father, like daughter.

Ted finally spoke up. "Well, that was fun."

"Loads."

His face turning serious again, he said, "Look, Rachel, I don't expect everything to be all fine and dandy now. I'm not that stupid. I'm not naïve. But...I'm an old man." He punctuated that line with a sort of guffaw, like it would be a ridiculous statement to make if it wasn't true. "I'm at that age where you start looking back at your life and at the things you did perfectly as well as the things you screwed up. More than anything, you want to fix those things, make them right somehow. I don't know that I can ever expect you to forgive me for being such a shitty father when you were a kid, but…" His voice trailed off. Wiping the sweat from his fresh bottle, he plunged ahead. "I'm glad we talked, no matter what happens. Even if we leave here and go back to the way we've been—hardly ever seeing each other and barely speaking—I'm still glad we had this conversation."

Rachel soaked in his words, soaked in the fact that she was actually spending uninterrupted time with her father for the first time since before high school, and felt her anger with him simply dissipate, melting away like a pat of butter on a steaming-hot roll. The lump returned, much to her chagrin, but she held it in check long enough to utter two words very clearly.

"Me, too."

CHAPTER NINETEEN

Rachel knew that April was a hit-or-miss month in upstate New York. You never knew what you were going to get from one day to the next. You could be plunged headlong into spring without an iota of looking back. Or you might be lassoed around the neck on your way to spring and be yanked roughly backward, back into the dark and icy cold of winter for several more weeks, Mother Nature's last laugh of the season, big tease that she is. Many a blizzard or ice storm has been written into the weather history books in the month of April. It was a crapshoot.

This particular early-April morning was gorgeous—unusually so—and Rachel took a giant breath of the crisp, fragrant air, filling her lungs with the promise of spring and flowers that were soon to bloom. It was a little bit too soon for the smell of fresh-cut grass, but the anticipation of it was enough to bring a smile to Rachel's face.

She folded her arms and leaned against the car, soaking in the silence as she watched Courtney from several yards away. The pleasantness of the air and the chirping of the birds helped to alleviate any discomfort Rachel was experiencing. Cemetaries were not among her top five places to visit on a Sunday morning, but as long as she didn't concentrate too closely on the scattered headstones, she could almost pretend she was in a park.

Courtney crouched down and Rachel watched as she patted the grass, obviously testing for wetness. She shed her nylon windbreaker and laid it down, then took a seat. Though curious about what was being said or thought about, Rachel respected Courtney's need to be alone, especially today.

April seventh.

Theresa's birthday.

So much had transpired in the past several months...so much and hardly anything. They'd fallen in love, that was certain. Rachel had fallen harder and faster than she ever thought possible and it took her a while to simply accept it as fact. Jeff had to beat her over the head on several occasions, but she finally learned to listen to him and to relax a little bit.

"Even control freaks need a break every now and then," he'd said, tossing a teasing wink her way.

"I'm not a control freak." She sounded completely unconvincing and she knew it.

"Yeah. Okay. Whatever you say."

Smiling now as she recalled the frequent conversation, she sent up a prayer of thanks for the people who loved her and looked out for her. Emily, Jeff, and now Courtney. Bless her heart, she'd never pushed, never demanded. Frankly, Courtney had issues of her own, and she told Rachel one night after they'd tiffed over Rachel's propensity to shut down that she never wanted to be the pot calling the kettle black...that the best they could do was talk to one another and try their best to understand the other side. It wasn't always easy, but they were managing.

The crunching of gravel under tires pulled Rachel from her ruminations and she watched as the dark Jeep coasted to a stop. Two familiar figures hopped out.

"Hey, Raich." Mark waved in her direction, a modest boquet of flowers clutched in his other hand, and headed off toward Courtney.

Lisa crossed the distance between the cars and leaned up against the BMW next to Rachel, folding her arms and mimicking her stance. "Hi."

"Hi."

"You okay?"

"Yep."

"It's kind of tough, huh?"

Rachel chewed on the inside of her cheek for several seconds, absorbing the words before giving an affirming nod. "A little." She felt Lisa's eyes on her, but didn't turn to meet her gaze. Across the grass, Courtney stood and Mark wrapped her in his arms.

"I mean, here's this person you love, who loves you, but a couple times a year, her focus goes fully and totally to some other woman."

Rachel didn't respond, tried not to bristle, not to let Lisa see how painful that truth sometimes felt. At the same time, she reminded herself that if anybody in the world had an accurate handle on Courtney's feelings with regard to this subject, it was Lisa. They stood in silence, watching their respective partners visit their lost loved one. Rachel wondered what was going through Courtney's mind, what she'd say to Theresa if Theresa could really hear her. At the same time, she wasn't sure she really wanted to know.

After a while, Mark turned away from the headstone and headed back their way, his eyes downcast, his demeanor somber. When he reached them, he held his hand out to Lisa. "Want to get some breakfast?" he asked as she entwined their fingers.

"Love to."

They bade Rachel their good-byes and strolled hand in hand back to Lisa's Jeep. As Rachel followed their departure, Courtney called to her. "Sweetie? Would you come here for a minute?"

When she arrived to stand next to her, Courtney took Rachel's hand and squeezed it. Tear tracks were visible on her cheeks and she sniffed once, quietly.

"How're you doing?" Rachel asked, her voice low as if she was afraid of disturbing the occupants of the grounds.

"I'm good," Courtney replied. "You?"

"I'm good, too."

"Good. I just wanted you here with me for a bit. Is that okay?"

"That's more than okay."

They stood holding hands in silence in front of a large, glossy, charcoal-colored headstone. Rachel read the words that were carved artistically into the granite.

Theresa Maria Josephina Benetti
April 7, 1971—January 18, 2004
Beloved Daughter, Sister, Partner, Friend

"She was lucky to have you." Rachel's tone was certain.

Courtney seemed to soak in the words. "I was lucky to have her."

"You were."

"And now I'm lucky to have you." She leaned against Rachel, holding her arm tightly and laying her head against Rachel's shoulder. "I can't believe she's been gone for more than three years." She blew out a heavy breath and was silent for several long moments. Finally, she spoke again, softly. "Thank you, Rachel."

"For what?"

"For being here. For being patient. For being you."

Rachel kissed the top of her head. "You're welcome."

"I get it. You know that, right?"

Rachel turned and looked at her. "Get what?"

"That it's hard for you. That it's unfair to you." Courtney cleared her throat, her focus on the headstone as she spoke. "That you sometimes feel like you have to share me with a ghost. That it makes you feel helpless because when I travel down Memory Lane, willingly or unwillingly, there isn't much you can do or say to bring me back to you until I'm ready. That you spend so much time waiting me out."

Rachel swallowed and looked off into the trees. Maybe Courtney did know how hard the waiting was for her, how difficult it was to just be patient.

"It sucks and I don't like that I do it," Courtney went on. "But Theresa was and always will be a part of me. And you know that and you do your best to accept it. And you have to know that I love you even more for your willingness to accept it. I just want you to know I'm so grateful that you do what you can to understand."

"Understanding doesn't always make it easier." Rachel's voice was low, barely above a whisper.

"I know. Believe me, I know."

Rachel turned toward Courtney and when their eyes met, she

spoke. "Do you know that I…that despite how hard it can be, I would never want to take her from you? That…I know you had some of the best years of your life with Theresa, that I know you loved her with all your heart?" She smiled. "Am I a little jealous about that? Of course I am. I'm human. But I'd never want to take it from you, that time, that love. Never."

"You wouldn't?" Courtney's voice was small. "I guess I just always figured it would make life so much easier on you if my relationship with Theresa had never existed, you know?"

"It doesn't mean that's what I'd choose."

"You wouldn't? How come?"

Rachel's voice cracked slightly as she responded. "Because I love you so much. Dummy."

A laugh burst from Courtney even as tears coursed down her cheeks. "I love you, too." Then she repeated her earlier line, sounding even more certain than before. "I am lucky to have you, Rachel. You're a keeper."

"Yeah, well." Rachel made a face. "Sometimes I'm a keeper. Sometimes, I'm just annoying."

They stood in the quiet, their arms around one another. After a few minutes, Courtney brought her fingers to her lips, kissed them, then pressed them to the top of the headstone. Turning to Rachel, she asked, "You ready to go?" She picked her jacket up off the ground and wiped the stray blades of grass from it.

Rachel remembered their next stop and growled low in her throat, which made Courtney laugh. "Yeah, I think so."

"Just concentrate on the Bloody Marys, baby, and you'll be fine. You've been doing great. I'm proud of you."

This would be the third Sunday brunch in the past two months that they'd enjoyed with Ted Hart and his girlfriend, Marie. As far as Ted and Rachel making amends, it was slow, achingly slow, progress, but it was progress nevertheless. Courtney and Marie had hit it off immediately, and Rachel suspected they did a lot of patting one another on the back after each successful get-together.

Rachel felt a satisfied glow wash over her as they sauntered back to the BMW, Courtney's pride warming her from the inside. "Marie does make a kick-ass Bloody Mary, that's for sure."

They piled into the car and Rachel turned over the engine. As Courtney buckled her seat belt, she asked with a mischievous grin, "Can I have your celery stick?"

Rachel smiled at her, feeling such a profound sense of love that it almost brought tears to her eyes. She reached across the center console to touch Courtney's face and stroked her thumb over her cheek. "You can have anything of mine you want, Courtney. Anything at all."

About the Author

Born and raised in upstate New York, so close to the border she's practically Canadian, Georgia Beers has been writing since she was old enough to hold a pen. Her first romance novel, *Turning the Page*, was published in the year 2000. Since then, she's written four more and has no intention of stopping anytime soon. Her fourth novel, *Fresh Tracks*, was presented the Lambda Literary Award, as well as a Golden Crown Literary Society Award, for Best Lesbian Romance of 2006.

She lives with Bonnie, her partner of thirteen years, and their two dogs. The eldest of five daughters, she has a slew of nieces and nephews to keep her on her toes. She is currently hard at work on her sixth novel, *Finding Home*, to be published by Bold Strokes Books in 2008.

You can visit her on the Web at www.georgiabeers.com.

Books Available From Bold Strokes Books

Queens of Tristaine by Cate Culpepper. When a deadly plague stalks the Amazons of Tristaine, two warrior lovers must return to the place of their nightmares to find a cure. (978-1-933110-97-4)

The Crown of Valencia by Catherine Friend. Ex-lovers can really mess up your life…even, as Kate discovers, if they've traveled back to the eleventh century! (978-1-933110-96-7)

Mine by Georgia Beers. What happens when you've already given your heart and love finds you again? Courtney McAllister is about to find out. (978-1-933110-95-0)

House of Clouds by KI Thompson. A sweeping saga of an impassioned romance between a Northern spy and a Southern sympathizer, set amidst the upheaval of a nation under siege. (978-1-933110-94-3)

Winds of Fortune by Radclyffe. Provincetown local Deo Camara agrees to rehab Dr. Bonita Burgoyne's historic home, but she never said anything about mending her heart. (978-1-933110-93-6)

Focus of Desire by Kim Baldwin. Isabel Sterling is surprised when she wins a photography contest, but no more than photographer Natasha Kashnikova. Their promo tour becomes a ticket to romance. (978-1-933110-92-9)

Blind Leap by Diane and Jacob Anderson-Minshall. A Golden Gate Bridge suicide becomes suspect when a filmmaker's camera shows a different story. Yoshi Yakamota and the Blind Eye Detective Agency uncover evidence that could be worth killing for. (978-1-933110-91-2)

Wall of Silence, 2nd ed. by Gabrielle Goldsby. Life takes a dangerous turn when jaded police detective Foster Everett meets Riley Medeiros, a woman who isn't afraid to discover the truth no matter the cost. (978-1-933110-90-5)

Mistress of the Runes by Andrews & Austin. Passion ignites between two women with ties to ancient secrets, contemporary mysteries, and a shared quest for the meaning of life. (978-1-933110-89-9)

Sheridan's Fate by Gun Brooke. A dynamic, erotic romance between physiotherapist Lark Mitchell and businesswoman Sheridan Ward set in the scorching hot days and humid, steamy nights of San Antonio. (978-1-933110-88-2)

Vulture's Kiss by Justine Saracen. Archeologist Valerie Foret, heir to a terrifying task, returns in a powerful desert adventure set in Egypt and Jerusalem. (978-1-933110-87-5)

Rising Storm by JLee Meyer. The sequel to *First Instinct* takes our heroines on a dangerous journey instead of the honeymoon they'd planned. (978-1-933110-86-8)

Not Single Enough by Grace Lennox. A funny, sexy modern romance about two lonely women who bond over the unexpected and fall in love along the way. (978-1-933110-85-1)

Such a Pretty Face by Gabrielle Goldsby. A sexy, sometimes humorous, sometimes biting contemporary romance that gently exposes the damage to heart and soul when we fail to look beneath the surface for what truly matters. (978-1-933110-84-4)

Second Season by Ali Vali. A romance set in New Orleans amidst betrayal, Hurricane Katrina, and the new beginnings hardship and heartbreak sometimes make possible. (978-1-933110-83-7)

Hearts Aflame by Ronica Black. A poignant, erotic romance between a hard-driving businesswoman and a solitary vet. Packed with adventure and set in the harsh beauty of the Arizona countryside. (978-1-933110-82-0)

Red Light by JD Glass. Tori forges her path as an EMT in the New York City 911 system while discovering what matters most to herself and the woman she loves. (978-1-933110-81-3)

Honor Under Siege by Radclyffe. Secret Service agent Cameron Roberts struggles to protect her lover while searching for a traitor who just may be another woman with a claim on her heart. (978-1-933110-80-6)

Dark Valentine by Jennifer Fulton. Danger and desire fuel a high-stakes cat-and-mouse game when an attorney and an endangered witness team up to thwart a killer. (978-1-933110-79-0)

Sequestered Hearts by Erin Dutton. A popular artist suddenly goes into seclusion, a reluctant reporter wants to know why, and a heart locked away yearns to be set free. (978-1-933110-78-3)

Erotic Interludes 5: Road Games, ed. by Radclyffe and Stacia Seaman. Adventure, "sport," and sex on the road—hot stories of travel adventures and games of seduction. (978-1-933110-77-6)

The Spanish Pearl by Catherine Friend. On a trip to Spain, Kate Vincent is accidentally transported back in time—an epic saga spiced with humor, lust, and danger. (978-1-933110-76-9)

Lady Knight by L-J Baker. Loyalty and honor clash with love and ambition in a medieval world of magic when female knight Riannon meets Lady Eleanor. (978-1-933110-75-2)

Dark Dreamer by Jennifer Fulton. Best-selling horror author Rowe Devlin falls under the spell of psychic Phoebe Temple. A Dark Vista romance. (978-1-933110-74-5)

Come and Get Me by Julie Cannon. Elliott Foster isn't used to pursuing women, but alluring attorney Lauren Collier makes her change her mind. (978-1-933110-73-8)

Blind Curves by Diane and Jacob Anderson-Minshall. Private eye Yoshi Yakamota comes to the aid of her ex-lover Velvet Erickson in the first Blind Eye mystery. (978-1-933110-72-1)

The Devil Unleashed by Ali Vali. As the heat of violence rises, so does the passion. A Casey Clan crime saga. (1-933110-61-9)

Dynasty of Rogues by Jane Fletcher. It's hate at first sight for Ranger Riki Sadiq and her new patrol corporal, Tanya Coppelli—except for their undeniable attraction. (978-1-933110-71-4)

Running With the Wind by Nell Stark. Sailing instructor Corrie Marsten has signed off on love until she meets Quinn Davies—one woman she can't ignore. (978-1-933110-70-7)

More Than Paradise by Jennifer Fulton. Two women battle danger, risk all, and find in each other an unexpected ally and an unforgettable love. (978-1-933110-69-1)

Flight Risk by Kim Baldwin. For Blayne Keller, being in the wrong place at the wrong time just might turn out to be the best thing that ever happened to her. (978-1-933110-68-4)

Rebel's Quest: Supreme Constellations Book Two by Gun Brooke. On a world torn by war, two women discover a love that defies all boundaries. (978-1-933110-67-7)

Punk and Zen by JD Glass. Angst, sex, love, rock. Trace, Candace, Francesca…Samantha. Losing control—and finding the truth within. BSB Victory Editions. (1-933110-66-X)

When Dreams Tremble by Radclyffe. Two women whose lives turned out far differently than they'd once imagined discover that sometimes the shape of the future can only be found in the past. (1-933110-64-3)

Stellium in Scorpio by Andrews & Austin. The passionate reunion of two powerful women on the glitzy Las Vegas Strip, where everything is an illusion and love is a gamble. (1-933110-65-1)

Burning Dreams by Susan Smith. The chronicle of the challenges faced by a young drag king and an older woman who share a love "outside the bounds." (1-933110-62-7)

Fresh Tracks by Georgia Beers. Seven women, seven days. A lot can happen when old friends, lovers, and a new girl in town get together in the mountains. (1-933110-63-5)

Too Close to Touch by Georgia Beers. Kylie O'Brien believes in true love and is willing to wait for it. It doesn't matter one damn bit that Gretchen, her new and off-limits boss, has a voice as rich and smooth as melted chocolate. It absolutely doesn't… (1-933110-47-3)

The Empress and the Acolyte by Jane Fletcher. Jemeryl and Tevi fight to protect the very fabric of their world…time. Lyremouth Chronicles Book Three. (1-933110-60-0)

First Instinct by JLee Meyer. When high-stakes security fraud leads to murder, one woman flees for her life while another risks her heart to protect her. (1-933110-59-7)

Erotic Interludes 4: Extreme Passions, ed. by Radclyffe and Stacia Seaman. Thirty of today's hottest erotica writers set the pages aflame with love, lust, and steamy liaisons. (1-933110-58-9)

Broken Wings by L-J Baker. When Rye Woods, a fairy, meets the beautiful dryad Flora Withe, her libido, as squashed and hidden as her wings, reawakens along with her heart. (1-933110-55-4)

Whitewater Rendezvous by Kim Baldwin. Two women on a wilderness kayak adventure—Chaz Herrick, a laid-back outdoorswoman, and Megan Maxwell, a workaholic news executive—discover that true love may be nothing at all like they imagined. (1-933110-38-4)

Unexpected Ties by Gina L. Dartt. With death before dessert, Kate Shannon and Nikki Harris are swept up in another tale of danger and romance. (1-933110-56-2)

Tristaine Rises by Cate Culpepper. Brenna, Jesstin, and the Amazons of Tristaine face their greatest challenge for survival. (1-933110-50-3)

Passion's Bright Fury by Radclyffe. When a trauma surgeon and a filmmaker become reluctant allies on the battleground between life and death, passion strikes without warning. (1-933110-54-6)

Sleep of Reason by Rose Beecham. Nothing is as it seems when Detective Jude Devine finds herself caught up in a small-town soap opera. And her rocky relationship with forensic pathologist Dr. Mercy Westmoreland just got a lot harder. (1-933110-53-8)

Sweet Creek by Lee Lynch. A celebration of the enduring nature of love, friendship, and community in the quirky, heart-warming lesbian community of Waterfall Falls. (1-933110-29-5)

Sword of the Guardian by Merry Shannon. Princess Shasta's bold new bodyguard has a secret that could change both of their lives. *He* is actually a *she*. A passionate romance filled with courtly intrigue, chivalry, and devotion. (1-933110-36-8)

Turn Back Time by Radclyffe. Pearce Rifkin and Wynter Thompson have nothing in common but a shared passion for surgery. They clash at every opportunity, especially when matters of the heart are suddenly at stake. (1-933110-34-1)

Promising Hearts by Radclyffe. Dr. Vance Phelps lost everything in the War Between the States and arrives in New Hope, Montana, with no hope of happiness and no desire for anything except forgetting—until she meets Mae, a frontier madam. (1-933110-44-9)

Innocent Hearts by Radclyffe. In a wild and unforgiving land, two women learn about love, passion, and the wonders of the heart. (1-933110-21-X)

Justice Served by Radclyffe. Lieutenant Rebecca Frye and her lover, Dr. Catherine Rawlings, embark on a deadly game of hide-and-seek with an underworld kingpin who traffics in human souls. (1-933110-15-5)

Justice in the Shadows by Radclyffe. In a shadow world of secrets and lies, Detective Sergeant Rebecca Frye and her lover, Dr. Catherine Rawlings, join forces in the elusive search for justice. (1-933110-03-1)

A Matter of Trust by Radclyffe. JT Sloan is a cybersleuth who doesn't like attachments. Michael Lassiter is leaving her husband, and she needs Sloan's expertise to safeguard her company. It should just be business—but it turns into much more. (1-933110-33-3)

Storms of Change by Radclyffe. In the continuing saga of the Provincetown Tales, duty and love are at odds as Reese and Tory face their greatest challenge. (1-933110-57-0)

Distant Shores, Silent Thunder by Radclyffe. Dr. Tory King—along with the women who love her—is forced to examine the boundaries of love, friendship, and the ties that transcend time. (1-933110-08-2)

Beyond the Breakwater by Radclyffe. One Provincetown summer, three women learn the true meaning of love, friendship, and family. (1-933110-06-6)

Safe Harbor by Radclyffe. A mysterious newcomer, a reclusive doctor, and a troubled gay teenager learn about love, friendship, and trust during one tumultuous summer in Provincetown. (1-933110-13-9)

shadowland by Radclyffe. In a world on the far edge of desire, two women are drawn together by power, passion, and dark pleasures. An erotic romance. (1-933110-11-2)

Love's Masquerade by Radclyffe. Plunged into the indistinguishable realms of fiction, fantasy, and hidden desires, Auden Frost is forced to question all she believes about the nature of love. (1-933110-14-7)

Honor Reclaimed by Radclyffe. In the aftermath of 9/11, Secret Service Agent Cameron Roberts and Blair Powell close ranks with a trusted few to find the would-be assassins who nearly claimed Blair's life. (1-933110-18-X)

Honor Guards by Radclyffe. In a wild flight for their lives, the president's daughter and those who are sworn to protect her wage a desperate struggle for survival. (1-933110-01-5)

Love & Honor by Radclyffe. The president's daughter and her lover are faced with difficult choices as they battle a tangled web of Washington intrigue for...love and honor. (1-933110-10-4)

Honor Bound by Radclyffe. Secret Service Agent Cameron Roberts and Blair Powell face political intrigue, a clandestine threat to Blair's safety, and the seemingly irreconcilable personal differences that force them ever farther apart. (1-933110-20-1)

Above All, Honor by Radclyffe. Secret Service Agent Cameron Roberts fights her desire for the one woman she can't have—Blair Powell, the daughter of the president of the United States. (1-933110-04-X)